"I'm asking you t...

Warning bells cla...

Because Kevin wa... ...s also a friend. And desp... ...y reminders to herself that he was ...rker and a friend, being around the man never failed to make her aware that she was still a woman, with a woman's wants and needs.

"Where's your date?" she asked.

They'd been seated at the same table, so she knew that he'd brought one to the wedding. Of course, it seemed to her that Kevin was always with a woman— and not usually the same one on Saturday that he'd been with on Friday.

"Dancing with yours," he told her.

Even if the music and the wine made her want to feel like her old self again, if only for three and a half minutes, she knew that the smart thing to do would be to decline his invitation.

Instead, she found herself accepting his proffered hand.

When Kevin drew her into his arms, her whole body started to hum with an unexpected—and unwelcome—awareness. And in that moment, Nat knew RSVP'ing "yes" to the wedding invitation had been a mistake.

And that she was about to make an even bigger one.

Dear Reader,

Kevin Dawson grew up in Haven, Nevada, and became a hometown success story. He's smart, good-looking, athletic and popular, and he's never had to chase after a woman—not until a sexy naval lieutenant crosses his path.

Natalya Vasilek grew up in a military family and never really felt as if she had a home—not until she resigned her commission and moved to Haven. Her work and volunteering (plus an adorable shepsky named Thor) keep her busy enough that she has no time—and even less interest—in romance. So why does she keep ending up in bed with Kevin Dawson?

Nat has a lot of reasons for fighting her growing feelings for her coworker and friend, not the least of which is that he's looking for the same kind of happily-ever-after that has already been stolen away from her, and that's something she can't give him.

Kevin knows it's not going to be easy to convince Nat that what he wants most is *her*, without qualification, but first, he has to convince her to go on a date with him. Thankfully, he has a plan—and a lovable mutt in his corner.

I hope you enjoy Kevin and Natalya's story—and if you want to learn more about the sale of Haven's favorite bakery, be sure to look for my next Match Made in Haven book, coming soon!

Happy Reading!

xo *Brenda*

HER FAVORITE
MISTAKE

BRENDA HARLEN

SPECIAL EDITION

Recycling programs
for this product may
not exist in your area.

ISBN-13: 978-1-335-40201-1

Her Favorite Mistake

Copyright © 2024 by Brenda Harlen

 Harlequin Enterprises ULC
22 Adelaide St. West, 41st Floor
Toronto, Ontario M5H 4E3, Canada
www.Harlequin.com

MIX
Paper | Supporting
responsible forestry
FSC® C021394

Printed in Lithuania

Brenda Harlen is a former attorney who once had the privilege of appearing before the Supreme Court of Canada. The practice of law taught her a lot about the world and reinforced her determination to become a writer—because in fiction, she could promise a happy ending! Now she is an award-winning, RITA® Award–nominated, nationally bestselling author of more than fifty titles for Harlequin. You can keep up-to-date with Brenda on Facebook and Twitter, or through her website, brendaharlen.com.

Books by Brenda Harlen

Harlequin Special Edition

Match Made in Haven

The Sheriff's Nine-Month Surprise
Her Seven-Day Fiancé
Six Weeks to Catch a Cowboy
Claiming the Cowboy's Heart
Double Duty for the Cowboy
One Night with the Cowboy
A Chance for the Rancher
The Marine's Road Home
Meet Me Under the Mistletoe
The Rancher's Promise
The Chef's Surprise Baby
Captivated by the Cowgirl
Countdown to Christmas
Her Not-So-Little Secret
The Rancher's Christmas Reunion
Snowed In with a Stranger
Her Favorite Mistake

Visit the Author Profile page
at Harlequin.com for more titles.

This book is dedicated to all service members,
with sincere appreciation.

And to Worf, who provides
(unofficial) emotional support to his family.

Prologue

July—six years ago

When Natalya Vasilek received the invitation to her coworker's wedding, her initial instinct was to RSVP with regrets. But she genuinely liked Matt Hutchinson and his fiancée, Carrie Morgan, and so she decided to put on a happy face for the blissful couple and try to forget about the fact that her own marriage had imploded not so long ago.

She suspected it wouldn't be easy, but she felt strongly that it was an important part of the healing process. A necessary step to prove—if only to herself—that she'd moved on.

And, for the most part, she'd succeeded. Throughout the day, she said and did all the right things, making no awkward steps that might have clued any of her colleagues in to the fact that the event might be just a tiny bit painful for her.

It helped that she'd decided to bring a plus-one to the event. She'd met Austin Manning, another local charter pilot, when she'd moved to Haven, Nevada, fourteen months earlier. He was interesting and fun and incredibly good-looking, and they'd spent a lot of downtime together over the past year. Early on, though, Nat had made it clear that she wasn't interested in any more than a flirtation—which might explain why her date was currently shaking and shimmying with another woman on the dance floor.

"…we could go dance."

Nat turned to Kevin Dawson, another one of her colleagues

at Adventure Village. Managing the family-friendly recreational park was a big change from flying missions for the navy, but she couldn't deny that she'd been sleeping better at night since her career change. "What did you say?"

A smile tugged at the corners of Kevin's mouth, making his already too-handsome face even more appealing. "I'm asking you to dance with me."

Warning bells clanged inside her head.

Because Kevin wasn't just a coworker, he was also a friend. And despite the almost daily reminders to herself that he was a co-worker and a friend, being around the man never failed to remind her that she was still a woman, with a woman's wants and needs.

"Where's your date?" she asked.

They'd been seated at the same table, so she knew that he'd brought one to the wedding. Of course, it seemed to her that Kevin was always with a woman—and not usually the same one on Saturday that he'd been with on Friday.

"Dancing with yours," he told her.

Her gaze shifted back to Austin and…Sydney, she remembered now.

"So why should we be left out?" Kevin said.

There were so many valid answers to that question, she didn't know that she could list them all. Even if the music and the wine made her want to feel like her old self again, if only for three and a half minutes, she knew that the smart thing to do would be to decline his invitation.

Instead, she found herself accepting his proffered hand.

Of course, by the time they joined the crowd on the dance floor, the last notes of "Shut Up and Dance" had faded away to be replaced by the opening bars of an Ed Sheeran ballad.

When Kevin drew her into his arms, her whole body started to hum with an unexpected—and unwelcome—awareness. And in that moment, Nat knew RSVPing "yes" to the wedding invitation had been a mistake.

And that she was about to make an even bigger one.

Chapter One

April—present year

"Unrequited love sucks."

Kevin Dawson looked, with a combination of amusement and exasperation, at the man sprawled on his sofa. He usually enjoyed hanging out with his brother, but over the past several weeks, every conversation with Steven managed to circle around to the pretty real estate agent who was currently the object of his infatuation.

Kevin lifted his bottle to his mouth and swallowed a mouthful of beer. "You're not in love with Thalia."

"How do you know?" Steven challenged.

"Because you've known her all of five minutes."

"I've known her five *months*," his brother said, scooping a handful of chips out of the bowl on the table between them.

"Same thing," Kevin said, his gaze fixed on the ball game playing on his seventy-seven-inch OLED TV. He'd invited a couple of buddies over to watch the game tonight, but though Jay and Matt had both expressed some envy over his new screen, they'd been busy with their families. And so Kevin was spending another night hanging out with his brother.

He didn't mind, really. Steven was smart and funny and an overall decent guy—despite the fact that he was a lawyer. He was also a huge A's fan, which meant that he didn't usually chatter too much during a game. And, true to form, he'd waited until the Padres called for relief from the bullpen before he made his proclamation about unrequited love.

Finally the batter stepped up to the plate and was retired on three pitches, ending the sixth inning.

"But I knew in the first five minutes," Steven said now, picking up their conversation again without missing a beat. "The minute my eyes locked with Thalia's, I knew."

"What did you know?" Kevin challenged. "That you'd be sitting in my living room lamenting your unrequited love five months later?"

"I knew that she was the one I was meant to be with."

"And yet here you are and she's…where?"

His brother collected the empty bottles and carried them to the kitchen, returning with two more beers. "I don't want to talk about it."

"You brought it up," Kevin felt compelled to remind him, as he twisted the cap off his bottle.

Steven sighed. "Okay, fine. She had a date with Anthony Serrano tonight," he said, naming one of the area's top-selling real estate agents. The agent who had, in fact, brokered the sale to Steven of his town house—just down the street—and then, six months later, this one to his brother.

"Please tell me you don't know this because you were eavesdropping on her conversation."

"I wasn't eavesdropping," Steven assured him. "Thalia told me about her plans."

"Now I understand," Kevin said. "And I'm sorry, bro."

His brother frowned. "What do you understand? And why are you sorry?"

"Because you're obviously in the friend zone."

"Why do you say that as if it's a bad thing?"

"Because it *is* a bad thing," he said, not without sympathy. "Because it means that she sees you as a pal or confidant—not as someone who's ever likely to see her naked."

Steven's frown deepened at that as he tipped his bottle to his mouth.

"Forget about her," Kevin advised.

"You don't think I've tried?"

"Try harder."

"You'll have to forgive me if I don't want to take advice from a guy who hasn't dated any one woman for more than three months in the past five years," his brother retorted.

"Three months is the relationship sweet spot," Kevin told him.

"Is that really the reason?" Steven mused. "Or is it that none of your recent…companions…has been able to make you forget about the one who got away?"

"No one got away," he denied.

But it was a lie.

The truth was, Kevin knew all about unrequited love.

He'd been living with it for more than five years.

After the five-hour drive from Auburn, California, following a weekend visit with her brother's family, Natalya was usually eager to get home and settle back into her own space. But despite having passed the Welcome to Haven sign more than fifteen minutes earlier, she continued to drive around town.

Mindlessly and aimlessly, while drops of rain pattered on the roof of her car and splattered against the windshield to be cleared away by the rhythmic sweep of the wipers.

Nat didn't mind wet weather—especially since she'd moved to northern Nevada, where rainy nights like this were few and far between. But she hadn't been thinking that it might rain when she'd left California, and she had neither a jacket nor an umbrella with her now.

Which was another good reason to go home.

Instead, she turned onto Juniper Street.

That's when she realized that her driving had perhaps not been as mindless or aimless as she'd believed.

But it was, nevertheless, decidedly ill-advised.

She eased up on the gas pedal as she made her way through the residential neighborhood that boasted an assortment of single-family homes and town houses. The unit numbers were inscribed on keystones above the garage doors, and the closer she got to number 55, the faster her heart started to beat.

She pulled up alongside the curb and shifted into Park.

His truck in the driveway and the light flickering through the blinds on the front window confirmed that he was home, probably watching TV.

She turned off the ignition and dropped her keys into her purse, staring at the front door.

She didn't have to wonder what would happen if she knocked on it.

She knew.

They'd done this dance before—more times than she wanted to admit.

But she wasn't at the point of no return just yet.

She could still go home.

She *should* go home.

But her house would be dark and empty, and there she'd be alone with the memories of everything she'd lost. Because as wonderful as it had been to spend the weekend with her sister-in-law and two adorable nephews, those few days had also been a reminder that all the hopes and dreams she'd once had for her future had slipped through her fingers, and she didn't want to deal with that stark reality right now.

Instead, she pushed open her door and stepped out of the car. Cool drops pelted down on her, and she tipped her head back to look up at the dark sky, letting the rain wash away any traces of the tears that she'd shed on her drive.

By the time she made her way to the front door, her wet hair was hanging in her face and her damp clothes were clinging to her body.

She pressed the button for the bell, heard the echo of its chime in the hall. Only a few seconds later, the door was pulled open and he was there.

"Natalya."

She tried to smile, but her lips trembled rather than curved. "Hi."

"Come in," he said, stepping away from the door so that she could enter. "*Jesus*, Nat—you're practically soaked through."

"It's raining."

"I can see that," he told her.

Her gaze shifted past him to the living room, where his brother was lounging on the sofa with his feet up on the coffee table.

"I didn't realize you had company," she said apologetically.

"Not company," Kevin assured her. "Steven." Then he turned his head to address his brother over his shoulder, "And he was just leaving."

"I can't leave in the middle of the eighth inning," Steven protested.

"You've got a TV at home," Kevin pointed out.

"I'm the one who should go," Nat said, feeling awkward and guilty and embarrassed.

"No." He caught her hand as she reached for the doorknob. "*You* should stay. *He* should go."

Steven obligingly rose to his feet and made his way to the foyer.

"I'm sorry I interrupted your evening," Nat said to him.

"Not a problem," he said, as he shoved his feet into the shoes he'd left by the door before picking up the jacket draped over the knob of the coat closet.

Obviously *he'd* been prepared for the weather.

Steven nodded to his brother. "See you."

"See you," Kevin agreed.

Nat toed off her shoes and left them on the mat by the door before following Kevin down the hall toward the kitchen at the rear of the house.

"Be right back," he said, and returned in short order with a thick fluffy towel.

"Thanks." She rubbed it over her head, wringing out her hair, then draped it over the shoulders of her wet shirt.

"I've got a bottle of that cabernet sauvignon you like, if you want a glass of wine first."

She quirked a brow. "First?"

He shrugged as he retrieved a bottle from the wine rack built into the granite-topped island. "We both know why you're here, don't we?"

She tightened her grip on the ends of the towel. "Am I pathetic or just predictable?"

He deftly uncorked the bottle of wine, poured a generous splash into a glass and offered it to her. "I wouldn't accuse you of being either of those things."

"Thanks," she said again. Then, "You're not having any?"

"I had a couple of beers with my brother."

"I really didn't mean to interrupt."

"You didn't interrupt anything," he assured her.

She sipped her wine, not sure what it meant that he'd had a bottle of her favorite label on his wine rack.

Or maybe it didn't mean anything.

Kevin would be the first to admit that he didn't know a lot about wine, so probably all the bottles had been recommended by friends or family—or the clerk at the local store.

She swallowed another mouthful of wine. "I should have called first."

"You never call first."

"I should," she said again. "It's rude to drop in on someone, unannounced and uninvited."

"You're always welcome here, Natalya."

She blinked back the tears that burned her eyes and brought her glass to her lips again.

He lifted a hand to tuck an errant strand of wet hair behind her ear. "I hate to see you hurting."

"I hate that you can tell when I'm hurting."

One corner of his mouth lifted in a half smile. "It's the only time you ever show up here."

She closed her eyes against the truth, the guilt. "I'm a horrible person, aren't I?"

"No." He dipped his head and brushed his lips over hers,

and her eyes opened again. "You are one of the most amazing women I've ever known."

But there was so much about her he didn't know.

So much that, even after more than six years of friendship, she hadn't told him.

Kevin could speculate—and he'd certainly done so—but he wanted to *know*. He wanted her to trust him enough to confide in him. And though there had been moments when he'd thought she was on the verge of opening up, those moments had quickly passed, and her secrets remained intact.

She set her half-empty glass of wine on the counter and lifted her hands to link them behind his head, drawing his mouth down to hers again.

There was nothing tentative or teasing about her kiss.

She was a woman who knew what she wanted, and right now, she wanted him.

She kissed him deeply, using her lips and tongue and teeth to communicate her desire. Her desperation.

When she came to him like this, their lovemaking was always a little wild. More than just a meeting and merging of their bodies, it was a clash of wants and needs. A fast-and-furious mating that hinted at desperation and recklessness.

He sometimes wondered what she was running away from. What she was trying to forget.

He'd made the mistake of asking her once—and learned his lesson when she completely shut him down.

So he told himself that it didn't matter what she was running away from, because she ran to him.

It didn't matter what she was trying to forget, because she let him help clear her mind.

"We should get you out of those wet clothes," he said, already unfastening the buttons that ran down the front of her shirt.

"Good idea," she agreed, sliding her hands beneath the hem of his T-shirt and up his torso.

"I've got another good idea," he said, lifting her into his arms and carrying her up the stairs to his bedroom.

One of these days, he might find the strength to turn Natalya away when she showed up at his door.

But today was not that day.

She was still there when Kevin woke up in the morning.

That was a bigger surprise to him than Natalya's appearance on his doorstep the night before.

Maybe it was because they'd been friends before they ever slept together that she let him pretend her late-night visits were more than booty calls. And she always hung around, at least for a little while, after they'd banged one another's brains out.

Sometimes they had another drink together and talked about any number of subjects (though never the forbidden one—which was whatever had brought her to his door). Sometimes they turned on the television in his bedroom to watch a movie. And sometimes a second (or even a third) bout of lovemaking followed the first.

But always—*always*—she was gone when he woke up in the morning.

So when Kevin opened his eyes to glance at the clock on his bedside table and realized Natalya was sleeping beside him, he was understandably surprised.

He wished he could interpret her morning presence as proof that she was starting to feel an emotional connection to him, but he knew it was more likely that she'd just been exhausted—physically and mentally—the night before.

She slept on her side, with her back to him, one hand tucked under the pillow, the other curled in a fist in front of her. The long sweep of eyelashes fluttered a little in her sleep, her lips were slightly parted, her breathing slow and even.

She wasn't a woman who played up her feminine attributes. She didn't fuss with her hair or dress in trendy clothes. If she wore makeup, it was subtle. Maybe some mascara to darken her lashes or a hint of color on her mouth that he suspected was courtesy of a tinted lip balm rather than cosmetic gloss. She rarely wore jewelry, aside from simple gold knots in her ears, and the "beachy waves" hairstyle that many women paid a fortune at a salon to achieve was natural to her.

Her shoulder-length silky tresses were splayed over the pillowcase now, the multihued flaxen color a stark contrast to his navy bedsheets. In so many ways, she was a contrast to him—the opposite of what he'd always thought he wanted.

But he knew the truth now—that she was the only woman he did want.

Unfortunately, she was as emotionally unavailable as several of his former girlfriends had accused him of being.

Those former girlfriends hadn't been wrong. Following the loss of both his parents, almost fourteen years ago, he'd put up walls around his heart. Because loving someone meant being vulnerable to hurting, and he never wanted to hurt like that again.

How Nat had managed to scale those walls—without even trying—he didn't know. And the irony of the situation wasn't lost on him.

He hadn't chosen to fall in love with her, but somehow it had happened. And he knew that if he confided his feelings to Nat, she'd be gone in the blink of an eye.

Of course, she might not manage to stay away for too long. Because it seemed that no matter how many times they agreed that their relationship wasn't going anywhere and that they should see other people (or disagreed on the same subject), they ended up finding their way back to one another again.

It was what gave him hope that she would someday realize they were meant to be together. And since he had the unexpected pleasure of awakening with her in his bed, he thought he might take advantage of the situation to make an argument in favor of his case.

He shifted a little closer and touched his lips gently to the jagged line on her forehead. She didn't stir. He trailed a hand along her side, following the curve of her hip and the indent of her waist, not pausing when he encountered any of the other scars she refused to talk about—scars he barely even noticed anymore, skimming over her ribs to cup her breast. Her nipple pebbled against his palm and a soft sigh slipped between her lips.

Her eyelids flickered, then opened slowly to reveal deep green eyes that were a little bit sleepy and a lot wary.

"Good morning."

She closed her eyes again and cursed beneath her breath.

"I'm not quite sure how to interpret that," he admitted.

"Just that it's later than I realized," she said. "And I need to be going."

"It's not yet seven, and you don't have to be at Adventure Village until noon."

"I need to go home, shower—"

"I've got a shower here."

"We don't do that, Kev," she said softly.

"Mornings after?"

She nodded.

"Just because we haven't before doesn't mean we can't start."

"Not a good idea." She started to slide out of bed.

He wrapped his arm around her and pulled her back. "You liked my ideas last night," he reminded her.

"I did," she agreed. "But I'm not interested in a morning tumble."

"You're not, huh?" He nuzzled her throat, rubbed his thumb over the peak of her nipple.

A low moan sounded in her throat—abruptly cut off as she pushed him away. "I said I'm not in the mood."

He immediately lifted his hands.

She threw an arm across her eyes and sighed. "I'm sorry."

"You don't have to apologize for not being in the mood," he told her. "I am a firm believer in 'no means no.'"

"I didn't ask you for consent last night, did I?"

"You know I'd never say *no* to you, Natalya."

"Maybe you should."

"Let's try something else instead," he suggested.

"What kind of something else?" she asked warily.

"I'm going to ask you a question, and I want you to say *yes*."

"What's the question?"

"Will you go out for dinner with me tonight?"

"We've been down that road before," she reminded him.

"Say *yes*, Natalya," he urged.

Her sigh sounded sincerely regretful. "I can't give you what you want, Kevin."

"All I want right now is for you to say *yes* to dinner."

"I work until six tonight."

"I could pick you up at seven," he offered.

"I haven't said *yes*," she reminded him.

"But you're going to."

She lifted a hand to his face, rubbing her palm gently against the stubble on his cheek. "I don't want to hurt you."

"It's just dinner."

"Is it?" she asked.

"For now," he said.

She didn't immediately reply, and he braced himself for another rejection. Not that being rejected one more time would change anything for him. When it came to his feelings for Natalya, he wasn't sure that anything could.

"Okay, then," she agreed.

Her response was so unexpected, it took him an extra second to realize that she hadn't said *no* this time.

"I want to hear *yes*," he told her.

She managed a smile. "Yes, Kevin. I will go out for dinner with you tonight."

He grinned. "I'll see you at seven."

She glanced at the Apple watch on her wrist. "It's seven now," she noted. "And I'm right here."

"So you are," he mused.

"And since I am—and since you're obviously a morning person—" she wrapped her fingers around his hard length to ensure he couldn't misinterpret her meaning "—perhaps we *should* take advantage of the fact."

He managed—barely—to hold back the groan of pleasure that emanated low in his throat.

"You said you weren't in the mood," he reminded her.

"I lied," she admitted, her gaze never wavering from his.

"I know."

Her brow lifted. "It doesn't bother you that I lie to you? Or that I use you for sex?"

"I don't think you lie to me as often as you lie to yourself," he said, reaching into the drawer of his bedside table for a condom. "And I'd rather you use me for sex than anyone else."

She plucked the square packet from his hand and tore it open. "I'm seriously messed up, Kev."

"So you keep telling me," he noted, trying to keep his voice level while she unrolled the latex over the rigid length of his erection.

"And I'm preparing myself—" she straddled his hips, positioning herself over him "—for the day that you wise up and kick me out on my ass."

"Why would I do that when it's such a nice ass?" he asked, sliding his hands around her bottom and squeezing gently.

He was surprised again—and pleased—when the combat-tested aviator's cheeks actually pinkened at the compliment.

Then she shifted her hips to take him inside her, and any thoughts of further conversation were abandoned.

Chapter Two

Nat didn't make it home that morning, either.

Because she still had her duffel bag from her weekend travels, she decided to accept Kevin's offer and make use of his shower, after all. Then she changed into a clean set of clothes and headed out to pick up coffee and a few treats on her way to visit a friend—who happened to be the wife of Natalya's boss.

"This is a nice surprise," Alyssa Channing said, when she opened the door and found Nat standing there with two large cups in a drink holder balanced on top of a bakery box from Sweet Caroline's.

"Me or the pastries?"

"Both," her friend said, taking the items from Nat as she stepped into the foyer.

"I got some of those doughnut holes that Lucy and Clara like."

"Jay took the girls to his parents' house this morning, so the doughnut holes are fair game," Alyssa said.

Nat had to laugh. "Spoken like a woman in her third trimester of pregnancy," she remarked, as she followed her friend to the kitchen where they'd shared countless cups of coffee and endless hours of conversation.

"Third trimester of my third—and last—pregnancy," Alyssa assured her, lifting a cup out of the holder. "I'm guessing the one marked 'decaf' is mine."

"You guessed right," Nat said, moving around her friend's kitchen with ease, finding dessert plates and forks and napkins and bringing them to the table where the expectant mom was perusing the offerings in the box.

"There's only one salted caramel brownie," Alyssa noted.

"It's all yours," Nat assured her, as she took a seat across from her friend and pried her own cup out of the grip of the paper holder.

Alyssa polished off half the brownie before she spoke again to say, "So tell me what's new."

Nat cut the raspberry bliss bar before transferring one half to her plate. "I slept with Kevin Dawson."

Her friend waved a hand dismissively. "That's old news."

"Last night." She peeled the lid off her cup and sipped. "And this morning."

"*New* news," Alyssa noted, her attention immediately shifting from her treat to the woman seated across the table.

"It was a mistake."

"Why do you always say that?" her friend asked.

"Because it's true," she insisted.

"And yet, it happens again and again."

Nat swallowed another mouthful of coffee. "Apparently he's my favorite mistake."

"Apparently," Alyssa agreed, sounding amused.

"He asked me to have dinner with him tonight. Like a date."

Her friend popped the last bite of brownie into her mouth. "Didn't you guys go down that road a few years ago?"

"That's exactly what I said."

"So you turned him down?" Alyssa guessed.

"Actually, I said *yes*," Nat admitted.

"Well now, *that's* an interesting turn of events," her friend mused.

"But I shouldn't have said yes." She frowned as she nibbled on her pastry. "I don't know why I did."

"Because you want to have dinner with him."

"Or maybe because going out for a meal saves me from having to cook."

"That's a possibility, too," Alyssa acknowledged with a laugh. "So where's he taking you?"

"He didn't say."

"If I was a betting woman, I'd put my money on The Home Station."

"Can we not talk about this anymore?" Nat asked. "I'm nervous enough about it already."

"You flew Super Hornets for the navy, probably without breaking a sweat, but you're nervous about having dinner with a smart, charming, attractive man?"

"I know it's crazy."

"Actually, it's kind of sweet," her friend said, helping herself to the other half of the raspberry bliss bar. "Because it proves that he matters to you."

Nat couldn't deny it was true.

Or that she had an even bigger worry: that he might already matter too much.

Kevin loved his job at Adventure Village, but it wasn't the only one he had. In addition to being an employee of and investor in Haven's family-friendly recreation park, he was an information security analyst for a handful of small companies. So after Nat was gone, he settled down at his computer to work.

He was running some remote diagnostic tests for a client when his bell rang, so he left the program running while he went to see who was at his door.

A few minutes later, he was sitting in the kitchen with Jason Channing, drinking the coffee his friend had brought from The Daily Grind—along with a couple of bear claws.

"What brings you out this way on a Monday morning?" Kevin asked.

"Early board meeting," Jay admitted, sounding none too happy about the fact.

His friend's surname might be Channing, but his mom had been a Blake, and that name was akin to royalty in Haven. The family had gotten rich mining silver and gold from the hills of Crooked Creek Ranch, and Blake Mining was now the single biggest employer in the northern Nevada town.

Over the years, Jay had worked various jobs for the family-run company, in the mines, in the lab and in the office, and he'd hated every single one. Eventually he'd left the company to start Adventure Village on two acres of dry, dusty terrain that included an old abandoned shoe factory.

At the time, his actions had caused several of the townsfolk to scratch their heads, but Carter and Matt and Kevin—Jay's three closest friends since high school—had complete faith in his plan. So much so that they'd contributed to the purchase of the undeveloped parcel of land directly behind the old factory.

As one of only three towns in the whole state where gambling was outlawed, Haven saw a steady exodus of residents to nearby cities on evenings and weekends. Adventure Village gave the residents another option, and now, in addition to keeping more of the locals at home, it drew visitors from other places, near and far.

But despite the success of AV—the moniker commonly used by those who worked at Adventure Village—Jay had yet to give up his seat on the board at Blake Mining, which necessitated his attendance at monthly meetings. And while Kevin knew that his friend didn't enjoy jumping through the required hoops of the family business, he also understood that a man with a wife and two kids—and a third on the way—would be foolish to walk away from that kind of job security. And Jason Channing was not a foolish man.

"There was a car parked out front that looked a lot like Nat's when I drove by earlier," Jay remarked now.

"It probably was hers." Kevin tore off a piece of bear claw and popped it into his mouth.

"Not any of my business," his friend admitted.

"Agreed."

"Except if it causes problems at our business."

"Has it ever?"

"No."

"So stop worrying about it."

"I wish I could," Jay said. "But you're the one who keeps telling me that you want to get over her."

"It turns out that getting over her isn't nearly as easy as I'd hoped it might be."

"Have you really tried?"

"Of course I have."

"Have you tried *not* sleeping with her?" his friend asked.

"Yeah, and let me tell you, that's a lot harder than you'd think."

Jay swallowed another mouthful of coffee. "As much as I'd like to see the two of you figure things out so that you can be together, I'm not sure that's ever going to happen."

"She stayed over last night."

"You say that as if it's significant," his friend noted.

"Because it is," Kevin confirmed. "Because it's the first time that I've woken up with her in my bed."

"You're kidding."

He shook his head. "Previously, she's always been gone before the sun comes up."

Jay frowned. "And that never bothered you?"

"Of course it bothered me." Though never enough to make him turn her away when she showed up at his door.

"And you think the fact that she finally spent a whole night in your bed is a sign that she might be ready to make a commitment?" his friend asked dubiously.

Kevin laughed, but it was without humor. "I took it as a sign that she might be ready to commit to a date."

"And did she?"

"We're having dinner tonight."

Even as he said it, he felt a niggling of doubt in his gut.

Because while Nat had, after much prodding, said *yes* to his invitation, she had a history of bailing at the last minute. It was as if she had an aversion to making—or at least keeping—plans. Almost as if she was warning him not to trust her.

But he did trust her.

Probably more than she trusted herself, and he suspected that was the real problem.

"Isn't she working tonight?" Jay asked him now.

"Only until six."

"So where are you taking her?"

"I made reservations at The Home Station."

"I guess, if you're going to be stood up, why not let it happen at the most exclusive place in town?"

Kevin frowned. "She's never stood me up before."

"You're right. She wouldn't be so rude as to leave you sitting in a restaurant, waiting for her. Instead, she'll call you later this afternoon and offer some kind of excuse that necessitates changing your plans."

Kevin hated that his friend's response so closely paralleled his own thoughts, but he was enough of an optimist—or maybe a fool—to let himself hope that Nat would prove them both wrong this time.

I should never have agreed to dinner.

That was the thought that kept circling through Nat's head as she took inventory in the stockroom.

Mondays were typically slow at Adventure Village, which meant they were the perfect time to catch up on all the little tasks that often got overlooked. And though they had a standing order for paintballs, air tanks, disposable coveralls and numerous other items that they went through on a fairly regular basis, with the summer season approaching, she wanted to ensure that they were prepared for bigger crowds and the summer camp programs they'd started running two years earlier.

Unfortunately, inventory didn't require a lot of focus, which allowed her mind to wander—and it had been recycling the same thought for most of the day.

I should never have agreed to dinner.

The problem was, when she was with Kevin, her hormones had a tendency to short-circuit her brain, impeding her ability to think clearly. And the fact that her hormones still jumped to attention whenever she was around him was another cause for concern.

They'd been sleeping together, on and off, for almost six years—shouldn't the attraction have started to wane by now?

Certainly no one else she'd dated in that same period had lingered in her thoughts after they'd gone their separate ways.

But she and Kevin never really managed to go their separate ways. Whatever else was going on in their lives, they worked together, so it was inevitable that their paths would cross. Add to that the fact that they had mutual friends, and it was rare for a day to go by that she didn't see him. So even when they were at an "off" period in their relationship, there was contact—and even the most casual contact was enough to stir her up whenever she was around him.

In any event, it wasn't the chemistry, per se, that worried her. She could handle the attraction. And she always enjoyed sex with Kevin.

What worried her was the possibility that her inability to quit their on-and-off-again relationship meant she was starting to have real feelings for Kevin. Because she'd had her heart broken once before and didn't want to go through that again.

She'd had other relationships since her breakup with Christopher, but she was always careful to keep things light and easy—and to step back if it seemed that either party was in danger of getting in too deep. The problem was, every time she took a step back with Kevin, she eventually stepped right back in again.

And as much as she never wanted to experience heartbreak again, she also didn't want to be responsible for breaking anyone else's heart. But Kevin didn't seem overly concerned about protecting his. He wore it right there on his sleeve, for everyone to see.

The bigger problem Nat had with Kevin was that, over and above the physical attraction between them, she *liked* him.

She'd felt the zing at their first meeting—and why not? The man sure was easy on the eyes, with a mouthwateringly handsome face and a body that made her own quiver.

But she'd ignored the quivering, because guys like Kevin Dawson—smart, athletic, attractive—rarely looked twice at women like her. She knew that she wasn't unattractive, but she didn't waste time fussing over her hair or putting on makeup. She was more comfortable in combat boots than high heels and the only time she looked at the labels when she was buying clothes was to ensure they were machine washable.

Over the course of the next few months following that first meeting, though, she'd started to suspect that the attraction she felt might be reciprocated. And if they hadn't worked together, she would have been happy to tangle the sheets with him until they'd both had their fill of one another. But they did work together, and that meant he was off-limits with respect to any naked extracurricular activities—not because their boss had a policy prohibiting fraternization between employees, but because she did.

So Nat occasionally went out with other men, and Kevin frequently enjoyed the company of other women. Lots of other women. Stunningly beautiful women. Which, of course, reinforced Nat's belief that he could never be interested in her.

For more than a year, that belief made it easy for her to respect the boundaries of their professional relationship.

Even if the attraction she felt whenever she was with Kevin continued to simmer beneath the surface.

And then, the night of Matt and Carrie's wedding, the attraction had boiled over.

All it had taken was one dance. A few minutes of music, their bodies barely touching, the air between them sizzling.

By the time the song ended, they both knew that their night together was only beginning.

Prior to that evening, Nat would never have believed it was possible to spend a whole night making love. Kevin showed her it was possible. And infinitely pleasurable.

When they finally managed to crawl out of bed the next morning—thoroughly sated and completely exhausted—they agreed that spending the night together had been a mistake, and one never to be repeated. Because as much fun as they'd had together, they weren't just colleagues but friends, and neither wanted to jeopardize that relationship for a tumble between the sheets—no matter how satisfying said tumble had been.

But the chemistry continued to sizzle.

Six months later, it boiled over again.

Another mistake.

Over the next few years, it was a mistake they made again and again, until finally Kevin managed to convince her that they should give dating a try.

The experiment had gone surprisingly well in the beginning, until Nat realized they had very different views of a potential future together.

And that was why she never should have said *yes* to his invitation to dinner. Because it was foolish to let herself hope they could have more than the occasional stolen night together.

The rattle of her cell phone vibrating against the metal shelf yanked her attention back to the present. After a quick glance at the screen, she connected the call. "Hey, Matt. What's up?"

"I need a favor..."

As Nat listened to her colleague explain his dilemma, she knew that she'd be happy to help.

When she finished talking to Matt, she sent a text message to Kevin.

Matt's kids are sick, so I'm stuck here until 10:00.

Then, in case the point of that message wasn't clear, she added:

Obviously dinner's not going to happen.

Kevin immediately replied:

I want a rain check.

Of course he did.

Because Kevin never gave up.

It was one of the things she loved about him—and one of the things that made her crazy.

Since she didn't want to get in a back-and-forth argument via text messages, she replied:

One can probably be arranged.

She would worry about wriggling out of *that* at a later date.

For tonight, she was just going to breathe a sigh of relief.

Except that she wasn't really relieved. She was frustrated that she couldn't let herself enjoy a relationship with a wonderful man who, for reasons she couldn't begin to fathom, seemed to want to be with her.

Because he didn't know her.

Yeah, they'd been colleagues and friends for close to seven years now—with a benefits component added for the last five-and-a-half of those—but he only knew what she'd been willing to share with him.

And while she'd let him see the scars on her body, he had no idea what kind of secrets were buried deep beneath them.

And if she had her way, he never would.

Maybe Jay was right to worry, Kevin acknowledged, as he carried a large pepperoni and mushroom pizza (Nat's favorite) out to his truck. Because while he was falling deeper and deeper, she was giving every indication of easing away.

He was ready to make plans for a life with her and she couldn't even commit to a meal. Of course, it wasn't her fault that Matt's kids were sick and he was needed at home to help take care of them.

But Kevin suspected that Nat had been more relieved than disappointed by the change of plans, and instead of taking the hint and giving her the space she obviously wanted, he was tossing aside his pride in favor of spending an hour with her.

But what good was pride, anyway?

It didn't race him to the top of the rock wall or debate the pros and cons of the Major League Baseball pitch clock. It didn't snuggle on the sofa with him to watch classic horror films on stormy nights or man the second oar in his two-seat kayak. And it certainly hadn't ever gone down on its knees in the shower while clouds of steam billowed.

So yeah, when it came to a choice between his pride and Natalya, she was going to come out on top every single time.

Chapter Three

Natalya glanced up when the bell over the door chimed, her eyes widening in surprise. "Kevin."

He gestured with the flat box in his hand. "Since you couldn't go out for dinner tonight, I decided to bring dinner to you."

"You didn't have to do that," she protested.

"I wanted to," he assured her.

"Well, thank you," she said.

"You haven't eaten already, have you?" he asked, wondering if that might be the reason she wasn't quite meeting his gaze.

"Only if you count Cheetos and Diet Coke from the vending machine."

He grimaced. "I don't."

"Then I haven't eaten."

He set the pizza box on the counter and made his way to the adjacent party room, returning with paper plates and napkins, a can of Coke for himself and another Diet for her.

"So how many showed up tonight?" he asked, referring to the usual group of Monday night climbers.

"Six."

"Hardly seems worthwhile to stay open late for six climbers."

"But sometimes there are twice that number. And if we weren't open, they'd find somewhere else to go, and we don't want them going somewhere else."

"True," he said.

"And I don't mind nights like this every now and again," she said. "Especially as there won't be *any* nights like this once summer hits."

"Also true."

She wiped her fingers on a paper napkin. "Anyway, I really appreciate the pizza."

"Man—or woman—cannot live on Cheetos and Diet Coke alone."

She toasted that statement with her soda can.

"But just to be clear," he continued, "I still want a rain check."

She folded her paper plate around the discarded napkin and dropped it into the trash can beneath the counter. "Doesn't this count as having dinner together?"

He shook his head. "I asked you to go out for dinner with me. We aren't out."

"We aren't at either of our respective homes," she noted.

"This doesn't count," he said.

She shrugged. "Well, I got Jo's pizza, so I'm not complaining."

"I'm not complaining, either," he assured her. "I'm just serving notice that I want a real date."

"Notice served."

"So how about Friday night?"

She opened the calendar app on her phone. "I'm working."

"Not here."

"No. I've got a flight. Winnemucca to Portland."

"Saturday?" he suggested as an alternative.

"You're working Saturday," she reminded him.

"Right," he acknowledged.

Usually the schedule was set so that each of Jay, Matt, Kevin and Nat only had to work one Saturday a month, but with Alyssa nearing the end of her pregnancy, Jay had asked his friends to cover Saturdays so he could spend some extra time with his wife before their lives were upended by the arrival of baby number three.

"But only until six," he pointed out.

"Why don't we play it by ear?"

"We can do that," he agreed.

"Anyway, thanks again for the pizza."

"Are you nudging me along?"

"Well, I didn't figure you planned on spending the rest of your night here."

"Not the rest of the night," he said. "Just until you close."

She looked amused. "Because you think I need a big, strong man to protect me in the dark?"

"No, because *I* need a sexy naval lieutenant to protect *me*."

She chuckled softly. "*Former* naval lieutenant."

"Still sexy," he said, wondering if he only imagined a hint of tension in her laughter—and if it linked back to her unwillingness to talk about her military career.

So he hung out with her, helped her inspect the climbing equipment that was returned before it was put back into inventory, wiped down the video game cabinets, gathered abandoned cups and discarded candy wrappers.

"Look what I found," Nat said, opening her palm to reveal half a dozen game tokens.

"What are you going to do with those?"

"Use them to regain my rightful spot at the top of the *Tetris* leaderboard."

"Who took your spot?" he asked, surprised to learn that she'd been toppled.

"ACC1992," she grumbled.

"Alyssa," he realized.

"She has to cheat. There's no way she could get a score that high without cheating."

"You mean there's no way she could beat *you* without cheating."

"That was *my* game," she reminded him. "I let her have *Frogger* and *Donkey Kong* and even *Pac-Man*. But *Tetris* was mine."

"Save your tokens for another day," he advised. "It's late."

She nodded and dropped the tokens in her pocket. "Thanks for your help tonight. And your company."

"It was my pleasure."

"But don't think I'm going to reciprocate by hanging out with you when you're stuck here Saturday night," she said.

He shrugged. "Then I guess I'll just have to buy a bucket of tokens and work on getting the top score in *Tetris*."

Nat tossed her hair over her shoulder. "You only wish you could."

Jake Kelly knew he was a lucky man.

He hadn't always thought so. In fact, he'd been wrestling with some pretty serious demons only four years earlier when Sky Gilmore walked into his life.

Or maybe it would be more accurate to say that he walked into hers.

Either way, meeting the woman who was now his wife had changed everything for him.

Prior to that, he'd never imagined himself as a husband or a father. He wouldn't have dared.

Now he was both.

Because wanting to be the man that Sky deserved had been his incentive to finally get the help he needed.

Though the truth was, he would never have been ready to fall in love with Sky if he hadn't met Natalya Vasilek first.

Like him, Nat had been a relative newcomer to Haven at the time. Unlike him, she'd made an effort to meet people and get involved in the community. Most notably, she'd joined—and eventually taken on the role of facilitator for—a veterans support group.

Jake had sat quietly through the meetings for a few months, but Nat never pushed him to open up. It wasn't her style to demand but rather invite participation. And there were plenty of others who wanted to share—and many who needed to do so. He'd come to understand that it was all part of the healing process, and that the process was different for each of the men and women who sat in the hard plastic chairs of Meeting Room 4 in the basement of the Haven Community Center on Wednesday nights.

Actually, it was the David M. Hastings Room now. That had been Nat's doing, too. She'd petitioned the town council to name the room in honor of the World War II vet who'd been a fixture at the meetings before he'd passed away the previous summer, days after his one hundredth birthday.

She was a tireless advocate for the causes near and dear to her heart; she was also a tried-and-true friend, and the one who knew him better than anyone, aside from maybe his wife. And it frustrated him that she could so clearly see when others were hurting and yet continue to ignore her own pain.

He didn't know all the details of her past. He did know that she'd been recovering from serious injuries suffered when engine failure forced her to eject from the F-18 she was flying during a RIMPAC training exercise when her husband decided it was a good time to file for divorce. And if Jake ever had an opportunity to meet the man, he'd happily beat the crap out of him—though he knew Nat wouldn't thank him for it.

In any event, she seemed to have moved on from her military career and her marriage. And she'd also introduced him to Connie—a friend who'd been planning to relocate to Nevada four years earlier. Connie trained emotional support animals under the PAWS banner (Pets Assisting Wounded Servicemembers) and had been looking to rent a property that would allow her to continue doing so. As Jake had the ranch he'd inherited from his uncle, Nat thought he might be interested in coming to an arrangement with her friend. Though most of Ross Ferguson's land was committed to a lease agreement with the Circle G—owned and operated by his wife's family—Jake still had a fair piece of property at his disposal, including an old barn that his uncle had used as a workshop where he made custom wood furniture.

That barn now housed more than a dozen kennels, a supply room, grooming area and office. And while Connie could usually be found at the ranch between 8:00 a.m. and noon Monday through Friday, somehow, while she'd been training the animals, she'd also been training Jake to manage the dogs and the facility in her absence.

But who wouldn't enjoy working with eager young pups?

Certainly Nat did, because despite working part-time as a charter pilot and full-time at Adventure Village, she still managed to put in a few hours at PAWS at least three days a week.

But Wednesday wasn't one of her usual days.

"I didn't expect to see you today," he remarked, when he walked into the barn and found her grooming Thor. The ten-month-old pup was a German shepherd and Siberian husky cross who'd been at PAWS for almost four months—which was already four weeks longer than any of Connie's trainees usually stayed. He'd also been in love with Nat since the day he arrived. In fact, Connie had remarked—not entirely jokingly—that she worried she might not be able to find a suitable placement for the shepsky, because he seemed to have decided that Nat was his person.

"I had some time, so I thought I'd spend it here," she said, as she continued to drag the brush through the dog's thick fur.

Thor gloried in her attention, as he always did.

Nat was a little less obvious about her affection for the dog.

Of course, for as long as Jake had known her, she'd been resistant to letting anyone get too close—a rule that apparently applied to canines as much as humans.

But unlike most humans, Thor wasn't easily rebuffed.

The dog loved her unconditionally, despite her determined unwillingness to love him back.

Nat looked up again, a smile—perhaps a little wistful—tugging at the corners of her mouth. "That looks good on you," she remarked.

Jake glanced at the baby carrier strapped to his chest and his daughter tucked contentedly inside. "It feels good," he said. "Which surprises me every single day."

"Where's Sky?"

"She had an appointment at the women's shelter." His wife, not unlike Nat, was dedicated to her causes, and the nearby woman's shelter had always been at the top of her list.

Nat finished brushing the dog and offered him a treat from her pocket.

"Okay," she said, after he'd gobbled his snack—the cue for him to scamper off to play with his friends.

Thor didn't move from her side, though his tail thumped against the ground.

"When are you going to put him out of his misery and take him home with you?" Jake asked her.

"You know I can't have pets in my apartment," Nat reminded him.

"Thor isn't a pet—he's an emotional support animal."

"I don't have a doctor's note saying that I need an ESA."

"You could get one easily enough."

"Which would require admitting to a professional that I'm not nearly as together as I want everyone to believe."

"There's no shame in acknowledging that you need help," Jake reminded her. "You're the one who taught me that."

"What's the old saying? Those who can, do, and those who can't, teach."

"Another option would be to find a new apartment," he said.

"Some place that isn't a tiny box filled with generic furniture in various shades of beige."

"When I moved here, I didn't have any stuff of my own," she reminded him.

"And you still don't."

"Because there's no point in buying new furniture when the apartment I live in is already furnished."

"That's a circular—and ridiculous—argument."

"It's also a valid one," she insisted.

Jake shook his head. "How long have you lived in Haven?"

"Almost seven years."

"Don't you think it's time to stop pretending that this is only a temporary posting?"

"I'm not pretending anything," she denied. "I just haven't decided if this is where I want to be for the long term."

"Well, you might want to print up some change-of-address cards, because clearly you're living in Denial."

"Ha ha."

"I didn't plan on staying here, either," Jake reminded her. "It was just supposed to be a temporary respite."

"A haven?" she suggested, with a wry grin.

He shrugged. "It certainly turned out to be."

"I'm glad."

"It could be for you, too, Nat."

"I guess we'll see."

"I know a placation when I hear it," he told her.

"Then you're more astute than most of the men I know," she responded lightly.

"Most men? Or one specific man?"

She glanced at her watch. "I need to be going."

Jake looked pointedly at the dog that remained sitting by her side.

"Go," she told Thor.

The shepsky looked up at her, his head tilted to one side, as if she was speaking a language he didn't understand.

"Go," she said again, frustration and impatience evident in her tone.

Thor whined low in his throat.

Nat shifted her attention to Jake again. "If I did want a dog—and I don't—I'd look for one that obeyed basic commands."

"Maybe he understands that what you say isn't the same as what you want."

"What I want is to not be late for work."

"When are you going to realize that making him stay here doesn't mean he's not your dog?" Jake pressed.

"Connie will find a good home for him," she said confidently.

"She's found two already," Jake told her. "Two different people who wanted to take him. Thor refused to engage with either of them."

"Third time's the charm," she said lightly.

"For Thor, you're the charm," Jake said.

Nat wished she could believe it was true. She wished she could take Thor home with her and know that he was as hers as much as she was already his—because she'd fallen for the silly mutt the first time she'd met him. The pup who was given up by his family because he was too much work seemed like a kindred spirit to the former naval lieutenant who'd been abandoned by her husband for the same reason.

And if she took Thor home, she'd never have to be alone again. Unfortunately, Nat wasn't in any position to keep the dog, and she doubted very much that changing her place of residence would solve any of her problems.

And anyway, she'd gotten used to being alone. Most of the time, she even managed to convince herself that she preferred it that way.

So all she said was, "Goodbye, Jake."

Then she patted Thor's head one last time and walked away, refusing to look back.

"How do you feel about a bachelor party on Saturday?" Jay asked, setting a pitcher of beer and a trio of glass mugs on the table at which Kevin was already seated.

"Who's getting married?"

"Not likely anyone you know."

"Then why would I care about the bachelor party?" Kevin asked his friend.

"Because the best man wants to have it at Adventure Village."

"Wants to have what at Adventure Village?" Matt asked, settling into an empty seat at the table. "And when?"

"A bachelor party," Kevin said, as Jay filled the mugs. "Saturday. And I'm not sure a bachelor party fits with our family-friendly image."

"It wouldn't be the first one we've had there," Jay pointed out, as he passed the mugs around the table.

"The first one was Matt's and the second one was yours," Kevin noted.

Jay nodded in acknowledgment of the point.

"And anyway, isn't Nat the one you should ask?" Matt said. "Doesn't she usually handle those kinds of group events?"

"She already said she wasn't going to touch it," Jay admitted. "Because she's got a team party the next morning. Fifteen minor hockey players, their coaches, parents and siblings."

"Or maybe she said *no* because she knows that putting guns—even the nonlethal kind—in the hands of drunk guys is a recipe for disaster," Kevin suggested.

"They promised there would be no drinking beforehand," Jay said.

"And after?" Kevin prompted. "We're not licensed to sell—or serve—alcohol on the premises."

"The best man has been so advised," Jay assured them.

"Who plans a bachelor party three days before the event?" Matt wondered aloud.

"A best man who's told, four days before the event, that the groom who'd previously insisted he didn't want a bachelor party suddenly wanted to do something fun with his friends."

"Isn't 'something fun' usually code for strippers?"

"Not when the best man is the brother of the bride-to-be."

"How many people are expected to attend this bachelor party?" Kevin asked.

"The groom and ten of his closest friends."

"Just paintball?"

"Laser tag, go-karts and paintball. I calculated what we'd usually charge and doubled it—the best man didn't blink. But I did tell him that I had to run it past my partners to ensure we'd have staff available. Sumera is available as field referee, but I need someone else at the front."

"In that case, and to answer your initial question, I have no objection to the event," Kevin said.

"Can you cover it?" Matt asked. "Because Saturday is Carrie's birthday."

Kevin narrowed his gaze. "I'm already working the day shift on Saturday. And didn't you get out of an evening shift just a few weeks ago because it was Carrie's birthday?"

"Carrie's *mom's* birthday," his friend clarified. "And if you've met my mother-in-law—and I know you have, because you were at the wedding—you'd understand why I wouldn't dare miss the occasion."

"I'll give you that," Kevin agreed, shuddering at the memory of his brief interactions with the woman who barked orders at anyone in her vicinity like a military general.

"And yes, I can cover the bachelor party," he decided. Because although he'd suggested Saturday evening as a potential date night to Nat, she'd been noncommittal, and he knew she wouldn't want him to turn down an event at AV for a dinner that she'd argue could happen anytime, even if he was increasingly doubtful that it ever would.

"Great, I'll get in touch with the best man tomorrow and let him know it's a go," Jay said. "Right now, I'm going to order some wings."

"Get potato skins, too," Matt said.

"I'm a little surprised to see you tonight," Kevin remarked to Matt, when Jay had gone to the bar to place their food order.

"Why's that?"

"I figured you'd be home with your wife and sick kids."

"How'd you know the kids were sick?"

"Nat told me she had to cover your shift Monday night because they had some kind of flu bug."

"Thankfully it was just a twenty-four-hour thing. And she didn't *have to* cover my shift," Matt said, a little defensively. "She offered."

Kevin swallowed a mouthful of beer. "Did she?"

"I only asked her to stay an extra half hour so that I could run to the pharmacy to pick up the prescription the doctor called in. It was Nat who suggested that my wife would probably appreciate it if I didn't leave her home alone with two sick kids."

"Nat's thoughtful that way," Kevin noted. And it was true—though not, he suspected, the only reason that she'd offered to cover her coworker's shift.

"And she was right. Carrie was very grateful."

"I'm sure."

Matt's gaze narrowed. "Did you have plans with Nat on Monday?"

"Nothing important."

"So...you guys are on again?"

"I don't know what we are," Kevin admitted.

"Well, for what it's worth, I'm sorry I mucked things up for you. Believe me, I would have preferred to be doling out climbing equipment than cleaning vomit off the bathroom floor, but that's life sometimes."

"Or at least life when you have kids."

"Your day will come," his friend warned.

"Maybe," Kevin said, deliberately noncommittal.

Because as much as he'd come to realize that he wanted the whole package of wife and kids someday, just like his friends had, what he really wanted was Nat—and he knew better than to take anything for granted where she was concerned.

Chapter Four

Nat never worked late on Wednesdays.

Not even in the summer months, when Adventure Village had extended hours, because on Wednesday nights, she was at the community center for the weekly veterans support group.

Her presence wasn't actually required at the meetings. Like anyone else, she could choose to attend or not from week to week. But she was the one who'd signed the rental agreement with the community center, who showed up early to set up the chairs and make the coffee. She was also the one who stopped at Sweet Caroline's to pick up a box of treats before each meeting.

Caroline—the namesake and daughter of the original owner of the bakery—had been incredibly generous to the group. After several weeks of Nat showing up on Wednesday afternoons to buy a selection of goodies, Caroline had asked where she was taking them. When Nat told her about the meetings, the proprietor had offered to donate a box of whatever pastries were left over at the end of the day.

Of course, "left over" meant that there were never going to be chocolate peanut butter banana croissants in the box—because whenever Caroline made those, they were snapped up within the first few hours of the bakery opening—but there was usually a pretty good selection. And after Nat had remarked that one of the regular attendees at the meetings loved Sweet Caroline's pecan tarts, there were always at least two of those in the box.

Nat wondered now what would happen when Sweet Caroline's was sold—because while Caroline remained tight-lipped, rumors were rampant around town that she was looking to sell the bakery. So far, those rumors were scarce on details—such as the identity of a potential buyer, a closing date and the purchaser's plans for the property.

Nat couldn't imagine anything but a bakery in the space. Sure, The Daily Grind had good coffee and a decent selection of doughnuts, but where would the residents of Haven get their Christmas cookies and birthday cakes if the new owner had another plan for the property?

Still, it wasn't a concern that would keep her up at night. The only thing that mattered to Nat was that the men and women who'd served their country had a place to connect one another and share their stories—if they wanted. Being able to offer them treats from the best bakery in northern Nevada was just icing on the cake.

It was a fairly small group of veterans who met and membership in the group was fluid. Only about half a dozen were in regular attendance—including Dirk and Leon, old buddies and army-navy rivals who argued about everything and especially football. They were usually some of the first to arrive for the meetings, to ensure they got first choice of goodies from Sweet Caroline's. A handful of others attended on a less regular but consistent schedule, and a few more dropped in a couple of times a year.

Still, Nat recognized them all. Which was how she knew that the woman with sharp blue eyes and short auburn hair hovering in the doorway was a first-timer.

"Hi." Nat offered a bright smile and a hand. "I'm Natalya."

The woman ignored her overture, keeping her hands stuffed deep in the pockets of her cargo pants. "Am I in the right place?"

"You are if you're looking for Veterans Supporting Veterans."

She responded with a short nod.

Nat tried not to take the woman's attitude personally. It was normal for newcomers to be reticent. For some, their first meeting was also their last, and that was okay, too. She'd been part of the group long enough to know that everyone's healing process was different; there wasn't a one-size-fits-all approach to dealing with the various traumas that each service member had endured.

"I don't know that I'm going to stay," the woman said now.

"That's your choice, of course," Nat assured her. "I hope you'll give us a chance, but if you decide you don't want to stick around tonight—for whatever reason—I hope you'll come back another time. We're here every Wednesday night."

"Yeah, I just don't think—"

"Raelynn!" Whatever else the woman intended to say was cut off by Jake Kelly's greeting. "I'm so glad that you made it."

The woman—Raelynn, apparently—turned to Jake, the deep furrow in her brow immediately smoothing, the tight set of her mouth softening.

"I told you I'd be here," she said. "But—"

"The coffee here isn't anything special," Jake said to Raelynn, winking at Nat. "But the contents of that bakery box will make you happy to stick around. Guaranteed."

Nat had to give him credit—within a few minutes, Jake had the reticent Raelynn sitting down with a cup of coffee in one hand and a glossy cruller in the other.

Several more people trickled in over the next half hour, and at seven thirty, Nat signaled Jake to address the group. She was usually the one who got things started, offering the standard welcome and inviting the members of the peer-led group to introduce topics of discussion, but she thought that Jake's new friend might be more comfortable if he took the lead.

As he did, she looked around the room, pleased to see that there was a decent turnout tonight. Nine men and three women and, aside from Raelynn, all were familiar faces. Most she recognized not just from the meetings but because she'd seen them around town, but there were a few—Darius, Shelby and Luka—who came to Haven from surrounding areas, either because there wasn't a similar group within their own community or it didn't offer them what they wanted.

Listening to Jake, she couldn't help but think about how fortunate she'd been to discover this group within the first few months of her move to Haven.

She'd gone into the navy right after her graduation from college, eager to serve her country. Her original plan had been to join the Marine Corps, following in the footsteps of her father and her brother before her. But at the time she was ready to enlist, there were still restrictions in effect that prevented women from fulfilling certain combat roles, so she'd opted to fly jets for the navy instead.

And it had been everything she'd always dreamed—until her dreams went up in smoke along with her F-18.

She'd recovered from the crash, but she'd resigned her commission. And though she'd had reasons—valid reasons—there were still times when she felt as if she'd let everyone down. Her family, her squadron and especially herself.

One of the reasons these Wednesday-night meetings meant so much to her was that they helped her feel as if she was doing something of service to her country again. And recently they'd performed the additional function of keeping her thoughts directed away from Kevin Dawson—at least for a few hours.

Nat spent enough time at Adventure Village when she was working that she usually stayed away on her day off, but she knew Kevin was working Saturday, tonight, and she wanted to make things up to him. Because she'd blown off his invitation to dinner and he'd brought dinner to her, anyway.

Of course, that was before he knew that she'd blown him

off. But even when he'd found out—courtesy of Matt's big mouth—he hadn't been mad.

Perhaps a little hurt, but not mad.

She would have preferred mad.

She hated knowing that she'd hurt him.

Hated that he'd given her the power to do so.

So even though she'd told Jay she had no intention of going anywhere near the bachelor party, and told Kevin that she wasn't going to keep him company on Saturday night, she found herself picking up pizza from Jo's (sausage and hot peppers— *his* favorite) and taking it to the park.

He wasn't at the desk when she arrived, so she set the pizza box on the counter and was heading to the party room to get drinks when the door over the bell tinkled.

She glanced up, a ready smile on her face for the customer.

"We need more paint." The man was dressed from head to toe in camouflage gear, with a bandanna covering the lower half of his face and protective goggles over his eyes, but there was something familiar about his voice that sent a shiver of unease snaking up her spine.

"How much paint?" she asked.

"You better give us another case."

She pulled a cardboard box from the shelf and set it on the counter.

As she did so, the man lifted his goggles onto his head to see her more clearly. "Natalya?"

She frowned, pretending not to know him.

But now that she could see his eyes, there wasn't a doubt in her mind.

Still, she hoped he'd let her feign ignorance and get back to his party as soon as possible.

"It's me, Cameron," he said, flashing a grin that was achingly familiar notwithstanding the grease paint smeared on his face.

"Cameron. Wow."

"Wow is right," he said. "I haven't seen you in…forever."

"It's been a long time," she agreed.

"So what the heck are you doing here?" he asked.

"I work here," she said, because her presence behind the counter apparently wasn't an obvious enough answer to his question.

"You're kidding."

"I'm not," she assured him.

He looked around the shop.

She followed his gaze, attempting to see the business that she'd helped build through his eyes. Maybe it didn't look like much to him, but it had been a lifeline to her when she most needed it, and she would forever be grateful to Jason Channing for not only the job but especially for inviting her into his group of friends.

"I heard you'd made a career change, but I didn't expect something this drastic," Cameron said now.

"Isn't *different* part of the definition of *change*?"

"I guess," he said dubiously.

"So what brings you to the desert?"

"Bachelor party."

"Yours?"

"Nah." He shook his head. "I tied the knot three years ago. Got one kid already and another on the way."

"Congratulations," she said sincerely.

Awareness flickered in his gaze, quickly chased away by remorse.

"Anyway." He cleared his throat. "The groom's my roommate from college. He moved back to Elko after graduation, proposed to his high school sweetheart and dragged all of us here to celebrate his imminent loss of freedom."

"By shooting at each other?"

He grinned. "Which we've been doing with much enthusiasm, hence the need for more paint."

"I'll add the extra case to your bill," she said, opening the file on the computer to do just that as she silently urged him to move along.

"Thanks," he said, but continued to linger. "So how'd you end up in the Middle-of-Nowhere, Nevada?"

"I decided a change of venue was in order along with a change of career."

"I guess I can understand that," he said, sympathy in his familiar blue eyes.

She didn't want his sympathy.

She didn't need him—or anyone else—to feel sorry for her.

She was doing just fine, thank you very much.

Except that right now, she wasn't feeling just fine.

She was feeling a little unsteady.

Her own fault, for letting down her guard. For trusting that this town could live up to its name and be a haven for her, too.

The bell over the door jangled again, and another man—dressed very much like Cameron—poked his head into the room.

"Dude," he said impatiently. "We're waiting on the paint."

Cameron lifted the box onto his shoulder. "I've got it right here."

"Well, we need it on the field."

"On my way," he promised.

"Have fun," Nat said.

Cameron hesitated half a beat, then nodded. "It was good to see you, Natalya."

She forced a smile. "You, too."

And finally breathed a sigh of relief when the door closed at his back.

Kevin had stepped away from the counter for five minutes—okay, it might have been closer to ten, because after he'd found the Tippmann pistol in the storeroom that Jay had called to ask about (ordered, at his wife's request, as a birthday gift for her nephew and mistakenly logged into inventory), Jay's four-and-a-half-year-old daughter had insisted on talking to "Unca Kevin"—and in that time Natalya had been and gone.

He knew she'd been there because he'd spotted her car through the window in Jay's office when he'd been putting the paintball gun in his friend's desk. She drove into the lot while he was being regaled by Lucy's story about a classmate who barfed all over the hopscotch grid at recess the previous day, and he'd watched Nat get out of the car—with a pizza box in hand—as Lucy described the various colors and shapes of her friend's ejecta, apparently all the more interesting because they'd had hot dogs for lunch at school that day.

Jay eventually managed to pry the phone away from his daughter again and end the call, and Kevin was smiling as he locked the office. But by the time he made his way back to what was referred to as the headquarters of the customer zone, there was no one there.

The pizza box he'd seen Nat carrying was behind the counter, and while he appreciated the quid pro quo, he was puzzled by her disappearing act.

The bachelor party emptied their third case of paint a short while later, and though there was a family of six about halfway through the eighteen-hole mini golf course and a group of teenagers lingering in the arcade, they were all regulars at AV, so Kevin didn't have any concerns about leaving Graeme—a recent hire—to lock up when everyone was gone.

It wasn't as late as he'd suspected it might be when he headed out, so he carried the leftover pizza to his truck and drove to Nat's apartment building.

Haven was generally a picturesque town, with some really nice places to live. And aside from the ultra-exclusive north end of town, where his brother had been nosing around in the company of his secret-crush-slash-real-estate-agent, it was predominantly affordable.

When Nat had been looking for a place, she hadn't seemed too worried about location or even aesthetics as much as finding something furnished, so that she wouldn't have to haul all her stuff from California to Nevada. She'd decided that The Square on Crescent (named for the shape of the building and the name of the street it fronted) met her needs.

Strictly speaking, there wasn't anything wrong with the apartment building in which she lived—but there was nothing unique about it, either. A traditional box shape, three stories high with six apartments on each floor, an elevator at the west end and stairs at the east.

Regina Tocchet, the building manager, had a unit on the ground floor, and the slatted blinds that covered her windows were almost always open so that she could see anyone entering or exiting the building. She was a self-proclaimed one-woman neighborhood watch—with all the sweetness of a Sour Patch Kid.

Tonight, he pulled into one of the two designated visitor parking spots just as Mrs. Tocchet was exiting her vehicle, parked in the "reserved spot" closest to the main entrance.

But Kevin knew how to play the game, and he smiled warmly as he approached. "Good evening, Mrs. Tocchet."

"Do you think so?" she asked, demonstrating her talent to argue about even the most uncontroversial topics.

"I do," he said. "The temperature is seasonal and the stars are bright in the sky."

She tilted her head to peer into the darkness, as if she'd never really noticed the stars before. Then, "It's a little late for a social call, isn't it?"

He didn't owe her any explanations, but he maintained his pleasant demeanor and replied, "Nat left her pizza at the park earlier today, so I thought I'd bring it by."

"Hmph," Mrs. Tocchet said, clearly seeing the box as nothing more than a ruse to get into the building.

He ducked into the lobby right behind her, before she could close the door in his face.

"Building rules require all visitors to be buzzed in, Mr. Dawson."

"Obviously you know who I am," he pointed out reasonably. "Just as you know that I'm a friend of Natalya's."

"I don't know that she's expecting you tonight."

"I'm not going to stay long," he promised.

"Hmph," she said again. "Natalya wouldn't let you. She's a good girl. Doesn't have different men spending the night all the time, unlike another tenant on the third floor—who shall remain nameless."

He considered shocking the prim Mrs. Tocchet by telling her that Nat didn't allow overnight visitors because she didn't want to deal with awkward morning-after conversations. It was the reason he knew that she preferred to have sex at his place—so she could sneak out in the middle of the night.

But, of course, all he said was, "Have a good night, Mrs. Tocchet."

"Make sure the latch on the door catches when you leave."

"I will," he promised.

"Did you get a new job as a delivery person for Jo's?" Nat asked, when she opened the door and saw him standing there with a pizza box in hand.

"Funny, that's what I was going to ask you when you dropped this off at the park earlier," he said.

"How'd you know it was me?"

"I was on the phone with Lucy when I saw your car pull into the lot."

"Jay and Alyssa's Lucy?"

"Aka Chatterbox," he confirmed, invoking the nickname his friend had bestowed upon his young daughter.

Nat managed a smile, but it didn't quite reach her eyes. "That girl does like to talk, doesn't she?"

He nodded. "And by the time I got off the phone—after

hearing her very detailed description of a classmate's vomit—
you were gone."

"I'm sorry I missed you, but I'm glad you got the pizza."

Kevin had never been accused of being particularly intuitive, but he could tell that something had happened to upset Nat. She was going through the motions—saying and doing all the right things—but her voice lacked its usual warmth, her eyes their familiar sparkle.

"So where did you rush off to that you couldn't hang around long enough to have a slice of pizza with me?" he asked, determined to get to the bottom of whatever was bothering her.

"I didn't rush off," she denied, not meeting his gaze. "I just had things to do…here."

He looked around her apartment, noting that everything was in its place, as per usual. What was unusual was the wine-glass on the table and a half-empty bottle beside it.

Of course he knew that she enjoyed a glass of wine every now and then, but he'd never known her to drink alone.

"You got another glass?" he asked, nodding toward the setup.

"Sure." She made her way to the kitchen and returned with a second glass, poured some wine into it.

"Thanks," he said, accepting the proffered drink.

She lifted her own glass and swallowed the last mouthful, then immediately refilled it.

The only time he'd ever seen her drink more than two glasses of wine was at Matt and Carrie's wedding, but that had been a celebration.

He didn't think she was in a celebratory mood tonight.

"Did something happen when you were at the park?" he asked cautiously.

"No." She shook her head. "Not really."

"What do you mean—*not really*?" he pressed.

"It was nothing," she decided.

"*What* was nothing?"

"It was my own fault," she said, contradicting her earlier claim that it was nothing. "I let my guard down and I was… blindsided."

"Blindsided by *what*?" he asked again.

"All that talk with Jake about this place being a haven for him… I think I started to believe it could be the same for me. Started to believe I could build a life and be happy here."

"Honey." He took the glass from her hand and set it on the table so that he could hold on to both of her hands. "Tell me what happened."

"Nothing really," she said. "I overreacted."

"Overreacted to *what*?"

"Seeing Cameron."

He tamped down on the jealousy that flared at her casual mention of another man's name. "Is he someone you were in the navy with?" he asked, certain he'd never heard her mention him before.

She shook her head. "I knew Cameron even before then."

"An ex?" he guessed, since she continued to be stingy with details.

"Of sorts."

"Of *what* sort?" he prompted.

Her gaze briefly lifted to meet his before dropping away again. "Cameron was my ex-brother-in-law."

Ex-brother-in-law?

"Your sister's ex-husband?" he guessed, though he was pretty sure she didn't have a sister. Just a brother, a marine, who'd died several years back.

"I don't have a sister," she said, confirming his suspicion. "Just a sister-in-law."

Which meant that—

"Cameron is my ex-husband's brother."

Kevin was certain he would have been less stunned if she'd hit him over the head with the wine bottle.

"You were *married*?"

Chapter Five

Nat frowned at the surprise in Kevin's voice. "You didn't know?"

"No, I didn't know," he assured her.

"Well, it was a long time ago," she said dismissively. "The divorce was final before I moved to Haven."

"Still—you'd think the fact that you'd been married might have come up in conversation at some point in time," he pointed out to her.

He was right, of course.

But it wasn't as if she'd consciously kept her failed marriage a secret. At least, she didn't think so.

"It's not something I like to talk about," she told him.

He hesitated a beat before he asked, "Because you're still in love with your ex-husband?"

Nat immediately shook her head. "No."

Definitely not.

"Then why?" he pressed.

"Because I don't like to fail," she admitted. "And obviously my marriage was a failure."

"I hardly think you're solely responsible for that," Kevin said.

"Christopher would argue differently."

"Clearly Christopher is an idiot."

She managed a smile, grateful for his unequivocal support. "You don't even know him."

"I don't have to know him to know that he was an idiot for letting you go."

"Maybe I didn't want to stay," she said lightly.

"Is that what happened?" Kevin asked.

Definitely not.

Instead of answering his question, she said, "I think you're forgetting the part where I said I don't like to talk about this."

"I'm not," he denied. "I just can't believe I've known you for almost seven years but never knew that you'd been married."

"Not just old news, but not very interesting news," she assured him.

"Still, you'd think it's the kind of news that you'd share with someone you're involved with."

She reached for her glass of wine again. "We're not involved."

"Obviously we have different opinions on the subject."

"Occasional sex is hardly the foundation of a relationship."

"I agree."

His unexpected acquiescence made her narrow her gaze.

"So…how long were you married?" Kevin asked her now.

Nat didn't know whether to be grateful or annoyed that he'd so willingly abandoned the topic of their present…*arrangement*, she decided, for lack of a better term, in favor of her romantic history.

"Three months," she said. "Well, technically, four years and three months. But for most of that time, I was deployed, so we actually only lived together as husband and wife for about three months."

"I guess that kind of separation can take a toll on a marriage," he noted.

"It can," she agreed. "Though not nearly as much as sleeping with another woman."

Kevin's brows lifted. "You or him?"

She rolled her eyes. *"Him."*

"Which substantiates my earlier assessment that your ex-husband is an idiot."

"I hope you don't expect me to disagree with that."

"I don't," he confirmed. "But I do wonder why, if you no longer harbor any feelings for your ex, you were so unnerved to see your former brother-in-law today."

"It was probably just the shock of him being *here*," she admitted. "Whenever I go back to California, I brace myself for the possibility that I might run into my ex or his new wife or his sister—who used to be my best friend. But it never occurred to me that I might cross paths with any of them in Haven."

"I guess I can understand that," he said.

"It just caught me off guard. And brought back a lot of... difficult...memories. I thought I'd put it all behind me, but—" she shrugged "—apparently not."

She tipped the bottle over her glass, frowned when only a few drops came out.

"You said that your ex-husband's sister was your best friend?" he prompted gently.

She nodded. "All through high school right up until the divorce."

"That would have been a double blow," he acknowledged. "Losing not just your husband but a friend."

"Two friends," she admitted. "The woman he cheated with was also a friend."

"I'm not so sure about that, considering she slept with your husband," he pointed out to her.

"You're right," she agreed. "But up until then, I thought she was a friend. She was even a bridesmaid when we got married. Victoria—Christopher's sister—was the maid of honor."

"I think I'm starting to understand why you don't like to talk about this," he said.

And it was true that she didn't.

But now that she'd started, she couldn't seem to stop.

"It gets better," she said. But, of course, she meant *worse*. "I found out about Christopher's affair when I was in the hospital."

"Hospital?" he echoed.

"I guess I never told you about that, either," she realized.

He shook his head.

"Well, you've seen the scars," she said, and left it at that.

Now he nodded. And while he still didn't know what had caused the scars, he'd learned not to push that subject.

"Anyway, I was recovering from surgery when a process server came to my hospital room and served me with the petition for divorce."

"And now I find myself wondering why in hell you ever married a guy who so obviously didn't deserve you?"

"I loved him," she said simply.

The words, so casually spoken, delivered a crushing blow to his heart.

And maybe she realized it, because her tone was almost apologetic when she said, "I was fifteen when I met him. He was seventeen—handsome and charming—and I was too young and naive to look beneath the surface polish."

"Are you so much older and wiser now?" he asked.

"At least old enough and wise enough to know that happy endings only exist in fairy tales."

"That's not wisdom, it's cynicism," he chided gently.

"It's realism," she countered.

"Well, I hope you won't share your realism with any of our happily married friends."

"Maybe they are happy," she said. "But still, any relationship is more like a job than a fairy tale. Loving someone is work. A never-ending shift of unpaid work."

"Tell me about it," he said dryly.

She swallowed. "I've always been honest with you about what I want—and what I don't."

"Maybe you have," he said. Then he lifted his glass to his lips, drained the last of his wine. "So what do you want from me now? Do you want me to stay or go?"

Something that might have been hurt flashed in her eyes, but it was there and gone so quickly he couldn't be sure. And when she responded, her voice was completely devoid of emotion.

"I want you to go," she said, and picked up the empty bottle and her glass to carry them to the kitchen.

And he left.

He blew that one, Kevin acknowledged, as he walked into Diggers' after leaving Natalya's apartment.

Pausing inside the doorway, he glanced around the bar, looking for a familiar face, though he knew it was unlikely that any of his friends would be here at such a late hour on a Saturday night.

Not that eleven was such a late hour—except when a man had a wife and kids, as most of his friends did. Well, it was too bad for them that they were stuck at home, snuggling on the sofa or spooning in bed with the same woman, night after night, for the rest of their lives.

Ten years ago, he would have shuddered at the thought.

At twenty-seven, he'd seen a world so full of beautiful women that he couldn't imagine ever wanting to settle down with just one.

He couldn't imagine that he'd ever meet a woman who might inspire him to think that "till death do us part" wasn't a death sentence but an opportunity to spend every day of the rest of his life with the woman he loved.

Because at twenty-seven, he hadn't met Natalya Vasilek.

Maybe his friends' lives weren't fairy tales, but he wanted

what they had. The problem was, he also wanted Nat, and it seemed that he couldn't have both.

He was going to have to choose one or the other.

It was the kind of choice that might drive a man to drink, he thought ruefully, as he scanned—unsuccessfully—for an empty seat at the bar.

So he slid into a narrow booth tucked against the wall and, not half a minute later, a server made her way to the table.

His first thought was that she was young—barely old enough to drink at the bar, he guessed. His second was that she didn't know the word *subtle*, as the T-shirt she wore with the word *Diggers'* scrawled across the front was about two sizes too small. But she was pretty, with long dark hair that tumbled over her shoulders and an easy smile.

"Hi there," she said, her crimson-painted lips curving as her thickly lashed eyes slid to the vacant seat across from him and back again. "Can I get you something to drink while you're waiting for your…date?"

"No date tonight," he said, and watched those dark eyes glint with interest. "And I'll have a pint of Icky."

"I'll be right back with that pint," she promised.

She was true to her word. He barely had a chance to decide which of the numerous TV screens over the bar he wanted to focus on when she returned.

"Did you have a chance to look at the menu or did you want another minute?" she asked, as she set the frosty glass on a paper coaster in front of him.

"I'm just here for the beer tonight," he told her.

She propped her tray on her hip and gave him a leisurely once-over. "You said you didn't have a date tonight, but a smart girl would have to wonder—is there someone waiting for you at home?"

He snorted. "Definitely not."

Her smile widened. "In that case, my name's Blair, and you

can let me know if you want anything else." She winked. "Anything at all."

"I'm Kevin," he said. "And I think I've got everything I need right now, but I'll be sure to let you know if that changes."

"Sounds good to me," she said, as Steven slid onto the bench across from him.

"I'll have what my brother's having," Steven said, gesturing to the beer in Kevin's hand.

Blair nodded and sauntered away.

"What are you doing here?" Kevin asked.

"Apparently saving you from yourself," his brother said.

"What are you talking about?"

"Blair was looking at you like she wanted to gobble you up in great big bites."

"There are worse ways to go," Kevin noted. "But how do you know her?"

"I don't really," Steven said. "But I met her a couple of times, when our firm represented her brother, who works security at the Maverick in Elko, on 'excessive force' charges."

"Suddenly my night looks a lot less promising," he lamented.

"Anyway, don't you already have the perfect arrangement of no-strings sex whenever you want it?"

It was more like no-strings sex whenever *she* wanted it, he mused, though he refused to acknowledge the details of his relationship with Natalya to his brother. Or admit that she was the one who'd insisted on the "no-strings" part.

He'd never wanted strings before. Certainly, he'd been quick to break them whenever any of his previous girlfriends wanted to tie him down. But the idea of tying Nat down—and not in a kinky way—held definite appeal.

He was saved from having to reply to his brother's question by the return of Blair with Steven's drink. She left the beer and gave Kevin another wink before she sauntered off again.

"Excessive force," Steven repeated.

"You mentioned that," he noted, appreciating the sway of the server's hips as she moved away.

"I'm reminding myself," his brother admitted. "Because a woman who looks like that could make a man forget his own name."

"And the object of his unrequited love?" Kevin asked dryly.

"Perhaps not so unrequited," Steven said, lifting his glass to swallow a mouthful of beer.

"You finally asked Thalia out?"

"She asked me out," his brother said smugly. "We're having lunch tomorrow."

"Lunch?"

Steven nodded.

"Lunch isn't a date," Kevin told him.

"Why not?"

"Because there's nothing romantic about lunch."

"Lunch can be just as romantic as dinner," Steven insisted.

"Only if it takes place the day after you've spent the night together."

"I don't know why I talk to you about stuff like this."

"Because no one else wants to hear it?" he suggested.

"*She* asked *me* out," Steven said again. "Which is probably more of an overture than Natalya's ever made toward you."

"I'm not talking to you about Nat." It was more a warning than a statement.

"And now I know the real reason that you're drinking alone."

"I'm not alone," he pointed out. "You're here."

"Yeah, but we both know that having company isn't a cure for loneliness."

It was a valid point, Kevin acknowledged, and one he was still pondering when Blair delivered a second round of drinks to the table.

"You're right," he said to his brother now. "And I don't just want someone to hang out with on a Saturday night—I want someone to share all my nights. And she's the one."

"Keep looking," Steven advised. "The world is full of beautiful, willing women who don't have brothers willing to go to jail to protect their honor."

"I know."

"Of course, you do," his brother acknowledged wryly. "You've dated more than your fair share of them."

"Which is why I know she's the one."

Steven looked puzzled. "How can she be the one? You just met her."

Kevin frowned. "What are you talking about? I've known her for years."

"*Who* are you talking about?" his brother countered.

"Natalya."

"I thought you were talking about Blair."

"Why would I be talking about Blair?" Kevin asked, baffled.

"Because she's the one who was flirting with you two minutes ago," Steven pointed out.

"Maybe," he allowed. "But she's not my type."

"Since when do you have a type?"

"Since I met Nat."

His brother gestured to the glass of beer in front of Kevin. "How many of those have you had?"

"I'm not drunk."

"Well, you're talking as if you are. Because you and Nat tried dating, remember? It didn't work out."

Yeah, he remembered. And what he remembered was that it had been working just fine until his sister and brother-in-law brought their twin boys to Haven for a visit that summer. He didn't know what happened when Eden and Phillip were there—and maybe whatever it was had absolutely nothing to do with their visit—he only knew that it was after they'd gone home that Nat had decided they were better off as friends.

A few months later, by mutual agreement, they'd amended their status to "friends with benefits" again.

"And anyway, you've got a good thing going," Steven reminded him. "All the fun with none of the commitment."

But that wasn't enough for Kevin anymore.

He wanted it all.

And Nat was everything to him.

She shouldn't have had the third—or maybe it was the fourth—glass of wine. Because if she hadn't drunk the better part of a bottle of wine—and let Kevin get under her skin—she might have looked at the clock and realized how late it was before she dialed her sister-in-law's number.

"Nat?" Margot said sleepily.

"Oh, crap," she said, squinting at the clock to bring the blurry numbers into focus.

11:14

"It's late. I'm sorry. Please hang up and just pretend this was a bad dream."

"No—wait!" Margot said, before Nat could disconnect the call. "It's fine. I'm awake. What's going on?"

"Nothing that warrants you losing sleep," Nat promised.

"I'm awake," Margot said again, using the achingly familiar and infinitely patient tone that always made Nat feel not just heard but loved. "Talk to me."

So Nat talked to her.

She told her everything—from her unexpected encounter with Cameron to the harsh words she'd exchanged with Kevin before he walked out the door.

"Can I ask you a question?" Margot said, when Nat had concluded her verbal dump.

"Of course."

"What are you most upset about—seeing Cameron or fighting with Kevin?"

"Seeing Cameron threw me off-stride for a minute," she admitted. "But I'd mostly bounced back from that before Kevin showed up."

"So it's the fight with Kevin that's got you all twisted up inside?"

"Yeah," she admitted.

"And now I'm wondering why you're letting the words of a man, who you claim you don't want a relationship with, impact your mood at all."

"I shouldn't," Nat agreed. "But we're friends…most of the time."

"Friendship does complicate a relationship when one party wants more than the other."

"I don't want to lose him," she confided, barely able to get the words out around the lump in her throat.

"As a friend? Or a lover?"

Nat didn't immediately reply. Whether out of indecision or something else, though, she wasn't entirely sure. "Both?"

"I think you're going to have to decide," Margot said gently. "Because your on-and-off-again relationship isn't giving either one of you what you want. And I'm worried it's going to lead to a world of hurt for you both."

Chapter Six

Kevin Dawson and Jason Channing had grown up together in Haven and become fast friends long before either of them was old enough to understand that Kevin's family was middle class and Jason's was seriously wealthy. And though Kevin had since built a successful career for himself as an information security analyst in addition to his work at AV, he didn't have the disposable income to charter a last-minute flight to Oakland to catch a ball game at the Coliseum. But Jay did, and so when he asked if Kevin wanted to go to the A's game the following Wednesday, he said yes.

"I'm a little surprised that your wife let you out tonight," Kevin said, as the A's took their positions in the field to start the game. "Isn't she about to burst?"

"She only looks like she is," Jay said. "Her due date is still seven weeks away." He tore open the bag of peanuts the vendor tossed to him, offered it to Kevin. "And this was her idea. Apparently I've been hovering."

"You doubt it?" Kevin cracked open a shell and popped the nuts into his mouth.

"No. I've been trying to be there more—and do more—because I know Lucy and Clara keep her busy," he said, referring to their two young daughters. "And that's after she gets home after being on her feet at school all day."

"I'm sure if she was overdoing it, her doctor would say so."

"That's exactly what she said," Jay admitted. "And why I'm here now."

"Well, as a beneficiary of you being kicked out of the house, can I say 'thank you' for hovering?"

Jay chuckled as the A's, having retired the first three Yankees batters in order, jogged off the field.

"Why are there two empty seats?" Kevin asked, as the Yankees pitcher threw some warm-up pitches. "Who else was supposed to come?"

"Devin and Claire," Jay said, naming one of his numerous cousins and his spouse. "But Claire bailed because she's got a colicky mare and Dev decided to stay behind with her."

"She's the one with the horse rescue?" Kevin guessed, as the leadoff batter stepped up to the plate.

Jay nodded. "Twilight Valley."

The crowd held its collective breath as the batter swung at the first pitch, connecting with a loud "thwack" and sending the ball sailing through the air to travel more than 370 feet…foul.

An audible groan reverberated through the stadium.

"No one else wanted the tickets?" Kevin asked, picking up the conversation where they'd left off as the batter squared up at the plate again.

"It was kind of last minute at that point," Jay said. "I thought about giving Nat a call, but it's Wednesday."

Kevin nodded, understanding that Nat would be at the community center, as she was every Wednesday night without fail. And as much as she loved the A's, he knew she'd never skip out on her veterans group for a game—not even prime seats on the third baseline.

He knew that because he'd gotten to know her pretty well over the last seven years. Though maybe not as well as he believed, considering recent revelations.

"Did you know that Nat was married?" he asked Jay now.

His friend shifted slightly to give him his full attention. *"Nat's married?"*

"Not *is*, *was*," Kevin clarified.

"No," Jay said, responding to his original question. "I never heard any mention of an ex-husband. Then again, Nat isn't exactly an open book when it comes to her past."

"Isn't that the truth?" Kevin agreed.

"So how'd you find out?"

"She told me. Just dropped it in conversation as if it wasn't any big deal."

"Is it a big deal?" Jay asked.

"Not the fact that she was married," Kevin said. "I mean, everyone has a past, right? But the fact that she never mentioned it to me… It kind of seems like a big deal."

"You think she's still hung up on her ex?"

"No." At least, nothing in her tone or demeanor had suggested to him that she had any residual feelings for the man she'd once loved.

But Kevin was more convinced than ever that the scars from her past were a lot greater in number than those visible on her physical body.

A week later, Nat was surprised to walk into the meeting room at the community center with a box of treats from Sweet Caroline's to discover that Jake Kelly was already there. Not only that, but the chairs had been set up, coffee was brewing and an identical white box bearing the embossed logo of the local bakery was on the table along with a stack of plates and napkins and a tray of mugs from the kitchenette.

"Did I know you were going to be here tonight?" Nat asked, in lieu of a greeting.

"Didn't I text you?"

She propped the box on her hip to free up a hand so that

she could pull her phone out of her pocket and scroll through the messages.

"No," she finally responded to his question.

"Sorry." He shrugged. "Guess I forgot."

"Then I guess I get to take my box of goodies to work tomorrow."

"I'm sure you won't hear any complaints from your coworkers."

"I'm sure you're right." She carried the box into the kitchenette. "So what's going on with you?"

"Why do you think something's going on?"

"Because you only show up this early when you want to talk to me," she pointed out.

"I should always come early. Or someone should," Jake said, still not answering her question. "How did this group become your responsibility?"

"Neal Sullivan moved to Tennessee."

"Who?"

"The vet who started this group. He moved to Nashville a few months before you moved to Haven."

"And left you in charge," Jake guessed.

She shrugged. "I wouldn't say in charge so much as responsible."

"Still, you shouldn't have to do everything on your own."

"I didn't do anything tonight," she pointed out.

"You need to ask for help."

"When I need it, I will. But everyone has busy lives—you probably more so than most, with your family and PAWS."

"I'm busy because my life is full of so many things I've got to be grateful for," Jake noted. "So many more than I ever imagined."

"But no more than you deserve," Nat told him.

"What about you?" he asked.

"What about me?" she asked warily.

"You deserve so much more than you're letting yourself have."

"I have everything I need. Two interesting jobs, a handful of close friends and, when I'm at the ranch, an overload of canine affection."

Jake's smile was a little strained. "Actually, that is something I wanted to talk to you about."

"You're firing me as a volunteer dog walker?" she asked, obviously teasing.

"Of course not," he responded in a serious tone. "I just wanted to let you know that…"

His words trailed off as voices sounded in the hall, drawing nearer.

Nat immediately recognized the bickering voices of Dirk and Leon. The two men nodded a greeting to Nat and Jake as they made their way to the refreshment table, still arguing about an alleged missed flag on a play in the Army-Navy game some five months earlier.

"Let's talk after the meeting," Jake suggested.

"I'll be here," Nat promised.

Since Jake was there, Nat let him take the lead. Raelynn hadn't said too much at either of the previous meetings that she'd attended, and Nat suspected that if the newcomer was ever going to open up, it would be Jake who persuaded her to do so.

So Nat made her way to the last row of chairs, where Charley was seated. At twenty-two, he was one of the youngest members of the group—and quite possibly one of the most damaged. The poor kid had been on his first tour overseas when his team was caught in an ambush. For the next three weeks, they were subjected to daily torture by their captors before they were located and liberated by a group of Navy SEALs.

Now Charley worked part-time at Adventure Village, when he could. Nat did the scheduling, to ensure that they were never caught short if he didn't show, and to ensure he had a job available to help give him a sense of purpose when he wanted it. As a result, they'd spent a fair amount of time together outside the group and begun to forge a tentative friendship.

He offered her a quick smile—a rare and priceless treasure—as she settled beside him.

Jake introduced Raelynn to the group, identifying her as a sergeant in the Third SFAB who was willing to share some of her story.

She stood up and began to talk. Her voice was a little shaky at first, but it grew in confidence and volume as she proudly recited the details of her service to the country.

"My last tour was Afghanistan, where my transport ran over a land mine," Raelynn continued. "I'm now what the doctors call a bilateral lower-limb amputee, with one transtibial and one transfemoral prosthesis. Loosely translated, I lost both my legs—one below the knee and one above.

"I lost both my goddamn legs," she said again. "But I was lucky. Two of the Joes with me were killed."

Her gaze snagged on Nat's for a brief second before cutting away.

"It took a long time—and a lot of therapy—for me to accept that the plans I had for my future weren't ever going to be realized." She shrugged. "But I'm sure all—or at least most—of us in this room have some experience with that. With reevaluating our goals and adjusting our expectations.

"Two years ago, I met Tim Brody at a crowded coffee shop in Henderson. It was a totally random, chance encounter. I was at the hospital to get my new legs. He was a radiologist desperate for a cup of coffee. The café was packed, so he asked to share my table.

"We chatted for a while, even flirted a little, but I didn't expect anything to come of it. Even when he asked for my number, I thought he was just being polite. I didn't expect that he'd ever use it. But he called and we talked, and we went out on a handful of dates. And when, six months after our first meeting, he told he loved me, I didn't believe it. I didn't trust that he—that any man—could love half a woman.

"I pushed him away. Through months of rehab and recovery, I'd learned a lot of tricks to push people away, to cut them out of my life before they started to mean too much. Before they became something else I could lose.

"But Tim refused to give up on me. On us. No matter how hard I pushed, he was there. I don't think it would be accurate to say he pushed back, because he didn't. He was just there. Every day.

"He stuck, and no matter how hard I tried, I couldn't shake him. Until finally, I realized that I didn't want to shake him. That I wanted everything he was offering to me, even if I was afraid to take it.

"I'd given up imagining that I'd ever fall in love or get married or have a family. Those long-ago dreams had blown up along with my legs. Tim helped me put the pieces of those dreams back together—and though we didn't waltz around the dance floor in quite the way that I'd imagined when I'd dreamed of my wedding as a little girl, that was more about my complete lack of rhythm than my prostheses."

There were a couple of quiet chuckles from the group that had fallen silent as she talked, and Raelynn responded with a shy smile.

"Anyway, Tim recently accepted a job at the General Hospital in Battle Mountain and we bought a house in Coopers' Corners. I was born and raised in Las Vegas, so to help with the transition, Tim decided that we should get a dog. His research led us to PAWS—that's where I met Jake and how I ended up here.

"I still have dark days," Raelynn confided. "Days I don't want to get out of bed. Days I don't think I can. It's a process—or maybe a long road. But I'm taking it one step at a time, and I'm finding joy in unexpected places.

"I didn't think I could be any happier than the day that I walked down the aisle to marry my husband," she continued. "Until six weeks ago, when I found out that I'm pregnant."

"Is this good news to you?" Jake asked cautiously, as Raelynn wiped tears from her cheeks.

She managed a small smile and a nod. "Very good news."

A smattering of applause sounded around the room, and her shy smile blossomed.

"I didn't actually plan to tell you that part," she confided. "We haven't even told our parents yet. But I guess I wanted to share my story to give some hope to those who might have lost it.

"Because I know what it's like to look in the mirror and see only what's broken. But we're more than just the sum of those broken pieces—whether the world can see them or not. We deserve to hope and dream and believe. We deserve to love and be loved. And if we're very lucky, we meet someone who can love all our parts, even—or maybe especially—the broken ones."

"Amen to that," Charley said, speaking quietly so that only Nat could hear.

She took his hand and squeezed it gently.

Her usual hours at Adventure Village and an unexpected charter flight added to her schedule at the last minute kept Nat busy throughout the week. Though she missed volunteering at PAWS, she'd didn't feel guilty about cutting that from her schedule, because the end of the college term always brought home students looking for volunteer hours who found their way to the ranch.

She finally made a trip out to Jake's place Friday morning, where she saw her friend Connie putting a group of new arrivals through their paces. Whereas service dogs were often bred for that express purpose, the dogs that ended up at PAWS mostly had less auspicious beginnings. From unregistered purebreds to indecipherable breeds, what many of them had in common was that this was their second chance to get some basic training and find their way home to a family who needed them.

Nat and Connie had been friends for more than eight years, having met when Connie brought Lacey, her yellow Lab, to the VA hospital where Nat was rehabbing after the injury that ended her career—and nearly her life. Nat liked Connie from the outset, and when the opportunity arose to help her friend at PAWS, she was glad to do so.

She'd worked with different dogs in various classes—mostly beginner. While ESA didn't require the same level of training as officially licensed service dogs, they needed to be socialized and taught to respond to commands and exhibit good manners so that their human companions could take them out in public and not worry that they'd behave inappropriately.

A sign-out sheet hung on a clipboard on a hook by the barn door so that volunteers could note which dog they'd taken and for what purpose—exercise or training or socialization. The local long-term care facility was a popular choice for socialization as both the residents and the dogs thoroughly enjoyed the visits.

There was also a fenced-in play area where dogs not otherwise occupied could play together, and when Nat didn't see Thor there, she headed into the barn to check his kennel. When he wasn't there, either, she examined the sign-out sheet, assuming one of the other volunteers must have taken him for a walk or on an excursion, but his name was absent from the list.

Just then, the side door of Jake's house opened, and he walked out with his wife. Jake carried Maya's car seat to Sky's vehicle, opened the back door to secure his daughter inside, then gave his wife a long kiss.

Jake had fought his demons and won, and he'd been rewarded with a beautiful wife and adorable child, and Nat was happy for him. But as she watched their lingering goodbye, she felt a pinch of something that she suspected might be envy.

"No Daddy duty for you today?" she asked, as Jake approached the barn.

He shook his head. "Friday mornings, Sky takes Maya to story time at the library."

"Sounds like fun."

"Maya seems to like it."

Nat nodded toward the corral. "The new recruits look good."

"Yeah. Connie should be starting another session with them in a few minutes, if you wanted to join in."

"Actually, I thought I'd take Thor for a run," she said. "I don't know if he needs the exercise, but I certainly do."

Jake glanced at the dogs wrestling in the play area, a furrow between his brows.

"Thor's not here," he finally said.

"I couldn't find him, either," she admitted. "But his name isn't on the sign-out sheet."

Her friend's gaze shifted back to her now. "He's not signed out, Nat. He's gone."

"Gone?" she echoed, unable—or maybe unwilling—to comprehend.

"You said you wanted Connie to find a good home for him," he reminded her.

It was his tone—not just gentle but almost apologetic—that finally clued her in to what he was saying.

Thor had found his forever family.

That had always been the end goal—as it was for all the

animals who spent time at PAWS—and Nat knew that she should be happy for him.

So why did she feel as if her heart was breaking?

"I wanted to tell you on Wednesday, before the meeting," he continued, in the same tone. "Then I decided the news should wait until after the meeting, but you were in the middle of a pretty intense conversation with Charley then and I didn't want to interrupt."

She nodded. "Of course."

"I'm sorry, Nat."

Now she shook her head. "There's no need to apologize," she said, pleased her tone was even so Jake wouldn't guess that there was an aching emptiness in the center of her chest where her heart used to be. "It's great news that Connie found a place for him. He deserves a real home."

"He does," Jake agreed, watching her steadily.

She fought valiantly against the tears that burned the back of her eyes.

She was *not* going to cry.

Not over some dumb dog.

And especially not in front of Jake.

"And since it looks like you've got plenty of help here this morning, I'm going to take off."

"Nat—"

"I'm fine, Jake," she said, cutting him off abruptly.

He nodded. "Okay."

But she wasn't fine.

She was at the complete opposite end of the spectrum from fine.

Which didn't make any sense, because she'd never had any intention of taking Thor home with her.

He had never been hers—so why did she feel as if she'd lost something important?

Chapter Seven

Nat went home, because she had nowhere else that she needed to be. And she busied herself cleaning the apartment, because she had nothing else to do. When the dusting and vacuuming were done, the toilet scrubbed and the stove gleaming, she realized it was past lunchtime.

She opened the fridge and frowned at the meager offerings. So she made a grocery list and headed over to The Trading Post. Then she wandered up and down the aisles, to ensure that she hadn't missed anything on her list, and returned home with twice as many bags as usual. After she'd put her groceries away, it was almost time for dinner—and there still wasn't anything in her apartment that she wanted to eat.

She considered forgoing food altogether in favor of opening a bottle of her favorite cabernet sauvignon, but she worried that drinking alone could become a habit—especially as she'd opened a bottle by herself not so long ago, and might have finished it by herself, too, if Kevin hadn't shown up.

Instead, she decided to head over to Diggers' and take a look at the menu there.

It was a pleasant late spring evening, she decided, as she traversed the familiar path to the local eatery. A nice night for a walk, which ensured that she wouldn't have to worry about driving home if one drink turned into two.

And, if she was being perfectly honest, another reason she

wanted to leave her car at home was that it was less likely she'd find herself driving around later—and ending up at Kevin's door.

Not that she couldn't walk to his place from the restaurant.

Certainly he'd walked home from Diggers' often enough, back in the days when the whole gang would go out for a bite to eat and a few drinks after a long day at Adventure Village. But that was when the business was fairly new and the six of them—Jay, Carter, Matt, Kevin, Hayley and Nat—were the entirety of the staff, juggling their hours at the park with various other jobs.

AV was no longer a fledgling business but a wildly successful one. And though most of the original staff remained, several other part-time employees had been hired, with the addition of extra seasonal staff to help out during the summer months.

Jay had a great group of people working for him, but there were still times that Nat missed Hayley, who'd moved with Carter to the East Coast after their wedding two years earlier. Or maybe she just missed those long-ago days when they were all just colleagues and friends, having fun at work and hanging out together afterward.

Matt had been the first to splinter from the group, when he met the woman who was now his wife. Jay had followed suit, falling head over heels for his pretty neighbor. And not long after Jay and Alyssa tied the knot, Carter and Hayley had done the same, leaving Kevin and Nat as the only two members of the original staff who were still single.

And even if they did hook up on occasion, they were still single. Their relationship—if it could even be called a relationship—was free of strings, expectations and promises. They'd always been in agreement on that.

Well, except for a six-month period almost three years earlier, when—in a moment of post orgasmic weakness—Kevin had convinced Nat to give them a chance at having a real relationship.

Things had been going well, until Kevin's sister and her husband brought their kids to Haven for a visit.

He'd been completely in his element with his nephews, and Nat had known then—even if he had yet to figure it out—that he wanted a child. He wanted to be a father. And she knew that he'd be a good one.

During the time she'd spent with Kevin, Nat had let herself hope that the question of having or not having children wouldn't matter to him. But of course it did, and she'd been foolish to let herself believe—if only for a short while—differently.

After his sister and her family had gone, Nat knew there was no way for her and Kevin to go back to the time before their visit—to fool herself into thinking that she could ever be enough for him.

He wanted something she could never give him, and that was why she had to let him go.

And this walk down memory lane wasn't serving any purpose except to highlight what she'd lost—any chance for a future with Kevin.

But that was okay, she decided, because she was happy with her life just the way it was.

As for a dog, she didn't have the time or space for a canine companion, which was one of the reasons that she'd started volunteering at PAWS. Because it gave her all of the joy and none of the responsibility.

She'd been spending a fair amount of her free time at the training facility for almost three years now without letting herself get too attached to any of the animals.

How had she grown so attached to Thor?

It was a question she didn't know how to answer, but the answer didn't really matter now, because he was gone.

* * *

Jake was settled in his favorite chair in front of the TV, Maya snuggled in his arms and Molly at his feet, when Sky came into the living room after tidying up the kitchen. They insisted on an even split of household chores and, since he'd cooked dinner tonight, his wife had tackled the cleanup.

"She's asleep already," Sky noted in a whisper, when she joined him in the living room.

"Before the middle of the second inning," he confirmed.

"How's she ever going to grow up to be a third baseman like her mom if she can't stay awake to watch the game being played?" his wife lamented.

Jake chuckled softly. "I think you should probably wait until at least her first birthday before you write off her potential baseball career."

"I guess I can do that," Sky agreed, as she lifted their sleeping daughter out of his arms to take her to the nursery.

Molly lifted her head from the floor, watching Sky carry Maya away. If Jake had had any concerns about the dog's reaction to a baby in the house, they'd been immediately dispelled by the Lab's doting and protective behavior toward the new addition to their family.

Sky was back in less than a minute, and she dipped her head to touch her mouth to his. "Thanks again for dinner."

"Wait," he said, as she started to draw away. "I need another one of those."

A smile curved her lips as she kissed him again—and she didn't resist when he drew her into his lap.

Molly, always ready to play, rose to put her front paws on Sky's legs.

"Not this time," he said, patting her head.

Molly sighed but dropped back down beside his chair.

"You've had a long day," Jake noted, as his wife tipped her head back against his shoulder.

"It was long," she admitted. "And…difficult."

He knew she wasn't referring to the story time session she'd enjoyed at the library with Maya that morning, but the hours she'd spent at April's House, the nearby women's shelter, in the afternoon.

"I know I've said this before, but I need to say it again— I wish you'd think about giving up your job at the shelter."

"I have thought about it," she said. "And if there was anyone else to take my place, I might actually do it."

"If you actually did it, they'd have more of an incentive to find someone to take your place."

"I'm lucky," she said. "I have an amazing husband and a beautiful daughter. The women who end up at April's House aren't nearly as lucky, so it seems the very least I can do is give them some of my time."

"It takes a toll on you."

"It does," she agreed. "And then I come home to my amazing husband and beautiful daughter and I'm instantly recharged."

"Instantly recharged, huh?" he echoed, as she lifted a hand to stifle a yawn.

"Okay, maybe not instantly," she relented. "Now tell me what I missed here while I was gone today."

"Not a lot," he said. "The new pups looked good going through their paces. Or at least enthusiastic."

Sky smiled at that.

"Also, Nat stopped by today."

"So she knows that Thor's gone."

Though it wasn't a question, he nodded.

"How'd she react to the news?"

"You know Nat—she's fine. She's always fine."

His wife sighed. "You mean, she always pretends that she's fine."

"Yeah," he agreed.

"I worry about her," Sky admitted.

"She wouldn't want to know it," he cautioned.

"I just wish she'd talk to me. Or someone."

"Maybe she does."

Sky lifted her head off his shoulder to meet her husband's gaze. "You think she talks to Kevin?"

He shrugged.

"Their on-and-off-again relationship seems more off than on," she said worriedly.

"I'd say that's her choice more than his."

"Which is why I worry that, one of these days, he's going to tire of being pushed away and decide not to come back."

"That's a possibility," Jake acknowledged, thinking of the way that Raelynn had described her husband at the recent meeting. "But if I had to describe Kevin, I'd say that he sticks."

"Hmm," Sky said, considering the implication of that brief description before nodding. "And that might be just what she needs."

Nat was sitting at the bar at Diggers', her finger tracing the base of the half-empty wineglass in front of her. The always affable Duke, attuned to his customers' moods, had poured the wine and moved away without making any effort to engage her in conversation.

So Nat drank her wine and tried not to think about the fact that she hadn't had a chance to say goodbye to Thor.

That was why the news of his departure had hit her so hard, she'd reasoned to herself. Because it was unexpected. If she'd known he was moving on, she would have said goodbye and gotten closure.

Instead, she was left to wonder what his new family was like and if they knew how much he loved ear scratches and belly rubs and bacon-flavored treats. So intent was she on these thoughts that she didn't immediately clue in to the fact that the previously vacant stool beside her was no longer vacant. It was only when the occupant spoke to the bartender, requesting "a pint of Rolling Rock—and another glass of whatever this pretty lady's drinking," that she glanced over to acknowledge his presence.

Duke looked at Nat, silently seeking her permission before acceding to the customer's request to pour her another drink.

She responded with a shake of her head.

"As soon as I'm finished with this one, I'm heading out," she told him.

"What's your hurry, honey?" the new arrival asked, sliding an arm across the back of her stool.

"Don't call me 'honey,'" she advised.

He smiled, undeterred by her clipped tone. "So tell me your name."

He wasn't unattractive, but that wasn't the issue. He could have been Ryan Reynolds and she would have responded the same way. She just wasn't in the mood to flirt with anyone, but especially not a man with a pale line around the fourth finger on his left hand that suggested he was either recently divorced or had removed his wedding band in an effort to pick up a woman.

"Okay, I'll go first," he said, when she remained silent. "Simon Menard."

Nat lifted her glass to sip her wine.

"I've been told that I'm quite charming," he said, brushing her shoulder with his fingertips. "Give me five minutes to prove it to you."

She shifted away from his touch. "I appreciate the effort, but—"

He lifted his other hand to her lips. "Five minutes," he said again.

She knocked his hand away. "Don't touch me."

A smart man would have taken the hint.

Apparently Simon was not a smart man.

"You're a feisty one, aren't you?" His smile widened. "I like feisty women."

"Unfortunately for you, I don't like aggressive, obnoxious men," she told him.

Years of experience behind the bar undoubtedly having given him a sixth sense about trouble brewing, Duke sidled over. "Is there a problem here?" he asked.

"Nothing I can't handle," Nat assured him.

"You know the rules," the bar owner reminded her.

She nodded.

Duke was a pretty easygoing guy, but he didn't tolerate fighting in his bar. The penalty for anyone who broke the rule: banishment from the premises for a full year. In a town with only four eating establishments, it was a harsh punishment, which might be why Nat hadn't heard of anyone daring to throw a punch inside Diggers' since Doug Holland had given Jerry Tate a black eye more than six years earlier.

"I don't know the rules," Simon said to Nat, inching his stool closer to hers. "Why don't you explain them to me?"

Nat was tempted to explain with her five fingers curled into a fist, but she really liked hanging out at Diggers'. Still, she was weighing the pros and cons of knocking Simon on his butt when Kevin walked into the bar.

Her bruised heart bumped against her ribs even as her brain urged her to proceed with caution.

She had a habit of acting impulsively when she was feeling raw or vulnerable, and she was feeling both tonight. She knew that Kevin could help her forget—at least for a little while— the emptiness in her heart, but she also knew that, if she let him, she'd be filled with regrets in the morning.

Not because Kevin wasn't good for her, but because she wasn't good for him—notwithstanding his refusal to believe it.

His gaze shifted from her to the guy seated beside her to the bartender with his arms folded across his wide chest. Quickly summing up the situation, Kevin breached the distance between them and dipped his head to touch his lips to her cheek.

"Hi, honey. Sorry I'm late."

Simon scowled at the intrusion.

"You know this guy?" he asked Nat.

"Of course she knows me," Kevin said, answering before Nat could. "I'm her fiancé." He frowned then as he held up her left hand. "Honey, what have I told you about going out without my ring on your finger?"

Though she didn't need his intervention, she appreciated that his efforts were well-intentioned and decided to play along. "You know I'm self-conscious about wearing a diamond that big."

Her uninvited neighbor finally took the hint—and his beer—and moved down the bar.

"You two practice that shtick?" Duke asked, sounding amused.

"Hardly," Nat said. Then to Kevin, "And I really don't need a man to rescue me."

"Nobody knows that better than me," he assured her. "But as much as I'm sure you wanted to drop that guy to the floor, I didn't want you to end up banned."

"What are you doing here, anyway?" she asked.

"I didn't feel like cooking tonight, so I came in to pick up some wings."

"Oh." The twinge of disappointment surprised her. After all, it's not as if she thought he'd come into the bar looking for her.

Kevin slid onto the stool abandoned by Simon. "Have you had dinner?"

"No," she admitted.

"I got a double order," he said, as Duke set a paper bag on the bar in front of him. "And garlic bread."

"You must be hungry—or expecting company."

He offered his credit card to the bartender. "I wasn't expecting company, but I wouldn't turn it down."

She hesitated, then shook her head. "It's been a crap day and I'm in a really lousy mood."

"And you're usually bubbling over with joy."

She didn't completely manage to hold back the smile that tugged at her lips in response to his dry tone.

"So…what do you say?" Kevin prompted, as he accepted the return of his card along with his receipt.

"I could probably eat something," she decided. "Especially if there's cheese on that garlic bread."

Kevin grinned. "As if I'd ever order it any other way."

Chapter Eight

Kevin rose to his feet and gestured for Natalya to precede him.

"Did you drive?" he asked, as they made their way to the parking lot behind the restaurant.

She shook her head. "I wasn't sure how many glasses of wine I was going to have."

"How many did you have?"

"Just one before you showed up."

"Anything you want to talk about?" he asked, as he opened the passenger door of his vehicle for her.

"It was a fairly decent Syrah out of Washington State with notes of blackcurrant and spicy plum and subtle earthy undertones."

"I wasn't asking about the wine."

"Then my answer's *no*."

Which was no less than he'd expected, he acknowledged, taking his position behind the wheel.

They rode the rest of the way to his house in silence.

He unlocked the door and carried the food into the kitchen, confident that she would follow. He set the bag on the counter, then opened the refrigerator. "Do you want beer or wine?"

"Wine, if you've got it."

"I do," he said, snagging a bottle of beer for himself before reaching into the cupboard adjacent to the fridge for a wineglass.

While he was getting their drinks, she gathered plates and

napkins. She'd spent enough time in his house to know where things were located, and they moved around one another in an easy rhythm that attested to the fact that they'd done this dance once or twice before.

Because despite Nat's insistence that their relationship was only about sex, they did spend a fair amount of time together outside the bedroom. (Of course, they sometimes had sex outside the bedroom, too, but that wasn't something he wanted to be thinking about right now.)

"Ball game or movie?" he asked, as they made their way to the living room.

"Are the A's playing tonight?"

Obviously she had more on her mind than he realized, or she would have noticed that the game had been playing on several of the screens around the bar.

"They are," he confirmed.

"Then let's watch the game," she decided.

He found the appropriate sports channel and settled back with his plate of food and his beer.

Nat didn't seem to have much of an appetite.

She put only three wings on her plate, along with a few carrot and celery sticks and a slice of garlic bread.

He didn't press her to talk about what was bothering her—though it was obvious to him that something was even before she told him that she'd had a crap day. Over the years, he'd learned that there was no quicker way to make her shut down than try to force answers. So now he respected her boundaries—which didn't mean that he didn't worry about her.

Nat dunked a carrot stick into the little tub of blue cheese dressing that Duke always packed with the vegetables and tried not to think about how much Thor loved carrots—something that she'd discovered completely inadvertently when she was munching on a snack that she'd packed to take to the ranch and accidentally dropped one of the carrots on the ground.

Thor had immediately pounced on the orange stick. Then he'd reared back from it and walked in a wide circle around it, as if assessing his prey before pouncing again.

It was the funniest thing she'd ever seen, and she'd found herself falling even more in love with the silly dog that day.

But she didn't want to think about Thor right now. She didn't want to admit that she'd never see him stalk and hunt inanimate objects again. And she'd accepted Kevin's invitation to come over not because she wanted to share his dinner so much as she wanted to not be alone.

"You've got the morning shift tomorrow, don't you?" she asked him now, as she reached for one of the wings on her plate.

"I do," he confirmed.

"I don't have to be in until noon."

He nodded. "I know. I'll try not to wake you."

"You should know better than to think I'll still be here in the morning," she cautioned.

He shrugged. "What can I say? I'm an eternal optimist," he said, with a hopeful smile.

"I sleep better in my own bed," she said.

But what she really meant was that she slept better alone, where she didn't have to worry that she might wake up from a bad dream with her body drenched in sweat and her heart pounding.

"Your call," he said easily.

She dropped the decimated bone onto her plate and licked sauce from her fingers. His eyes grew dark as they followed the movement of her tongue, and an answering heat rushed through her system.

She used a paper napkin to finish cleaning her fingers, then reached for her glass of wine.

"Was the park busy today?"

"The high school kids were off because teachers had a Professional Development Day, so yeah, it was busy."

"How's Trish doing?" she asked, naming one of the new hires who had been on the schedule.

"She's a quick learner and a hard worker," he said. "I think she's going to be okay."

"Jay asked me to sit on interviews with him next week," she said.

"Why do you sound surprised?"

"I guess I just figured it should be you and Matt making the hiring decisions—you're his partners."

"We might have put some money into the business when Jay was getting it off the ground," Kevin acknowledged. "But you've been part of AV since day one—and everyone knows the day-to-day operations wouldn't run as smoothly as they do without you."

"Now you're flattering me because you think it will get you into my pants," she said teasingly.

"I *know* how to get in your pants," he assured her. "I just wish you wouldn't assume it's always my end goal."

"You're not going to get all touchy-feely on me now, are you?" she asked warily.

"I wouldn't dream of it," he assured her.

"Good," she said, and turned her attention back to the ball game.

She continued to pick at the food on her plate while she watched the A's battle in a tight contest against the Mariners.

When the ninth inning ended with the score tied, Kevin rose to his feet. "As you reminded me, I've got the early shift at AV tomorrow, so I'm going to bed."

"But the game's not over."

"You're welcome to stay up and watch the end," he told her. "But I can't. Not if I'm going to keep up with a dozen ten-year-olds in the morning."

"I don't understand," she admitted.

"Ten-year-olds have a ridiculous amount of energy and—"

"That part I understand," she interrupted impatiently. "What

I don't understand is why you invited me to come over tonight if it wasn't to have sex."

"I invited you to come over because I enjoy your company—and because I didn't like the idea of you hanging out at the bar by yourself. I liked the idea of you hanging out with that creep who was hitting on you even less."

"So you *don't* want to have sex with me?"

"I always want to have sex with you," he acknowledged ruefully. "But it's not the only thing I want to do with you. And when I spend time with you, I don't have any expectations that we're going to end up in bed together."

"Really? Because I usually assume that we will."

He brushed an easy kiss over her lips. "Good night, Nat."

She lifted her arms to link them behind his neck and drew his mouth to hers again, kissing him longer and deeper.

"Take me to bed with you, Kevin."

It wasn't a request he could ever refuse, but still, he had to ask, "What are you trying to forget, Nat?"

When she looked at him, her beautiful green eyes were filled with a pain that made his heart ache for her.

"That I'm alone," she said.

"You're not alone, honey," he promised, drawing her to her feet and into his arms. "Not tonight."

"I need you."

"I'm here."

It was more than a statement of fact—it was a vow.

The loss of his parents had been a shocking lesson in mortality and a stark warning to Kevin to hold those he loved close. At the time, that had meant his siblings and his closest friends. Everyone else, he'd kept at a distance, reluctant to let himself form new attachments, unwilling to risk loving—and losing—anyone else.

Until he'd met Nat. Somehow, without even trying, she'd obliterated all his defenses and taken up residence in his heart. And now there wasn't anything he wouldn't do for her.

He carried her up the stairs to her bed, though she'd told him—on more than one occasion—that such romantic gestures were wasted on her. It was more likely, he thought, that she hadn't had enough romance in her life, and he wished he could make up for the lack.

But she didn't want hearts and flowers, candlelight dinners or walks on the beach. She wanted to live life on her own terms—even in the bedroom.

The first time they'd spent the night together, their mating had been frantic. They'd come together in a clash of wants and needs. An inevitable realization of desires too long denied.

He prided himself on his creativity in the bedroom, but when it came to the moment that two bodies finally joined together, he was a fan of the missionary position—or reverse missionary—because he liked to be able to look into the eyes of his partner when they were making love, to know that she was with him in the moment and ensure her pleasure.

Nat always attempted to manipulate things , so that he was behind her. At first, he'd deferred, assuming it was a more pleasurable position for her. It hadn't taken him long to realize that the reasons he enjoyed watching his partner were the same reasons she didn't want him looking at her. Because it was easier for her to focus on the physical and ignore the emotional aspects of the act.

They'd had their first real argument when he confronted her about it. He'd told her that he didn't mind if she was using him for sex, but he wanted her to be damn sure that she knew she was using *him*.

She'd finally relented, and intimacy was a familiar dance between them now, though no less urgent than it had been in the beginning. He knew where and how to touch her to bring her the greatest pleasure, and she returned the favor.

Their clothes were quickly discarded, and they tumbled onto the bed together, a tangle of limbs and needs. She brought his head close enough to fuse her mouth with his, her tongue mimicking the intimate act of lovemaking as her naked body writhed against his.

Control was a slippery thread already sliding through his fingers when he reached out a hand, fumbling blindly in the drawer of his nightstand for a condom. When he had the square packet in hand, she hooked her legs around him and twisted, rolling him over to reverse their positions.

He didn't complain. It was easier to see her this way, and now his hands were free to touch.

She held his gaze as she opened the packet and unrolled the latex over his erection, her lips curving in satisfaction when he jerked in her hand.

Well, two could play that game, he decided, and lifted his hands to cup her breasts, brushing his thumbs over the already turgid peaks of her nipples.

He didn't notice the marks on her body anymore. The first time he saw her naked, he'd admittedly been jarred by the scars from what he knew must have been a serious injury. They weren't clean surgical lines, but rough and jagged, almost as if her flesh had been torn. There were several of the irregular marks on her torso, front and back, one on her right bicep, another on her right thigh. But they did nothing to mar her beauty. In his eyes, she was perfection.

Her eyes darkened as her smile widened, and she shifted her hips to position him at her entrance. But she didn't take him inside. Not yet. Instead, she rubbed herself against his tip, testing, teasing, her eyes never leaving his. He continued his own ministrations, confident that he could bring her to orgasm with only his hands on her breasts, because he'd done it before.

After minutes—or maybe hours—of mutual torture, she took him inside. Just a fraction of an inch, at first, her eyes never leaving his. Then a little bit more…and a little bit more… continuing to watch him as he watched her draw out the pleasure of their joining.

Though it was killing him, he let her set the pace. And when they were finally, completely linked, when he was buried as deep inside her as he could be, she began to move. Slowly at first, then increasing the pace until her head fell back and her breath was coming in short, shallow pants as she rode him. Faster. Harder.

He slid a hand between their bodies, finding the ultrasensitive nub at the center where they were joined, using his thumb to create some added friction.

He knew the tension was building inside her, saw it in her face, heard it in her breath and finally…felt it as she plunged into the abyss…and he followed.

He fell asleep with a satisfied smile on his face and a warm woman in his arms—and woke up alone.

Nat knew it said something about her that she was always sneaking out of Kevin's house in the middle of the night, but she was more worried about what it might say to him if she stayed—and what it would say *to her*.

It scared her to think about how often she turned to him when she was feeling sad or scared or alone, and how often he succeeded in lifting her out of her mood.

She'd tried to quit him, so many times, but eventually, inevitably, she always went back for more.

It wasn't a healthy relationship for either of them.

She knew that.

Because while she couldn't let herself want anything more than what they had, she knew that he looked at his friends with their wives and their kids and hoped that his life would follow the same path.

And she couldn't give him that.

But no matter how many times she told him, she knew that he didn't believe her. Or maybe he thought he could change her mind.

Because he didn't know it wasn't her mind that was the problem.

Or even her heart.

In any event, she was glad that she had to work the following day. The arrival of spring meant busier weekends at the park, which limited the time for uncomfortable introspection.

Even better, Matt and Jay were on the schedule with her, which meant that she didn't have to worry about uncomfortable conversations with the man who'd help her reach an earth-shattering climax the night before.

But her reprieve lasted only until the end of the day, when she arrived home and found his truck parked outside her building.

He climbed out of the cab at the same time she exited her vehicle.

"Hi," she said cautiously.

He returned her greeting, then said, "I want to redeem my rain check."

"Right now?"

"It's almost dinnertime and I'm hungry."

It was a perfectly reasonable statement, in a perfectly reasonable tone of voice. Nothing in his expression indicated that he was annoyed with her for leaving his bed in the middle of the night—again—but still she was wary.

While she was trying to decide how to respond, her stomach rumbled. Audibly.

"Apparently I'm hungry, too," she said.

He grinned, and her foolish heart turned over inside her chest.

"I'll call The Home Station and book us a table."

She glanced at her watch. "You're not going to get a table at The Home Station at six thirty on a Saturday night."

"Let's find out," he said, pulling his phone out of his pocket.

"Wait!" She gestured to the T-shirt and jeans that she'd donned before work several hours earlier. "I'm not dressed for The Home Station."

"You have other clothes upstairs, don't you?"

"Of course I do. That isn't the point."

"What is the point?" he asked.

"You can't just show up at a woman's apartment and tell her that you want to take her for a meal in a fancy restaurant *five minutes later.*"

"What should I have done?" he asked. "Suggested a future date and time so that she'd then have the opportunity to cancel closer to that date and time?"

She folded her arms over her chest. "I'm just saying that some notice would be nice."

"I'll see if they've got anything available around seven," he said.

She huffed out a breath as he found the number for the restaurant in his contact list and tapped the screen to initiate the call. And tapped her foot while he exchanged basic pleasantries with the hostess, nodded a couple of times, then covered the mouthpiece with his fingertips to say to her, "They have a table for two available at nine forty-five."

"You said you were hungry now," Nat reminded him. "And so am I."

He declined the reservation and disconnected the call.

"Do you want to drive into Battle Mountain?" he asked.

"I'd rather just grab a bite at Diggers'."

"Or we can do that," he agreed. "In which case I'm hanging on to my rain check."

"I don't think you can do that," she protested. "Offer it up and then take it back."

"It's my rain check. I can do what I want with it."

"Fine," she said. "Hold on to your rain check. But you invited me to dinner, so you're buying."

"Seems fair to me."

"And I want ten minutes to go upstairs and change my clothes."

"What you're wearing is perfectly fine for Diggers'."

"I want ten minutes," she said again.

"Okay," he relented.

She was gone twelve minutes, and when she came back down, she was not only wearing different clothes—having exchanged a red Adventure Village T-shirt and faded denim for a scoop-neck T-shirt in a deep green color tucked into snug black jeans—she'd also brushed out her hair, put on some makeup and dabbed on a scent that nearly brought him to his knees.

He whistled approvingly.

She rolled her eyes. "Are we driving or walking?"

"Driving," he said, opening the passenger side door for her.

She stepped onto the running board, drawing his attention to the sexy low-heeled boots on her feet and making him wonder what the odds were that he'd get to see her wearing those boots—and absolutely nothing else—later in the evening.

"Restaurant or bar?" Nat asked, as they walked through the double doors into the enclosed foyer that held separate entrances to each.

"Restaurant," he said, opting for the slightly more upscale setting.

The hostess welcomed them to Diggers' and told them to expect an approximately forty-five minute wait for a table in the restaurant.

Kevin and Nat looked at each other and, at the same time, said, "Bar."

The hostess seated them on the other side and left them with menus, promising that their server would be with them shortly.

It turned out their server was Blair, and she sidled up to their table with a smile that widened in recognition.

"Kevin," she said. "It's good to see you again."

"Hi, Blair." He glanced across the table at Nat, who was watching the exchange with interest. "This is my, um, friend, Natalya."

"Hi, Natalya."

"Hello," Nat said.

"I know you've just sat down," Blair said. "So I'll give you a couple of minutes with the menu, but can I bring you any drinks while you're deciding what you want to eat?"

"I'll have a glass of the Washington State Syrah," Nat said.

"And Icky for you?" Blair prompted Kevin.

"Sure. That would be good." He cleared his throat. "Thanks."

He opened the menu, as if he hadn't eaten here often enough to have the contents memorized, then glanced up to see Nat watching him, a smile playing at the corners of her mouth.

"What?"

"I was just wondering if it's awkward for you—flirting with another woman while I'm sitting at the table?"

"I wasn't flirting with her," he denied.

"She was definitely flirting with you."

"She was not."

"'Kevin,'" Nat said, in a surprisingly accurate mimic of the server's breathy tone. "'It's good to see you again.'"

He closed his menu and set it aside.

"And then there was the way you introduced me."

"I said you were my friend. Aren't we friends?"

"You said I was your '*um*, friend.'"

"I was tempted to say girlfriend, but I suspect Duke would bill me for the Nat-shaped hole left in the wall when you bolted."

"It's called an impact silhouette," she said. "And I wouldn't have bolted, but I would have pointed out that I'm not your girlfriend."

"Hence the 'friend,'" he said, as Blair returned with their drinks.

She served Nat first, setting a coaster on the table, then the glass of wine on top. Then she gave Kevin his beer, tapping a crimson-painted fingernail on the paper mat where she'd written her name and number.

Nat lifted a brow. "Still think she wasn't flirting with you?"

Chapter Nine

"I'm sorry tonight was such a complete disaster," Kevin said to Nat, as they walked out of Diggers' together.

"It wasn't a complete disaster," she denied. "The food was good."

"As soon as I realized Blair was working, I should have put us on the wait list. Or taken you somewhere else."

"It's fine, Kevin."

"It's not. You have every right to be annoyed. I know that I would be if Marcus had been our server tonight and he'd flirted with you," he said, naming another member of Duke's serving staff.

"Neither one of us has the right to feel possessive or jealous, because we don't have that kind of relationship."

She took a few more steps, then turned to face him. "But I was annoyed," she admitted now. "Because she couldn't know that we don't have that kind of relationship. Which means that she either didn't care about flirting with a man who was possibly on a date with another woman, or she figured—why would you want to be with me when you could be with someone like her?"

"I could give her a whole list of reasons that I want to be with you," Kevin said.

She waved off the suggestion. "I'm not fishing for compliments. I just wanted you to know why I'm annoyed." The furrow in her brow deepened as she sniffed the air. "I smell smoke."

He could smell it, too, but wasn't concerned. "Lots of people burn yard waste this time of year," he noted.

"Is that legal?"

"With a permit."

She seemed to accept that response, because she nodded and turned away.

"Where are you going?" he asked. "My truck's parked in the back."

"I'm in the mood to walk."

"Then I'll walk with you," he said.

"I can find my own way home."

"I know you can," he said patiently. "But I want to walk with you."

"You should go back inside and wait for Blair to get off work."

"I'm not interested in Blair," he said, frustrated by her apparent willingness to hand him over to another woman, as if all that they'd shared didn't mean anything to her.

Or maybe it meant too much to her.

Because if he'd learned nothing else about Nat in the past almost seven years, he'd learned that she had a tendency to pull back when she felt as if she was getting too close.

"Well, you should be," she told him now.

"Why?" he challenged.

"Because she's a gorgeous twentysomething whose breasts haven't yet made the acquaintance of gravity."

The irritation in her tone eased some of his own, and he didn't completely manage to hold back the smile that tugged the corners of his mouth—or maybe he didn't try.

"You're jealous," he realized.

"I'm not," she denied. "But I'm also never having sex with you with the lights on again."

"Does that 'never' start tonight?" he asked hopefully, as they approached the doors of her building.

She tilted her head to look at him, amusement glinting in her eyes. "You are an eternal optimist, aren't you?"

He shrugged. "What can I say?"

"You can say that you forgive me for not being very good company tonight—" she trailed a fingertip along the row of buttons that ran down the front of his shirt "—and let me make it up to you."

"I'm not sure you can make it up to me," he said. "But I'm willing to let you try."

She kissed him then, right there on the sidewalk, illuminated by the streetlight for any passerby to see, then took him by the hand and drew him into the building.

And though he knew that loving a woman who wouldn't—or couldn't—love him back would only lead to heartache, he wasn't ready to give up on her yet.

Something jolted him awake.

He didn't know if it was a sound or a motion, but he immediately pushed himself up in bed and noticed that Nat was awake, too—sitting up and hugging her knees to her chest.

The blinds on her window were only partially closed, allowing the light from the street to filter between the slats and into the room.

"Nat?" he said gently. "Are you okay?"

Her only response was a shake of her head.

"Bad dream?" he guessed.

She hesitated a brief moment, then she nodded.

He'd never seen her like this.

He'd never even seen her flinch.

She was the toughest woman—maybe the toughest person—he'd ever met.

And she was trembling.

He wanted to draw her into his arms, to offer her comfort. But for the first time since he'd known her, she looked so fragile, he was afraid to touch her.

"Can I get you anything? Water?"

"Water." She nodded. "Water would be good."

He went to the kitchen and filled a glass.

Her hands were unsteady as she took it from him, and water sloshed over the rim.

He covered her hands with his and helped her lift the cup to her lips. She managed to swallow a few sips, then pushed the drink away.

She was still trembling.

Or maybe shivering.

He didn't know what she usually slept in or where he might find a nightshirt or pajamas, so he picked up his discarded shirt from the floor and draped it over her shoulders.

She slid her arms into the sleeves. "Th-thanks."

"Do you want to tell me about your dream?" he asked, as he fastened the buttons.

"No."

The abrupt response invited no further conversation, but he pressed forward, anyway.

"You don't always have to be the toughest person in every room, Nat," he said gently.

"I'm never the toughest person in the room." The confession was a quiet whisper in the dark. "I've just learned to fake it."

"Well, I hope you don't fake it with me."

"Are you honestly questioning your prowess in the bedroom?" She'd tried for a light tone, but it fell flat.

"No," he said. "I'm only worried about you, because I've never seen you like this."

"And I wish you weren't seeing me like this now."

He took her hands in his. "Are you ever going to tell me what happened to you? Why you left the navy?"

She stared at their linked fingers. "Maybe nothing happened. Maybe I just decided it was time for a career change."

"We've been friends for almost seven years, Nat."

"And you think that gives you the right to pry into my past?"

"No, but I'd hope that gives you the confidence to trust me."

Her sigh was weary. "I do trust you. There are just some things I don't like to talk about."

"How often do you have bad dreams?"

"Not very often," she said. "But they come at completely random times, with no schedule or warning."

"That's why you prefer to sleep alone," he realized.

"Or maybe I just don't like to share the covers."

"Well, that's true, too," he acknowledged with a wry grin.

"If you were smart, you'd stay far away from me."

"Well, nobody ever accused me of being smart."

She tried to smile, but her lips trembled rather than curved. "I'm a mess, Kevin."

"Maybe," he allowed. "But you're a hot mess."

She choked on a laugh that turned into a sob.

He wrapped his arms loosely around her and touched his lips to the top of her head.

"It's the smoke," she finally told him. "They say that smell has the strongest connection to memory. For me, it's the smell of smoke."

He kept his jaw tightly shut, unwilling to utter any kind of sound that might cause her to shut down.

"We were in Hawaii for RIMPAC, participating in war games designed to keep us sharp for the real thing. It was all standard stuff—nothing I hadn't done hundreds of times before.

"But this time, one of my engines failed. Again, challenging but not catastrophic, and something I was trained for. I was still in control of the aircraft, running various options through my head to complete the mission, when the second engine went out.

"At that point, there really wasn't anything else to do. I had to eject. Still, even when a pilot knows it's absolutely necessary, punching out isn't an easy decision to make. Not just because of the potential for something to go wrong when your seat is rocket propelled out of an aircraft, but because you're ditching an incredibly expensive piece of military equipment.

"I was flying at about six thousand feet—a reasonable altitude for ejection. Anything over ten thousand feet and lack of oxygen is a concern. Anything below two and there's a possibility your chute won't have time to open."

She recited the facts dispassionately, as if responding to a hypothetical question on a test rather than recounting a terrifying, true-life experience.

"So I pulled the ejection handle, less worried about punching out than getting my ass chewed by my commander for losing the plane. But for some reason, I blacked out after I pulled the handle.

"Transient loss of consciousness, the doctors called it. What it meant for me was that I couldn't control my landing and crashed hard into a canopy of trees."

"How badly were you injured?"

"I was impaled by a broken branch. Or maybe it was a tree limb. Either way, it went right through me, from here—" she pointed to her abdomen, a few inches to the side of and below her belly button, and then to her back "—to here."

Though she was wearing his shirt now, he could picture the scars clearly. He'd seen and touched them, along with every other inch of her body. He'd even ventured to ask about them once. But she hadn't wanted to talk about them, and he hadn't wanted to make her self-conscious.

He'd never before let himself consider that the injury that created those scars might have killed her.

Even now, knowing that she had fully recovered, the possibility made his blood run cold.

"I came to as they were cutting me out of the tree, and all I could smell was burning jet fuel."

He tightened his arms around her, more for his own comfort than hers.

"As you can see, I survived," she said lightly.

"I know. But I can't stand to think about how differently things might have gone."

"You didn't even know me then," she reminded him.

"Maybe not," he allowed. "But I know you now, and I know there would be a huge hole in my life if you weren't in it."

She tipped her head against his chest and was silent for a moment, maybe considering his revelation or maybe just gathering her own thoughts.

"I worked my butt off to get through rehab and get back to my squadron," she finally said. "And then, when the opportunity was finally presented to me, I didn't take it."

"That kind of accident would have shaken anyone," he said.

"It wasn't the accident," she said now. "It was that my brother died."

He'd heard her mention her brother before—a marine, like their father. "Was he killed in action?"

She shook her head. "He completed more than fifty missions in a dozen different countries without mishap—then he was diagnosed with glioblastoma and was dead within three months."

"That sucks."

Now she nodded. "It was a blow to all of us—he always seemed so invincible. When we got the news, my mom begged me to quit the navy, terrified by the possibility that she might lose a second child. At first, I balked at the request, because I felt as if my career was all I had left after my marriage imploded. But then, at the funeral, I realized that I still had my family, and that they needed me. Not my parents so much as my sister-in-law, who was seven months pregnant with a toddler at home.

"So I resigned my commission and I moved in with Margot and Alex, went to prenatal classes with her, coached her through labor and delivery, and was the first person—after the new mom and the doctor—to hold baby Levi."

"You must have been a huge help to her."

"We helped each other," she said. "We grieved together and, eventually, moved toward healing."

"But you still have bad dreams," he noted.

She shrugged. "It's a process."

"When did you decide to leave California?"

"When I saw the announcement for the birth of my ex-husband's baby."

"You wanted to have a family with him," Kevin guessed.

"That was the plan," she agreed.

"Instead, he went on to have a family with someone else."

She nodded.

"I'm sorry, Nat."

"There's no reason to be," she told him. "I got over it."

"Did you?"

"The dreams I had when I was married to Christopher were a young woman's dreams. They're not mine anymore."

"You're only thirty-four," he pointed out. "There's still plenty of time to get married again, have a family. If that's what you want."

"It's not."

"I don't understand," he admitted. "I've seen you with Jay and Alyssa's girls and Matt and Carrie's boys and with countless kids of all ages who come to AV, and you do a pretty good imitation of a woman who likes kids."

"Of course I like them," she said. "But just because I like kids doesn't mean I feel compelled to have any of my own."

He knew there was something more behind her decision, something that she wasn't telling him. But she'd told him a lot more tonight than ever before, so he decided that was enough for now.

Instead, he tipped her chin up and brushed his lips over hers gently. "Do you think you'll be able to go back to sleep now?"

She nodded.

He drew her into his arms and under the covers, where she slept all the way through to the morning.

"Why are you scowling at your coffee?" Sky asked, sliding into the booth across from Nat at Sunnyside Diner.

"I wasn't." Nat looked up at her friend. "Was I?"

Her friend nodded. "As if that poor cup of joe was responsible for all the evils in the world."

"Sorry. I guess my thoughts were wandering." She lifted her cup and sipped.

"But where did they wander? That's what I want to know."

"Here and there."

Sky dumped two packets of sugar into her coffee. "Is there a man anywhere in the vicinity of here and there?"

"Maybe," Nat hedged.

"Details," her friend demanded.

"I had a date last night. Sort of."

"What's a 'sort of' date?"

"A last-minute 'we're both hungry so let's grab a bite' thing."

"Okay."

"We went to Diggers'."

Sky made a face. "Not that they don't have great food there," she hastened to clarify. "But it's not my top pick for a romantic evening."

"'Sort of' date," Nat reminded her friend. "But we've been there—both of us—hundreds of times before. So maybe I'm balking a little at the idea of calling it a date, but it's a Saturday night, and I'm wearing my best jeans and my favorite perfume and I'm sitting across from a great-looking guy who makes my body tingle in all the right places, and our server starts flirting with him. Blatantly."

"How blatant?" Sky wondered.

"She wrote her name and number on his drink coaster."

"That's blatant," her friend agreed.

"I don't know why it bothered me," Nat admitted. "I mean, it's not as if we were seated beneath a flashing sign that announced we were on a date."

"But it was a date?"

"Technically a rain check for a date I canceled a few weeks back."

"So you and Kevin are dating?"

She frowned. "I didn't say it was Kevin."

"You didn't have to."

"And anyway, one date does not equal dating."

"So not dating," Sky concluded. "Just sleeping together. Again? Still?"

"We tried the dating thing," Nat reminded her friend. "It didn't work."

"And yet you keep ending up in his bed."

"Well, the sex thing works." She couldn't prevent the smile that curved her lips. "We've never hit any snags there. But that's just chemistry."

"There's no *just* about that kind of chemistry," Sky said.

"You know why it can't lead to anything more," Nat told her.

"No, I don't," her friend denied.

"Yes, you do," she insisted.

"I know why you *think* it can't lead to anything more, but it's not fair for you to make that decision without letting Kevin know the reasons."

"He'd say the reasons don't matter."

"Maybe they don't."

"I'm not going to argue with you about this," Nat decided. "It's bad enough that I have to argue with him about it. And that's why I'm so annoyed about the way I reacted to the server flirting with him—because I have no right to be jealous."

"A logical point—except that jealousy isn't a rational emotion."

"Anyway, I told him that he should call Blair—and I hope he does."

"Do you really?" Sky sounded skeptical.

"Yes. And I think, if he starts dating someone else, we'll finally be able to break this cycle we're in."

"So maybe you should take the first step toward breaking it," Sky suggested.

"How?"

"If you want to convince him that you're not interested in a relationship with him, you could start dating someone else."

"I don't see how dating someone else will prove to Kevin that I'm not interested in dating."

"It's the *someone else* part that matters," her friend insisted. "Because so long as you're not involved with anyone else, he's holding on to the hope that you might, one day, fall in love with him."

She waved her hand dismissively. "He knows that's never going to happen."

"Does he?" Sky asked gently.

"I've told him often enough," Nat assured her.

"And then you sleep with him again."

She sighed. "You're right. I need to stay out of his bed—and keep him out of mine."

"Which might be easier if you were dating someone else."

"Maybe," she said, lifting her cup to her lips.

"Speaking of," Sky said. "Whatever happened to that guy you were seeing last fall? The gardener."

"You mean Brent? The landscape architect?"

"That's the one."

"We had three dates," Nat told her friend. "And early in our third date, right after our appetizers were delivered to the table, he decided it was an appropriate time to enumerate his criteria for a relationship."

"Third date?"

She nodded.

"He told me that he was thirty-nine years old and didn't want to waste two or three years dating a woman only to find out that they wanted different things. 'So I'm telling you right now,' he said, 'I want to get married and have kids. At least two. Preferably three.'"

"That's...bold," Sky decided.

"Maybe. But I get not wanting to put too much time in a relationship that can't go anywhere."

"Except that there aren't any shortcuts to getting to know someone. You need to put in the time and figure things out together."

"Well, he was honest with me, so I was honest with him."

"Uh-oh."

"There wasn't any *uh-oh*," Nat denied. "I simply told him that I didn't want the same things he did."

"How did he respond to that?"

"He said that he was open to negotiating the number of kids, and I said that I really didn't see kids in my future."

Sky looked troubled by this revelation, so Nat opted not to detail how the rest of the conversation unfolded.

"What kind of a woman doesn't want to have kids?" Brent had demanded.

"A woman who likes her life exactly the way it is," she'd responded bluntly.

"We parted ways before dessert," Nat said.

And three days later, she'd ended up in bed with Kevin again. She didn't tell Sky that part, either.

"Okay, forget about the landscape guy," her friend said. "Because I've got the perfect someone else in mind. I met him the other day when he was at the ranch. His name's Ian. Dr. Ian Payne."

"That's a rather unfortunate name for a doctor, don't you think?"

"Thankfully, most of his patients don't get the irony."

"How can you know that?"

"Because he's the new vet that Brooke Stafford hired to help out at the clinic."

"I hadn't heard that she hired someone new."

"Well, she did," Sky confirmed. "I'd guess that he's in his late thirties or early forties, about five ten, dark hair with just a hint of silver at the temples, dark eyes and a great smile."

"Sounds like you might be interested in dating the doctor."

"I might be, if I wasn't completely in love with my husband— which is why I think, for you, he might be just what the doctor ordered."

Chapter Ten

"How was your weekend in Lake Tahoe?" Kevin asked, when his brother slid into the booth across from him at Sunnyside Diner Thursday morning.

Steven was originally supposed to be in a trial all week, but a last-minute settlement had opened up his schedule and he'd invited his brother to join him for breakfast.

"It was amazing," Steven said. "I got to hike some trails, do some kayaking and even play some golf."

"I thought it was a working weekend."

"It was," his brother confirmed with a grin. "Is it any wonder I love my job? And especially clients who own waterfront resorts."

Kevin nodded his thanks to the server who topped up his mug of coffee.

Steven turned over his cup so that she would fill it, too.

"Need a minute with the menu?" she asked.

"Nah," Steven said. "I always have the same thing, anyway—sausage and egg sandwich on a multigrain bagel."

"Home fries?"

He shook his head. "No, thanks."

She wrote down his order, then looked at Kevin.

"I'll have the big breakfast—eggs scrambled, bacon crispy, with home fries, white toast and a side of sausage."

"I'll get that order into the kitchen right away," she promised.

"How can you eat like that every day?" Steven asked his brother, when the server had set their plates in front of them.

"I don't eat like this every day," Kevin said, picking up his fork to dig into his food. "And I burn off a lot of calories at work."

"I prefer to burn off calories in more pleasurable pursuits."

"Like hiking and kayaking and golfing in Lake Tahoe?"

"Those, too." His brother grinned. "But even better than my weekend…is that Thalia called while I was out of town."

"Did she invite you to have lunch again?"

Steven ignored the question as he chewed on his sandwich. "She was calling about the house on Miners' Pass."

"The one you made an offer on in the fall?"

"Yeah."

Kevin sprinkled some salt on his home fries. "I thought the owners took it off the market."

"They did. But the wife recently got a promotion that necessitated a move to San Jose. They're already gone and the house is empty. It hasn't been relisted yet, but they reached out to Thalia and told her that if I was still interested, they'd sell it to me on the same terms as the original offer."

"It sounds as if you're still interested," he noted.

"It's a nice house."

"You really want to live in a McMansion?" he asked dubiously.

"It's not a McMansion," Steven protested. "It's custom-built."

"It's ostentatious."

"I make a ton of money."

Kevin knew his brother's statement wasn't a boast so much as a statement of fact.

"I might as well spend some of it," Steven concluded.

"I thought that's why you bought the Audi Q8."

"A ton of money," Steven said again.

"No wonder people hate lawyers."

"You can hate us all you want, but you still need us."

"Well, since you make a ton of money, you can buy breakfast."

"I'm pretty sure it's your turn."

"You're right," Kevin agreed, snatching the check when it arrived. "I'll get this one. Because the next time I'm having steak with my eggs."

"I thought you were supposed to be at a barbecue with Sky's family tonight," Nat said to Jake, when he walked into the community center the following Wednesday night.

"That was the original plan," he agreed. "But an old friend came by the ranch today and saved me from an evening with the in-laws."

"I've been to more than one barbecue at the Circle G," she reminded him. "And I'd be disappointed to miss one."

"The Gilmores do know how to feed people," he agreed. "But I had something more important to do."

"With this old friend of yours?"

"Well, he's not really old. And he's a friend of yours, too."

"It's not like you to be deliberately cryptic," Nat remarked.

"You're right. I skipped the barbecue to come here tonight to bring you—" he sighed "—an obviously poorly trained dog who doesn't understand 'stay.'"

Nat had caught sight of the familiar furry head poking through the doorway at the same moment Jake did, and her breath stalled in her lungs.

The shepsky, realizing he was busted, froze in place.

"Okay, Thor," Jake said.

The dog didn't need any further invitation. He bounded through the door and across the floor to greet Nat, his tail wagging furiously. Though he was fairly trembling with excitement, he came to an abrupt halt in front of her, dropped to his haunches and lifted a paw.

"Oh, Thor," she said, falling to her knees to put her arms around him.

He pressed his head against her shoulder, returning her embrace.

Nat gave herself a minute to regain control of her emotions—though she wasn't entirely successful because when she looked at Jake again, it was hard to focus through the tears that blurred her eyes. "I don't understand... What happened? Why is he here? I thought Connie finally found a home for him."

"So did she," Jake agreed. "But apparently he kept trying to run away. He would barely eat or drink and had zero interest in playing. The family took him to their local vet, then to a pet psychologist and finally brought him back this morning—before returning home with Hawkeye, who was already in love with his new family."

"So Thor was returned," Nat noted sadly. "Again."

"This time, I'd say it was his choice. He certainly seemed happy to be back at PAWS. He ran around the barn, sniffing everywhere, looking for any sign of you—and finally finding a sweatshirt that you'd left behind a few weeks back."

"How do you know it's my sweatshirt?"

"It says Go Navy on the front."

"I've been looking for that one," she admitted.

"Well, Thor found it—and he brought it to me, which seemed a pretty clear signal about what he wanted."

"You have to know I'm happy to see him, but...I don't want a dog."

"You're a horrible liar," Jake said, a smile tugging at his mouth.

She sighed. "Maybe I am. But I can't keep him. You know I can't."

"When are you going to realize that it doesn't matter where he lives, Nat? He's yours."

"I can't have a pet," she said, though without very much conviction.

"You'll figure it out," he said confidently.

Jake had brought Thor's bed and a bag of food, so Nat really had no reason to refuse to take him home with her. No reason except her pet-averse building manager, but Nat would deal with her in the morning, if she had to.

She breathed a sigh of relief when she didn't see Mrs. Tocchet's ancient Chrysler Sebring in its reserved spot by the main doors, which meant that she likely wasn't back from Wednesday night bingo in Coopers' Corners.

Still, Nat felt compelled to caution Thor. "You have to be quiet," she told him. "No barking at the neighbors—or Mr. Barrymore's cats, if you see one of them roaming the halls. Mrs. Tocchet has a very strict rule about no pets—except, apparently, Mr. Barrymore's cats."

Thor whined quietly in his throat, perhaps a sign that he understood—or maybe disapproved of—the building rules.

"Which means that we're going to have to find another place to live," she continued. "Maybe a ground-floor apartment in a building near a dog park."

Thor's tag wagged.

She picked up her mail from the slot in the lobby, then walked Thor down the hall to the stairwell, trusting they were less likely to run into other tenants there than in the elevator.

As soon as she unclipped his leash inside her apartment, he started to explore, his tail wagging as he sniffed all the nooks and crannies. When he found her bedroom, he leaped onto the bed and rolled around on the comforter.

"I'm going to have to draw the line there," Nat said, as he burrowed his head beneath her pillows. "Off."

Thor didn't move.

"That's my bed—" she set his doggy bed on the floor beside her dresser "—this is yours."

The dog's tail thumped against the mattress.

"Okay, we'll work on that tomorrow," she decided, making her way back to the kitchen.

Thor hopped off the bed and followed.

She found a can of Diet Coke in the refrigerator, popped the top.

"I'll bet you're thirsty, too," she said, filling a stainless steel mixing bowl from the tap.

Nat lowered herself to the ground, leaning back against the cupboards as Thor shoved his face in the bowl and began lapping up water. When he'd drunk his fill, the dog sat down beside her and laid his head in her lap.

"I know this place is small," she acknowledged, as she scratched behind his ears. "And maybe it's a little lacking in character. But it's home—at least for now."

His tail wagged.

"Jake gave me some food, so you won't go without breakfast in the morning, but I'm obviously going to need to make a trip to the pet store to stock up on supplies. You're going to need proper bowls. And treats and toys."

He looked up at her adoringly.

"I'm not sure you know what you're getting yourself into," she said to the dog, as she continued to stroke his soft fur. "But you're stuck with me now."

Thor let out a short, happy yip.

And for the first time in more years than she could remember, Nat let the tears fall.

"Natalya."

Nat paused in midstride and turned to face Mrs. Tocchet, breathing a quiet sigh of relief that she'd taken Thor to AV with her earlier that morning and left him there with Sumera while she ran some errands for the business—after which she'd made a quick stop at her apartment to pick up a book that she'd borrowed from her coworker and needed to return.

"Hello, Mrs. Tocchet."

"Do you remember when the front door was kicked in by those teenage hooligans last fall?"

"I remember when the door was damaged," Nat said.

The culprits had never been apprehended, but Mrs. Tocchet remained convinced that it had been the work of the same "teenage hooligans" that she blamed for everything that was wrong with society.

"Then you should also remember getting the notice that was sent to all tenants about security cameras being installed in all common areas."

"I do," she confirmed.

"Those security cameras are how I know that you took a dog up to your apartment last night."

"Then you must also know that I brought him back down again this morning."

Mrs. Tocchet's mouth thinned. "Is it your dog?"

"Yes."

"Pets are not permitted in your lease agreement," the building manager reminded her.

"Did Mr. Barrymore sign the same lease agreement?" she asked, naming the man who lived directly beneath her. "Because there are at least four cats in 202."

"Cats don't bark."

"Did you hear any barking last night?"

"I'm on the ground level," Mrs. Tocchet reminded her. "So it's unlikely that I'd be the first to hear any ruckus from the third floor. But the tenants have certain expectations and it's my job to ensure the high standards of this building are maintained. I can't have dog hair on the carpet or unwelcome deposits in the grass."

"I understand."

"So you're going to take that dog back to wherever it came from?" Mrs. Tocchet pressed.

"No," she said. "I'm giving you my notice that I'm moving out."

Nat had high hopes when she opened the browser on her iPad and began searching for a new apartment during her lunch break the next day.

Jake was right—she should have moved out of The Square years earlier. And now that her hand was being forced, she realized she was excited about the prospect of a new place.

Or she had been, half an hour earlier, before her high hopes were thoroughly dashed by a quick scan of the listings.

"Why are you looking at apartments for rent?" Kevin asked, when he came into the lunchroom and saw the screen of her tablet.

"I'm moving."

"Really?" he asked, obviously surprised. "You always said your apartment had everything you needed."

"Because it did."

"And now it doesn't?"

"Well, the building has a strict 'no pets' policy, and apparently I now have a dog."

His brows lifted. "Thor?"

"Yeah."

He grinned. "I'm glad that you finally decided to keep him."

"It's more like he decided to keep me," she confided.

"German shepherds are known to be smart dogs."

"He's a shepsky," she clarified, though most people, upon first glance, assumed he was a shepherd because he'd definitely inherited more of the physical characteristics of that breed. "And anyway, he might decide to give me back after a few weeks—or maybe it won't even take him that long."

"I can't imagine that happening," Kevin said. "Sure, you can be a little bit prickly at times, but beneath that don't-mess-with-me attitude is a soft, squishy heart."

She sent him a pithy look that only made him grin.

"There's that don't-mess-with-me attitude," he noted.

"Anyway, Thor's not only a dog, he's a pretty big dog," she said, choosing to ignore his remark. "So even if I didn't have to move, I could probably use an apartment with a little more space."

"A house would give you more space than an apartment," he pointed out. "With the added benefit of a yard."

"I don't need *that much* space," she told him, though the prospect of a yard where Thor could run freely was undeniably appealing. "Besides, there aren't a lot of houses available on the rental market in Haven. At least not in my price range."

"It so happens that I know of one not yet on the market," he said.

"You do?" she asked, equal parts curious and wary.

He nodded. "Steven just bought a new place on Miners' Pass and he mentioned wanting to rent out his town house rather than selling it right away."

"Your brother's moving to Miners' Pass? I guess lawyers really do make the big bucks," she mused.

"A ton of money, so he claims," he agreed.

"Isn't his current place close to yours?"

"Just down the street," he confirmed.

"So if I rented his place, we'd be neighbors?"

"In a manner of speaking."

She nibbled on her bottom lip.

"What's your hesitation?" he asked. "Are you worried that the proximity will challenge your ability to resist me?"

"That's the least of my concerns," she told him.

"So what *is* your concern?" Kevin challenged.

"That it's a really nice neighborhood and likely way out of my price range."

"Maybe it is, maybe it isn't," Kevin said, with a shrug. "But you won't know if you don't ask."

"You're right," she agreed. "But I also need something that's going to be available soon."

"I'm helping him move the last of his stuff this weekend."

"You'd think a guy who can afford a place on Miners' Pass could afford to hire movers."

"You'd think," he agreed, with a chuckle.

Then he pulled his brother's business card out of his wallet and set it on the table beside her iPad.

Nat stared at it for a long time before she finally picked up her phone and dialed the number.

She didn't know that it was a good idea to take Thor when she went to view Steven Dawson's town house, but she knew that she couldn't leave him alone in her apartment. He wasn't an especially vocal dog, so far as she could tell, but he was a dog—and dogs barked. And if she wasn't there to reassure him that everything was okay, he might cause a "ruckus." True, Mrs. Tocchet couldn't evict her without notice—and certainly not in advance of the notice Nat had already given—but she didn't want her last few weeks at The Square to be marred by unnecessary conflict.

So she drove to the off-leash dog park in Kevin's neighborhood to let Thor burn off some of his seemingly endless energy before they walked over to 45 Juniper Street, in the hope that he wouldn't be too excitable when they got to Steven's house. The last thing she needed was her dog jumping on the furniture or running into walls while she was trying to convince her potential landlord that she'd be a good tenant.

"You have to be on your best behavior," she said to Thor, as they turned onto Spruce Street. "Because if Steven's house is anything like Kevin's, it might be just what we're looking for. But I don't want to get my hopes up."

Another turn and they were on Juniper.

"Of course, even if this doesn't work out, I'm not going to be disappointed. Because I have you now, so my life is already infinitely better than it was three days ago."

As they approached Kevin's house, she noted that his truck was in the driveway. She considered knocking on the door and asking him to keep Thor while she toured his brother's house, but she decided that Steven was going to want to meet the dog before he agreed to let her rent his place, so it might as well happen now.

She didn't see Steven's car, but if she drove an Audi, she'd probably park in the garage, too.

"Okay," she said, pausing at the bottom of the steps leading to the front porch to draw a deep breath, hoping to calm the butterflies that were suddenly winging around in her belly.

She looked at the dog, who was looking at her with his head tilted, as if he was trying to figure something out.

"Best behavior," she reminded him.

He wagged his tail.

She mounted the steps and lifted her hand to knock, but the door opened from the other side before her knuckles could make contact.

"Oh," she said, when she found herself face-to-face with Kevin. "Am I at the right house?"

"Number forty-five," he confirmed, already down on his haunches to meet the dog.

"You must be Thor," he said, offering a hand for the shep-sky to sniff.

Thor responded by putting his paw on Kevin's hand, offering a shake.

The man chuckled as he shook, then he straightened up again. "Impressive."

"Connie knows what she's doing," Nat said, giving the credit for her dog's training where it was due.

He nodded. "Steven had a deposition that ran late, so he asked me to let you in and show you around."

"Okay," she said.

"Don't worry," he said. "I promise to give back my key if he ends up renting the place to you."

"I'm not worried," she said. "I know a good locksmith."

That earned another chuckle. "Do you really?"

"Well, I know that Glenn Davis from the hardware store replaced the locks on Frieda Zimmerman's house after she lost her keys at The Trading Post last week."

"It turned out she didn't actually lose them," Kevin told her, confirming that he was also privy to the latest town gossip. "They'd just fallen into one of her grocery bags."

"But she didn't find them until after she'd called Mr. Davis out to change the locks."

He nodded an acknowledgment of the point. "So—do you want the tour?"

"That's why we're here," she confirmed. "Assuming it's okay that Thor comes in, too?"

"He should get to see his new home, too, don't you think?"

"I think you're jumping the gun," Nat cautioned.

"Let's find out."

Chapter Eleven

Nat removed her shoes at the front door but continued to hold tight to Thor's leash so he wouldn't wander off, because she could see his nose twitching at all the new smells inside Steven's home.

Not that she could smell anything, except the subtle scent of cinnamon, but she didn't have the nose of a bloodhound—or even a shepsky.

From her position in the tiled foyer, she could see that the layout was a reverse footprint of Kevin's, with the coat closet on the right and the living room—with a wall of built-in bookcases and a gas fireplace—on the left. Following the short hallway, past the curving stairs to the second level, was the kitchen and dining room.

The maple cabinets in the kitchen were fronted by Shaker-style doors and offered under-cabinet lighting to illuminate the workspace. The appliances were stainless steel and gleaming. And the island included a breakfast bar with a trio of padded stools.

Looking around, Nat nodded her head slowly. "I think I could actually learn to like cooking in here."

"Or at least learn to cook?" he suggested. "Because chopping up vegetables for a salad isn't cooking."

"I can cook," she assured him. "I just don't bother most of the time."

"Well, as you can see, the kitchen isn't that much different than mine. Though he went for the quartz countertops, which are an upgrade from granite, and he got new appliances about six months ago."

The Shaker style and maple wood carried over to the dining room, where a table surrounded by eight chairs was centered beneath a trio of bronze pendant lights. The cabinet on the wall was flanked by a pair of Cezanne prints.

"I don't know why, but I expected your brother's taste to run more to beer posters than impressionist masters," she confided.

"Don't give him too much credit," Kevin advised. "He hired a decorator when he bought this house. There were plenty of Budweiser posters and neon bar signs in his previous place."

She hit the switch on the wall once to turn on the lights, then again to turn them off.

"Are you ready to see the upstairs now?" he asked, when she continued to linger in the dining room.

"I don't think so," she said regretfully.

He frowned. "Why not?"

She sighed. "Because I'm already in love with the place and there's no way I can afford it."

"Did you already talk rent with Steven?"

"No," she admitted. "We only exchanged a couple of text messages to pinpoint the time for me to come over."

"Then why are you so sure you can't afford it?"

"Because it's at least three times the size of my current apartment, a hundred times nicer and in a much more desirable neighborhood—all of which adds up to way out of my price range."

"Except that Steven isn't looking to rent this place as a moneymaker. He just wants a tenant who will take care of the property and cover expenses until he's ready to sell."

"Why isn't he ready to sell now?" she asked curiously.

He shrugged. "Something about market trends being more favorable to buyers than sellers right now."

"So I could move in here and, six months later, he could decide that the market's right to sell?"

"He's not going to sell the place out from under you," Kevin assured her.

Still, she hesitated. "Maybe I could buy it."

"Not two minutes ago, you were worried that you couldn't afford the rent, and now you want to buy it?"

"Not now," she said. "But maybe, when he's ready to sell, I'd be ready to buy."

"Why don't we take it one step at a time?" he suggested, gesturing to the staircase leading to the second story.

Though she still had reservations, she couldn't resist the opportunity to see what else the house had to offer.

At the front of the house on the upper level were two decent-sized bedrooms—though Steven had set one up as a home office—with a four-piece bath shared between them. At the back of the house was the master bedroom—almost the size of her current apartment—with a wide window overlooking the backyard, a spacious walk-in closet and luxurious en suite bathroom.

"I'd need to get a bigger bed." It was the first thought that came to mind when she saw the king-size bedroom suite that Steven had in the space.

He winked. "Haven't I been saying exactly that for years?"

She pointedly ignored his remark, but she couldn't prevent the flush of heat that crept up her face.

"Of course, I'll need a lot of new furniture—or furniture, at least," she clarified. "Since nothing in my apartment is mine."

"I know Steven's planning to leave some of his stuff. The dining room set and living room furniture, for sure. I think he mentioned the bedroom suite, too."

"I like the bedroom suite," she admitted.

But she'd definitely want a new mattress, because the idea

of sleeping in the same bed that Kevin's brother had undoubtedly done a lot more in did *not* appeal at all.

"Can we check out the backyard now?"

"Of course."

The yard wasn't overly big, but it was fenced, which would be convenient for Thor. There was also a patio. And even patio furniture.

She ran a hand along the back of a dark blue cushion.

"I want it," she said.

"The patio furniture?"

"All of it," she admitted.

Kevin grinned. "I thought you might."

"Obviously I'll need to work out the details with your brother," she said, mentally crossing her fingers that the amount of rent Steven wanted wouldn't be a huge stumbling block. "But first, I want to know if you think things might be weird between us if we were neighbors."

"Why would they be weird?"

"I don't know," she hedged. "But I don't want you to be afraid to invite Blair—or anyone else—back to your place because you're worried that I'll see a strange car in your driveway when I take Thor for his morning run."

"Or maybe you're worried about how *I* might react if I see a strange car in *your* driveway overnight."

"I don't foresee that being a problem."

"That's right—because you don't invite men to your place. You prefer to go to theirs and leave in the middle of the night."

"Is it a crime that I prefer to sleep alone?"

"No," he agreed. "But it's a shame that you won't let anyone in."

She turned to walk back through the French doors into the kitchen. "I should have waited until your brother was available to give the tour—I might have gotten through it without an amateur psychoanalysis."

"You're right. That was out of line. I'm sorry."

Kevin had never been afraid to own his behavior or apologize for it. And that was probably why she was never able to stay mad at him for long.

Thor strained at his leash, growling low in his throat just as Nat registered the sound of a key turning in the lock.

"It's okay," Nat told him, as the homeowner walked in.

But Thor wasn't willing to take her word for it when confronted by a stranger—and while Kevin might have been accepted as a friend, his brother was still an unknown quantity, as evidenced by the dog's cacophony of barking.

"Sounds like someone's feeling a little proprietary already," Steven noted, sounding amused.

"I'm sorry," Nat apologized automatically.

"No need." He paused a respectable distance from the dog and offered a hand to be sniffed.

Nat slackened the leash so that Thor could make friends.

He immediately did so, sniffing the human's feet, then plopping to his haunches and offering a paw.

"Clever dog," Steven said, shaking.

"He's pretty much a one-trick pony—or shepsky," Nat confided. "But despite being occasionally loud, he's friendly and really great with kids."

"That's good, because the neighbors on each side have lots of them."

"Lots?" she queried.

"Maybe only a couple each," he admitted. "Although when they're outside playing, it sounds like dozens. But the backyard is fenced all around, so they don't wander over, although the occasional ball or Frisbee does breach the barrier."

"New toys for Thor," Kevin suggested.

"Or you could toss them back over, which is what I usually do," his brother suggested as an alternative.

"Probably a better plan," Nat agreed.

"So…what do you think of the place?" he asked.

"To be honest, I'm wondering why you wanted to move," she admitted.

"I'm not sure he wanted to move so much as he wanted to hit on the new real estate agent in town," Kevin said.

"Thalia Morales?" Nat guessed.

"I'm on the fast track for a partnership at my law firm," Steven said, ignoring his brother's remark. "It was suggested that I should have a home that reflects my status in the community."

"Congratulations," she said. Then to Kevin, "Would you mind taking Thor outside for a bit?"

"Sure," he said, taking the leash from her hand.

Thor happily trotted behind him as he went through the French doors again to the back deck.

"Something you wanted to talk to me about without my brother overhearing?" Steven guessed.

"I just want to know if you're offering to rent to me because I'm friends with Kevin," she told him.

"I'll admit it's a factor," he said. "Because it's through your friendship with Kevin that I've gotten to know you and can feel confident that you'll take care of this place."

"I would," she assured him. "But I can't make any promises about Thor."

"He's not housebroken?"

"He is, but this is only his third day with me, so I don't really know if he likes to chew furniture or if his nails will mark the hardwood floors."

"Most of the hardwood is covered with area rugs."

"You're not planning to take the rugs?"

He shook his head. "They don't fit the house in Miners' Pass."

She arched a brow. "Not fancy enough?"

He chuckled. "No, they literally don't fit."

She had to smile back. "Okay, so I guess the only question remaining is—how much?"

Steven tossed out a number that was higher than what she was paying currently, but definitely—and shockingly—well within the price range she'd established on the basis of her current budget.

"That's less than some of the apartments I was looking at online," she said, a note of suspicion in her voice.

"You'll have to arrange and pay for your own TV service and internet."

"Which is pretty standard across the board," she noted.

He shrugged. "I'm not looking to make money off the property, Natalya. I just don't want it to cost me anything. I've crunched all the numbers and even added a little bit of a buffer and that's what I came up with."

"In that case...where do I sign?"

Steven had his assistant draft up the lease agreement and send it to her to DocuSign.

"That's it," she said to Kevin, when she'd clicked to send the executed document back to her new landlord. "It's official now."

"How do you feel?" he asked. "Excited? Queasy?"

"Yes."

He chuckled. "Do you have an official move-in date?"

She shook her head. "Steven said that he'll finish moving everything he wants to take by Sunday, so I can pick up the keys from him on Monday and move in any time after that. Of course, my apartment's paid up until the end of the month, but I think the sooner I can get Thor out of there, the happier we'll both be."

"Well, let us know when you pick a date," Kevin said.

"Us?"

"Me, Matt, Jay," he clarified. "We'll give you a hand moving."

"Oh. Um, thanks, but I planned to call a local moving company."

"Save your money," he advised. "This is what friends do, Nat."

"Okay," she relented. "Thank you."

"The usual way to thank a friend for help moving is pizza and beer," he said, with a wink.

"I really don't have a lot to move," she reminded him. "Most of the stuff in my apartment isn't even mine."

"Then it won't take us too long," he said easily.

Jake had suggested—and Nat agreed—that she should take Thor to see the local vet. Although the shepsky had been given a wellness check when he first arrived at PAWS and was up to date on all his shots, she knew it was important for him to get used to visiting the veterinarian clinic, so that it became a familiar and comfortable place to him and the prospect of going to the vet wouldn't instill fear.

And if Nat had some curiosity about the man who Sky had suggested she should consider dating, well, that *might* have been a factor in her decision to take Thor in sooner rather than later.

Still, she knew it was just as likely that Brooke Stafford would be the veterinarian on duty that day, so Nat didn't really have any expectations one way or the other when she checked in at the reception desk.

She led Thor to the platform scale, as directed, to verify his weight, before they were taken into an exam room.

Definitely not Brooke, Nat noted, when the doctor walked in a few minutes later.

And Sky's description had been fairly accurate, she mused, though she would lean toward early forties over late thirties, factoring in the creases around his eyes in addition to the hints of silver in his hair.

"Hello, Thor," the doctor said, standing in front of the metal exam table that Nat had managed to maneuver the dog onto—but only with the enticement of several treats.

Thor responded appropriately with the offer of a paw to shake—and the doctor's answering smile transformed him from moderately handsome to incredibly appealing.

His gaze shifted to the dog's human companion then, and she thought she saw a glimmer of interest there.

"Is he from PAWS?" the doctor asked.

She nodded. "I volunteer there sometimes. That's how Thor and I found one another."

"I've been out to the ranch a few times," he said. "I don't think I've ever seen you there."

"I'm usually an early morning visitor, before I have to be at one of my real jobs."

"One of?" he asked curiously.

"I'm the manager of Adventure Village and a part-time charter pilot. Natalya Vasilek," she said, realizing that she'd neglected to introduce herself. "'Nat' to my friends."

He offered his hand. "Ian Payne."

He had a good handshake—and a really nice smile.

"So what brings you in today?" he asked, returning to the matter at hand.

"I made the appointment just to meet you. I mean, for Thor to meet you," she hastened to clarify. "So that he wouldn't get freaked out when he has to come in for a checkup or vaccinations and other stuff like that."

"Something I recommend to all my patients," Dr. Payne said. "Unfortunately, not many of them actually do it."

"Well, that was my plan when I called," she said. "But over the past couple of days, I was glad we had the appointment, because his behavior's been a little off."

"How long has he been with you?"

"Not quite a week," she said. "But I spent a lot of time with him at PAWS before he came home with me, so I know what I'm talking about when I say he's acting out of character."

"Can you give me specific examples?"

"He follows me everywhere I go. He doesn't just want to be in whatever room I'm in—which is normal for him—but right beside me. He's even followed me into the bathroom."

"He might have some separation anxiety," Dr. Payne said. "Does he bark excessively?"

"He barks at strangers—or strange animals. But I wouldn't say excessively."

"How's his appetite?"

"He eats the prescribed amount of food, twice a day."

"Any destructive behaviors? Excessive licking? Chewing? Urinating in the house?"

She started to shake her head, then paused. "I did catch him chewing on a box yesterday."

"A regular cardboard box?"

She nodded. "I had two boxes beside my desk, and while I was filling the first, I noticed that he'd dragged the second box into the hall and was gnawing on the flaps."

"You were packing?"

"Yeah. My current apartment isn't pet friendly, so we're moving to a town house. I just signed the lease yesterday, but I wanted to get a head start."

The doctor smiled a little. "Are you excited about the move? Stressed?"

"Both," she admitted.

"And you're aware of what's happening," he pointed out.

If she'd been a cartoon character, a light bulb would have illuminated above her head. "You think he's stressed about the move?"

"Or, at the very least, confused."

"I should have thought of that," she said. "Especially considering the number of moves that he's already made in the short span of his life."

"Seems to me you've got a lot on your mind right now—a new dog, an upcoming move, two jobs, volunteering at PAWS."

Still, she felt foolish that she hadn't considered the most obvious trigger for the dog's behavior.

"Are you worried about the move?" Nat asked Thor now. "Because you know you're coming with me, right? In fact, you're the reason we're making the move."

The dog tucked his head under her arm and looked up at her with big dark eyes, making her smile.

"Silly dog."

"And now that we seem to have solved that mystery, what can you tell me about Thor's daily routines?"

"We go for a quick run—about twenty minutes—every morning, then he has breakfast when we get home."

"Do you feed him right after you get back?"

"No. I usually shower and get ready for work, giving him about half an hour to cool down before I feed him."

He nodded. "So you're aware of the dangers of gastric dilation and volvulus?"

"Is that the official term for a twisted stomach?"

"It is," he confirmed.

"I don't understand exactly how it happens, but I know what not to do so that it doesn't happen to Thor."

"That's good enough," the vet assured her.

"After he's eaten, I take him outside again to do his business, and then we go to work."

"You take him to work with you?"

"Sometimes, if I'm working at the park. Obviously, he can't be with me when I'm flying, so I'll likely take him to PAWS so he can hang out there.

"And then, at the end of the day, we go home, have dinner and, about half an hour later, enjoy a leisurely walk."

"Sounds like a good routine," the vet agreed, as he lifted the lid off a clear glass canister and took out a handful of bite-size treats. "Is there anyone else involved in his care? Husband? Boyfriend? Roommate? Kids?"

She shook her head.

"Well, if you ever need to leave him in the care of another trusted adult, just make sure they understand the importance of sticking with your schedule. Routines are as important to dogs as they are to humans—maybe even more so."

She nodded.

"Can you stand up for me, Thor?" the vet asked, using the same hand gesture for "up" that was used in training at PAWS.

The shepsky immediately complied.

"Good boy." The vet gave him one of the treats.

Thor's tail wagged.

"His weight is in the healthy range and he's got good muscle tone and a thick, shiny coat," Dr. Payne said, as he ran his hands lightly over the dog's torso. "How about we try 'sit' again?"

Thor sat and earned another treat.

"Very food motivated, I see." The vet smiled at the wagging dog.

"Very," Nat confirmed.

"There's nothing wrong with that." While he talked, the vet continued to examine Thor—checking out his eyes and ears and teeth. "So long as you're giving him healthy treats and scaling back his food to compensate for extra indulgences."

Nat nodded as Dr. Payne removed the stethoscope from around his neck. "I'm just going to take a quick listen to his heart—just to get him used to me and the equipment."

Thor continued to be still while the doctor pressed the stethoscope to his chest, and then his back, beneath his shoulder blades.

"You're a very good boy," the doctor concluded, offering Thor another treat.

"No cause for concern?" Nat asked.

"None at all," he assured her.

"That's great. Thanks."

Nat gestured to the floor and Thor nimbly hopped off the table.

"The reverse process wasn't nearly as easy," she noted dryly.

"It never is," the doctor said with a chuckle.

Then he reached into the pocket of his coat and pulled out a card. "Any questions, give me a call."

"I will, thanks."

"That's my direct number, not a service—so don't be afraid to use it," he said, ending with a friendly wink.

"Thanks," she said again, wondering, as she led Thor out of the exam room, if the new doggy doctor had been flirting with her.

And wondering, too, if she'd flirted back.

Chapter Twelve

Maybe it was a sign, Nat mused, when she walked into The Daily Grind the following Monday and found herself in line directly behind Dr. Payne.

Of course, it might have been a sign of nothing more significant than that they both enjoyed coffee, but he smiled and seemed pleased to see her.

After they'd exchanged greetings, he shifted his attention to the muffins and doughnuts in the display case and asked, "What would you recommend?"

She leaned a little closer so the staff behind the counter wouldn't hear her response. "The raspberry bliss bar at Sweet Caroline's."

Ian chuckled. "I've heard good things about Sweet Caroline's, but I haven't been there yet."

"It's worth the trip," she assured him.

"And where would you recommend that I go for real food?" he asked, moving down the line.

"That would depend on what kind of food you want," she said. "Sunnyside Diner has fabulous breakfasts, Jo's is the only place to go for pizza and Diggers' has a lot of good options on their menu. There's also The Home Station, for a more upscale meal."

When it was his turn to order, Ian asked for a large Americano and a banana nut muffin, then gestured for Nat to add her request.

"Large coffee, black," she told the server, then added, "Thanks," to the doctor.

"One of the technicians at work mentioned a good steak place in Battle Mountain," he said, as they waited for their beverages.

"The Chophouse?" Nat guessed.

"That was it," he confirmed.

"I've only been once, but it was excellent," she assured him.

"It would be nice to have company to check it out, if you're interested."

She felt something in her belly—more a knot of anxiety than a flutter of anticipation. She really wasn't good at flirting—or maybe she just didn't have a lot of experience.

She'd fallen in love with Christopher when she was a teenager, and after the implosion of their short-term marriage, she'd had a lot of stuff to work through. She'd gone out on dates, of course, and even had physical relationships, but everything had been rather superficial. Her choice, always, but not one that any of her temporary lovers had objected to.

Not until Kevin.

And she definitely didn't want to be thinking about him right now while an attractive doctor might be asking her out.

But since she wasn't entirely certain that was his intent, she felt compelled to ask, "Are you asking me out?"

"I guess I'm not doing a very good job of it, am I?"

"I wouldn't say you're doing a bad job," she said. "I'm just…surprised."

"Me, too," he said. "I haven't dated much since my divorce, more than two years ago. But maybe that's because I hadn't met anyone who made me want to put myself out there again."

"Or maybe you don't want to go to a fancy restaurant alone."

"That might be part of it," he acknowledged. "But another part is that I'd like an opportunity to get to know you better."

"A tempting offer," she said.

He grinned. "How's Friday night?"

"I'm working late."

"Saturday?"

"Working," she said again, a note of apology slipping into her voice. "It's a busy weekend at the park."

"You still have my card?"

She nodded.

"Give me a call when you're free."

Of course, before she could move, Nat had to finish packing.

And so, with her boss's approval, she gathered up a bunch of boxes from the storeroom that were earmarked for recycling and set them aside to take home—and then left without them.

"You're on your way out," Kevin realized, when Nat opened the door in response to his knock. And *damn*, if the sight of her in her pilot's uniform didn't rev his engine.

"Did I know you were coming over?" she asked.

"Nope," he admitted, offering Thor—attached to the other end of the leash that Nat held in her hand—a friendly scratch. "I just stopped by to drop off the boxes that you forgot at work."

"Thanks, but I don't have time to deal with them right now."

"You're not taking the dog to the airport, are you?"

"No, I'm taking him to Jake's ranch, so that he can hang out at PAWS, before I head to the airport."

"The ranch isn't exactly on your way."

"I know," she admitted. "But I can't leave Thor here when I'm not—I can only imagine what Mrs. Tocchet might do if she heard him bark."

"Yeah, she might evict you," Kevin said dryly.

"Anyway—" she glanced at her watch "—if you could hold on to the boxes, I'd appreciate it, because if I don't leave right now, I'm going to be late."

"Here's a better plan," he suggested. "You go directly to the airport and I'll stay here with Thor and get started on the packing."

"I can't ask you to do that."

"You didn't ask—I offered."

"You don't have anything better to do tonight?"

"I had no plans at all."

"Okay, then," she agreed, after another quick check of her watch. "Thank you."

"Not a problem."

"I don't know if I've got much in my fridge, but you're welcome to anything you find. And don't worry about Thor—he's had his dinner."

Kevin took her by the shoulders and gently turned her toward the door. "Drive safely, Nat."

"If I'm not back by ten, can you take him outside?"

"I can do that."

"And don't forget to scoop, if necessary. The waste bags are in a dispenser attached to his leash."

"I'll figure it out," he promised. "Go."

"I'm going." But first she bent to kiss the top of the dog's head. "You be a good boy for Kevin, okay?"

Thor responded by licking her chin.

"Seriously," he said, when she reached for the doorknob. "The dog gets a kiss and I don't?"

"Oh, alright," she relented, turning back. "Since you saved me having to make a trip out to the ranch."

She pursed her lips and kissed him as chastely as she'd kissed the dog.

"I'm also going to help with your packing," he said, sliding his arms around her waist and drawing her toward him.

"And you think that earns you another kiss?"

"At least one more."

Then he was kissing her, and she was kissing him back. When his tongue swept along the seam of her lips, she opened for him willingly. When his hands slid up her back, she pressed herself against him, and made that soft humming sound low in her throat that never failed to drive him wild.

"You're going to make me miss my flight," she protested, when she finally eased out of his arms.

"Then I guess you better be on your way," he said.

Because he didn't want her to miss her flight—he just wanted her to want to.

And when she gave him a lingering glance over her shoulder as she walked out the door, he thought he might have succeeded.

Throughout her drive home after the quick charter to and from Salt Lake City, Nat told herself that, even if Kevin was still at her apartment, she absolutely was *not* going to sleep with him.

When she pulled into the parking lot behind her building and saw his truck still occupied one of the visitor spots, she suspected that she was lying to herself.

She also suspected that Sky was right. That the only way she was going to convince Kevin that there was no future for them together was to start seeing other people. And to encourage him to see other people.

They'd been in this relationship limbo for too long already, and while she knew that he'd be happy to move forward, she couldn't. There was no forward and definitely no future with Kevin, and the sooner she made that clear to him, the better off they both would be.

So resolved, she opened the door to her apartment and walked inside. Kevin was on the sofa watching TV, Thor curled up beside him, sleeping with his head on Kevin's thigh.

"Looks like we've got a couple of slackers here," she said.

Thor immediately lifted his head, barked with joy and leaped off the sofa to greet her.

Kevin rose to his feet a little more slowly. "How was your flight?"

"Uneventful, which is always a good thing," she said. "How was your evening?"

"Productive, I think." He gestured to the boxes stacked in the corner of the living room.

"Wow." Nat was impressed. "You got a lot accomplished. Either that, or you just folded and taped the boxes to make it look as if you got a lot accomplished."

He opened the doors fronting two of her kitchen cupboards to reveal that they were empty.

"You got a lot accomplished," she said again.

"I left you a couple of plates and bowls, a coffee mug and a few utensils, but the rest of your kitchen stuff is packed, the boxes labeled.

"I also emptied the bookcases in the living room and have to ask—why do you have so many books? Haven't you heard of Kindle?"

"I'm an old-school kind of girl," she said.

"Well, because of all those books, you're going to need more boxes."

"So noted."

"I didn't touch anything in the bedroom or bathroom. I didn't want to…intrude…on your personal space."

She felt her lips curve. "You've never had any problems intruding on my personal space before."

"Maybe not," he allowed, an answering smile tugging at the corners of his mouth. "But you've always been right here with me when I intruded on your personal space."

"I'm here now," she noted.

"So I see."

"It occurred to me, on the way home, that you hadn't really been clear on whether you intended to stay until I got back."

"I wasn't sure if I should stay or go," he told her. "But I knew you were concerned about Thor being alone, so I stayed."

She took a step closer, so that she was standing directly in front of him. So close that he could touch her, if he wanted to touch her. "Is that the only reason you stayed?"

"No," he admitted, drawing her into his arms. "It's not the only reason."

"This was never supposed to be anything more than a fling," she reminded him.

"Just one night," he recalled, unfastening the buttons of her jacket.

She nodded. "One night to let the attraction burn out."

He slipped the jacket off her shoulders, draped it over the back of a chair. "When was that supposed to happen?" His voice was thick with desire and tinged with a hint of amusement.

"Almost six years ago," she admitted, sliding her hands beneath his T-shirt, eager to touch his lean, hard body. The man spent a lot of hours sitting in front of a computer, but he played as hard as he worked and kept himself in prime physical condition through various activities at AV.

"Six years," he echoed, his brow furrowed. "Maybe we're doing something wrong."

She was laughing as she unsnapped his jeans. "You think so?"

"It's the only explanation that makes sense." He'd already made quick work of the buttons that ran down the front of her shirt, and draped it over her jacket now. "Unless…"

"Unless what?" She dipped her hand into the front of his pants, eager to move things along.

"Unless—" He sucked in a breath as her fingers wrapped around him. "Unless you've fallen in love with me."

She immediately stilled and slowly lifted her gaze to meet his.

"I haven't," she said, in a voice that was gentle but firm, worried that he was projecting his feelings onto her.

He shrugged, but she'd seen the flash of hurt in his eyes before he managed to conceal it.

"Then it must be that we're doing something wrong," he said lightly, before she could call him out.

She knew they needed to talk—to set the record straight once and for all. But he was already touching her again, and the desires of her body were clamoring a lot louder than the caution in her mind.

"I guess that's possible," she allowed, as her pants joined the pile of clothes.

"So maybe we need to keep at it until we get it right," he suggested, leading her to the bedroom.

"Maybe we do," she agreed.

Thor whined once when the door was closed almost against his nose, keeping him on the outside. Then, thankfully, he fell silent.

Kevin eased Nat onto the bed. She drew him down with her, savoring the weight of his body pressing her into the mattress, glorying in the delicious friction of his skin against hers that wiped any remnants of concern from her mind.

He covered her mouth again as his hands stroked over her, making her skin vibrate with need. He peeled away her bra and panties, his mouth following the path of his hands.

Touching. Tasting.

Heating her blood.

Melting her bones.

She arched beneath him, a wordless plea for more.

For everything she knew he could give her.

She wanted the familiar clash of needs and the desperate mindless pursuit of release.

But Kevin had something different in mind this time.

Though desire pounded in his veins, he held it in check, determined to take his time, to show her how much she was cherished. How much she was loved.

It frustrated him that she still wasn't ready to hear the words, but he could no longer hide his feelings. Or maybe he no longer wanted to.

He captured both of her hands in one of his and lifted them over her head, holding them there while he feathered kisses over her cheeks, along her jaw, down her throat. Making her sigh. Making her shiver.

"Kevin." His name was a whisper on her lips. A plea.

"I'm here," he said. "I've got you."

"I need..."

"I know what you need," he assured her, as he resumed his leisurely—and very thorough—exploration of her body. He worshipped every dip and curve, every inch of silky skin, including those that bore evidence of the trauma she'd only recently, finally, shared with him. His lips touched on her scars—not lingering, just loving, as he loved every other part of her.

When she was quivering in his arms, as desperate for him as he was for her, he took a quick moment to sheath himself with a condom before joining their bodies together. She came apart almost immediately. He felt the intensity of the waves that rippled through her, found himself caught up in the current and dragged into the abyss of pleasure along with her.

It was a long time after that before either of them spoke, and it was Natalya who eventually broke the silence to say, "I think we should see other people."

"You really need to work on your timing."

The ice in Kevin's voice made her shiver.

"I didn't mean to blurt it out like that," Nat said, immediately chagrined.

"You mean while our bodies were still tangled together after sex?"

"You're angry," she acknowledged. "And I'm sorry that you're angry, but we can't keep going on like this."

"I didn't hear any complaints ten minutes ago."

"I don't have any complaints at all," she assured him in a gentle tone. "You're an amazing man, an incredibly skilled lover and one of my best friends."

"I appreciate the glowing reference," he said, not sounding appreciative at all. "But if I'm all that, why do you want to see other people?"

"It's not just me," she said. "We *both* need to see other people."

"I can't figure you out," Kevin admitted. "You were a lieutenant in the navy. You flew missions in the dead of night in enemy territory—probably without breaking a sweat—but the prospect of having a real relationship with someone who cares about you sends you into a tailspin."

"I told you, from the very beginning, that I didn't want a relationship."

"So you did," he acknowledged. "But a lot has changed since then."

"Nothing has changed."

"There you go—lying again," he noted, his tone casual. "But this time, you're lying to yourself."

"I *don't* want a relationship," she insisted.

"And yet, you keep showing up at my door and waking up in my bed."

"You're in my bed right now," she pointed out. "And sometimes sex is just sex."

"Sometimes it is," he agreed, in that same maddeningly patient tone. "And sometimes it's a lot more."

"I don't want more."

"And yet," he said again.

She shook her head. "And yet *nothing*."

"So why did you turn down the doggy doctor's invitation to dinner?" he challenged.

Her gaze narrowed. "How did you hear about that?"

"You should know it's not possible to have a private conversation in the middle of The Daily Grind."

"Isn't that the truth?" she muttered.

"So why did you say no?" Kevin asked again.

"Because I had to work."

"Is that the only reason?"

"What other reason possible reason could there be?"

"I think that's something you need to figure out for yourself," he said. "When you do, you know where to find me. And if you're lucky, I might be waiting for you."

"So I've been thinking," Jay said, addressing the group of senior staff that he'd invited to Diggers' for a bite to eat after work Friday afternoon.

"Is this an official staff meeting?" Nat asked. "Should someone be taking notes?"

"Someone else can take notes," Matt said, surveying the platters of food that had been delivered to the table. "I'm starving."

"No notes required," Jay assured them.

"So what have you been thinking about?" Kevin asked, transferring some wings to his plate.

"The summer camps."

"We've still got a few weeks before they start," Nat pointed out. "And all the groups are full already."

"That's because we have great programs," Matt said.

"And that's why I've been thinking that we should expand our schedule to six weeks of camps instead of four next summer," Jay told them.

Kevin looked at his colleagues around the table, as if gauging their reactions to the boss's announcement.

"Can we take him out to the paintball field and shoot him?" he wondered aloud.

"That's the best idea I've heard since I sat down," Nat said.

"This is a *great idea*, guys," Jay insisted, refilling his glass from the pitcher of beer on the table.

Kevin, Matt and Nat exchanged looks.

"But perhaps this wasn't the right time to bring it up," their boss finally acknowledged.

"You think?" Nat responded dryly.

"Okay, so we'll table the discussion until early fall, when the anticipation and chaos of the summer crowds has faded from your memories," he decided.

"Good idea," Kevin said, reaching for a slice of garlic bread.

For the next several minutes, they chatted about other upcoming group events.

When the platters of food were almost empty, Matt wiped his fingers on a napkin and said, "Thanks for this, boss, but I've gotta get home for dinner."

Nat looked pointedly at his empty plate. "Because you didn't just eat?"

He shrugged. "Carrie's making meat loaf tonight—not my favorite."

"And I promised to help my brother fix some loose panels in his fence," Kevin said.

Jay looked at Nat. "What's your excuse for cutting out before the check comes?"

"I don't need an excuse," she said. "You were always going to pick up the check and expense it, anyway. I do, however, have a dog waiting for me to pick him up from PAWS before I head back to AV."

"Do you think he can he wait another half hour?" Jay asked, as their colleagues headed off.

"Sure," she agreed easily. "Sumera's on the clock until six, anyway. What's up?"

"I know you take on a lot of extra work when we run the summer camps, and I just wanted to assure you that, if we decide to expand our offerings next summer, we'll hire more seasonal staff to compensate."

"Have you considered the expense of more staff?" she asked. "I don't just mean their wages but the insurance premiums. You need to be sure the additional registration fees will offset the extra costs."

"I figured you'd have questions," he admitted, opening the folder she hadn't noticed was by his elbow and passing a page across the table to her.

She frowned at the chart. "These numbers don't just reflect an extra two weeks of camp but twice as many groups."

Jay nodded. "We had almost three applications for every spot we had available this summer," he said again. "And every time I had to explain to a disappointed parent that our camps were already full, I had a mental image of money—stacks of money—flying out the window."

"Lucky for you, you were born with a silver spoon in your mouth and probably have stacks of money under your mattress," Nat said. "Maybe your mattress is even made of stacks of money."

"Is the comedy act over? Can we get back to having a serious conversation now?"

"Sure," she agreed with a shrug. "You know I was only kidding about the silver spoon thing, right? Not that it's not true, but I know you work harder than any of us and—"

"Can you shut up for one minute, Nat?"

"Sure," she said again.

"You've been my right hand for almost seven years," he said, his expression as serious as his tone. "And I've talked to you before about my plans to further expand Adventure Village."

She nodded. "A ropes course, zip line, indoor trampolines."

"The trampolines were your idea."

"And a good one," she insisted. "We need more indoor activities to keep customers showing up in inclement weather. Something more than laser tag, mini golf and video games."

"If we want to add more indoor activities, we need more indoor space, which will require a significant investment of time and money."

"I've got some money set aside," she said, surprising her boss. "Not stacks of it, but a modest investment fund."

"I don't want your money, Nat. I want you."

"Um…"

Jay laughed. "Yeah, that didn't come out the way I intended. What I meant to say is that I want to know that you're committed to the park. Before I give the go-ahead for any of the expansion plans, I need you to be onboard one hundred percent."

"Have I given you any reason to think that I wouldn't be?"

"No," he admitted. "But I can't help feeling that you could be doing so much more than this."

"There are plenty of people who would say the same thing about you," she noted.

"And most of them are members of my own family," he confirmed.

"There you go."

"But I'm me, so I know what I'm thinking," he said. "You hold your cards very close to the vest."

"Do you think I'd walk ever out and leave you high and dry?"

"No," he said. "But I want to know that you're here because you want to be here and not because you're worried that I'd struggle to keep my head above water without you."

"I don't believe for a minute that you couldn't do this without me," she said. "But I don't want you to do it without me."

"I heard that Harry offered you a full-time gig with Mountain Charters."

"The same gig he's offered to me for each of the last three years."

"You're not going to take it?"

She shook her head. "In fact, I've given him notice that I plan to cut back my hours."

"Why?"

"Because I want to stay in one place—I don't want to be flying here and there and sleeping in hotels and worrying that I'm leaving you in the lurch because a mechanical problem or unexpected weather system stranded me out of town for an extra night or two."

"That hasn't been a problem in the past."

"But I've got Thor now, so I can't take that chance. And I love my job at AV, so the decision was a no-brainer."

Jay didn't look convinced. "You could probably make three or four times more money as a pilot than what I pay you."

"More like five times," she told him.

"Seriously?"

She nodded.

"Maybe I should get my pilot's license," he said.

"We both know if you only cared about making lots of money, you'd be sitting behind a desk at Blake Mining right now instead of here with me."

He lifted his glass of beer. "This is only one of the reasons that I know I made the right decision."

"Day drinking?" she teased.

"Doing something I love and doing it with my friends."

"I'll drink to that," she said, tapping her glass against his.

"I'm glad to hear it," he said, "because I want to offer you a stake in the business."

She carefully centered her glass on the paper coaster. "Why?"

"Because Adventure Village would never have become the success that it is without you."

"I think you're giving me more credit than I deserve."

"I'm not," he insisted. "And I'm aware that this acknowledgment is coming late in the game, but you deserve it."

"I'm a little confused," she admitted. "Not two minutes ago, you said that you didn't want my money."

"I'm not asking you to buy in," he said. "I'm offering you a five percent stake in the company."

She eyed him warily. "There's no such thing as a free meal."

"This isn't free—you've earned it with hard work."

"And yet you want something else from me," she guessed.

"I'd like you to sign a three-year contract."

"You don't need to give me five percent of your business to entice me to sign a contract. Considering the current economic climate, I'd be a fool to reject that kind of job security."

"Well, that's the offer," he said. "You sign a three-year contract and you get five percent of the company as a signing bonus."

She lifted her glass to her lips, swallowed the last mouthful of beer. "What if I said I wanted ten percent?"

Jay grinned. "I told Alyssa that you'd counter."

"Glad I didn't disappoint."

"You never could," he told her.

"So?" she prompted.

"Ten percent and a five-year contract."

"You keep handing out shares and you'll be in danger of becoming a minor partner in your own business," she cautioned.

"You let me worry about that," he said.

"I have one more question."

"What's that?"

"Why now?"

"As I already noted, I needed to know that you were one hundred percent committed before I moved ahead with any kind of expansion. But also, and more important, because I think you're finally ready."

"What's changed that you think I'm ready for something now that I wasn't a year—or even six months—ago?" she wondered aloud.

He grinned. "You got a dog."

Chapter Thirteen

Jake had suggested that Thor could hang out at PAWS on the day of Nat's actual move, so that the dog wouldn't be underfoot while people were in and out. But since realizing that her canine companion was likely feeling stressed and uncertain about what was happening, she insisted on keeping him with her, so he wouldn't have any reason to worry that he might get left behind.

"I thought you said you didn't have much stuff," Jay remarked, when he walked into her apartment Saturday morning and saw the stack of boxes.

"Apparently I've acquired a few things over the last several years," she told him, breathing a quiet sigh of relief when both Matt and Kevin entered behind their boss.

After the way he'd stormed out of her apartment the last time he was there, she hadn't been sure Kevin would show up for the move. She'd seen him since then, of course. Their paths had crossed several times at AV and they'd both attended the unofficial staff meeting at Diggers', but they'd always been careful to keep their personal relationship separate from their work and continued to do so.

Which brought to mind another question—

"If you're all here, who's in charge at the park?"

"Sumera's manning the shop. Marcus is on-site at the fields and Charley will be at the go-kart track when it opens at ten."

Obviously Jay had such complete faith in all his employees that he had no concerns about operations running smoothly in the absence of the entire senior staff—even on a Saturday.

"Any of this furniture yours?" Matt asked, as Jay and Kevin started loading boxes onto the dolly they'd brought.

"Just the blanket chest in the bedroom. And the desk and desk chair."

The blanket chest was the one piece of furniture that she'd brought with her from California. It was old—and it looked it, having been passed down to her from her paternal grandmother and namesake, and it was the only thing she'd taken out of the house that she'd briefly shared with her ex-husband when she left.

Jay, Matt and Kevin all had pickup trucks, so it wasn't long before Nat's apartment was empty of everything that needed to go. When it was, she turned in her key to Mrs. Tocchet and—after the building manager did a walk-through inspection of the unit—accepted the refund of her damage deposit.

By the time she loaded up Thor and made her way to her new town house, Jay and Matt and Kevin had already started unloading their vehicles. Nat let Thor loose in the backyard so that she could lend a hand.

She picked up a box marked "Master Bedroom" and carried it up the stairs, following Steven, who had a box marked "Office."

"Don't tell me there aren't things that need to be done at your new place," she said.

"Of course there are," he agreed. "But I heard that this is where the pizza and beer were going to be."

"Later," she promised.

The rest of the day passed in a whirlwind of activity.

She honestly hadn't expected so many people to be willing to do so much. She would have been grateful to have the boxes transferred to her new home—and thrilled if any of them actually ended up in the appropriate rooms. But her friends went above and beyond, helping to unpack and put away, freeing her of the heavy lifting while she kept busy supervising their efforts.

"I almost forgot about these," Jay said, returning to the house with a platter of brownies covered in plastic wrap. "Alyssa apologizes for not being able to help, but she sent these to help fuel your workers."

"When did your eight-months-pregnant wife have time to make brownies?" Nat wondered.

"Last night. She always goes on a baking binge in the nesting stage."

"Well, I appreciate the brownies. And especially your help. But maybe you shouldn't have left her alone at home to chase after two other kids.,"

"Three other kids," he said.

Her eyes went wide.

He laughed. "No, the baby didn't pop out last night. The third is Maya. And Sky's there with her, too."

The two women had become good friends when they both worked at Diggers', Nat recalled. Sky had been a steady fixture behind the bar since she was of legal age to serve, and had, in fact, been working there when she met the man who would become her husband. Alyssa had moved to Haven to accept a teaching position at the high school, but she had some experience tending bar in college and decided to apply for a posted job to fill some of her spare time.

Though it wasn't surprising that the coworkers had become friends, it was perhaps surprising that they'd remained so in light of the fact that Sky was a Gilmore and Alyssa had married a Blake.

Nat had been fascinated to hear the local folklore alleging that, more than 150 years earlier, a shady developer had sold a 100,000-acre parcel of land in Nevada to Everett Gilmore, a struggling farmer from Plattsmouth, Nebraska. And apparently that same developer also sold 100,000 acres to Samuel Blake, a down-on-his-luck businessman from Omaha. Both men then proceeded to pack up their families and their worldly possessions and head west for a fresh start.

Everett Gilmore arrived first, and it was only when Samuel Blake showed up with his deed in hand that the two men realized they'd been sold the exact same parcel. Since both title deeds were stamped with the same date, there was no way of knowing who had a legitimate claim to the land. Distrustful of the local magistrate's ability to resolve the situation to their satisfaction—and unwilling to admit that they'd been duped—the two men agreed to share the property, using the natural divide of Eighteen-Mile Creek as the boundary between their lands.

Because the Gilmores had already started to build their home on the west side of the creek, the Blakes were relegated to the higher elevation on the east side, where the land was mostly comprised of rocky hills and ridges. So while the Gilmores' cattle immediately benefited from grazing on more hospitable terrain, the Blakes struggled to keep their herd viable—at least until gold and silver were found in the hills on their side of creek and they gave up ranching in favor of mining.

The bad blood between the two families had eventually comingled, though there were still several members on each side who remained distrustful of the other. Obviously Sky and Alyssa were not.

A few hours later, just after Nat had pilfered the last brownie, her pregnant friend walked through the door with another plate of treats.

"I thought supplies might be running low," Alyssa said, laughing as she kissed Nat on the cheek still stuffed with brownie.

"I'm so glad you're here—but where are the kids?" Nat asked, after she'd finished chewing and swallowing her snack.

"At home with a babysitter. I wasn't sure about coming, but I figured it might be my last chance to get out of the house without a baby attached to my boob."

"Any day now?" she asked sympathetically.

"I'm hoping any day now," Alyssa confided. "My doctor says I've still got another two weeks—at least."

"Well, I'm really glad you're here," Nat said sincerely. "Now if I'll just excuse me for a minute, I'm going to order some more pizzas."

Before she could reach for her phone, the door opened again and Sky and Jake walked in. She was carrying a stack of pizza boxes and he had a case of beer in each hand.

"That's quick service," Alyssa noted.

"Obviously I need to tip the delivery people," Nat agreed, surprised—and touched—to see that her friends had made the trek into town for her.

"I can't believe you guys are here," she said, hugging first Sky then Jake, after they'd deposited the food and drink on the counter in the kitchen.

"I can't believe you thought we'd miss your housewarming party," Sky chided.

"It's hardly a party," Nat protested.

"Maybe it *wasn't* a party," Jake said, with a wink. "But that was before we got here."

Nat smiled at her friends, then muttered something about needing to check on Thor as an excuse to duck out of the house.

She just needed a minute—maybe two—to catch her breath and corral all the unexpected emotions that were coursing through her system.

"What's going on?" Sky asked, lowering herself onto the back step beside Nat a short while later.

"I just wanted some air."

"Feeling a little overwhelmed?"

She nodded.

"In a good way or a bad way?"

"In a good way, I think," Nat said.

"Okay. Because I can clear everyone out, if it's too much."

"I expected Jay and Matt and Kevin today, because they told me that they'd be here. Then other people started showing up, and I thought it would be too much. But actually... It's kind of perfect."

"'Other people' meaning more of your friends?"

"Yeah."

"You've lived in Haven almost seven years," Sky pointed out. "Are you really surprised to realize that you've made so many friends?"

"A little," she admitted. Then she shrugged. "I know that I sometimes come across as a cool and standoffish."

Sky's expression grew dark. "Who told you that?" she demanded, her gaze narrowing as she realized the answer to her own question. "Jake's right—your ex-husband needs to have his ass kicked, and I'd like to be the first in line.

"Not that I don't believe you're capable of doing it yourself," she continued. "But I wonder why you haven't done so."

"Well, at the time that he was becoming my ex-husband, I could barely get my own ass out of bed," Nat confided. "And when I'd recuperated enough to be able to do it, I realized he wasn't worth the effort."

"I hope you really believe that."

"I really do."

"Then prove it," Sky challenged. "Get back in there and enjoy your party."

By the time everyone was gone—and Sky had supervised to ensure that the house was cleaned up before they all cleared out—Nat's new home was in order.

And it really did feel like a home.

She'd spent much of her life as a nomad, moving from post to post with her family, as dictated by her dad's military career, before choosing to follow the same path herself.

Sure, she'd had a home base in California when she married Christopher. They'd bought a place together when they were engaged, lived in it for a few weeks before the wedding—and a few more weeks after the honeymoon, before she was deployed.

In fact, the almost seven years that she'd lived in The Square was the longest she'd ever stayed in one place. And Jake was right—when she moved in to that apartment, she'd assumed it was only temporary. In fact, she'd negotiated a six-month lease instead of the usual twelve, because she hadn't been sure she wanted to stay in Haven—or maybe she'd just been unwilling to admit that she did.

But somehow, over the next several years, she'd put down roots in the Nevada town without ever intending or even realizing it. And now she was happy to let those roots spread and grow.

"Well, I think that's it," Kevin said, tying up the last bag of garbage and adding it to the pile in the garage.

Things had been a little awkward between them earlier in the day. Or maybe *stilted* was a better term. But they'd been friends for a long time and thankfully the foundation of that friendship seemed to hold strong beneath the weight of their recent conflict.

And when he lingered after everyone else had gone, it wasn't awkward at all.

"I can't believe we got everything unpacked and set it in only a few hours," she said now.

"Not quite everything," he pointed out. "Your new mattress isn't going to be delivered until Monday."

"I forgot about that," she admitted. "I guess it's a good thing your brother didn't want to take his sofa."

"You're going to sleep on the sofa?"

"I'm betting it's more comfortable than the chair."

"There is another option," he told her.

"What's that?"

"A bed at my place. And before you pull a muscle jumping to the conclusion that I'm trying to take advantage of your exhausted state," he hastened to clarify, "I was referring to the spare bed."

"I appreciate the offer," she said. "But I think I should spend the night here. Poor Thor's confused enough without moving him to yet another place tonight."

He looked for the subject of her concern and found "poor Thor" snoring away on his doggy bed beside the fireplace hearth.

"Your call," Kevin said with a shrug, before he made his way to the door.

"But thank you again, for the offer and for everything else you did today. And this week."

"It was my pleasure." He gave her a quick hug, releasing her far too soon. "See you around, neighbor."

She smiled, grateful that their friendship was back on track—and maybe just a little bit sorry that he finally seemed to have given up on the possibility of something more. "See you around."

She slept like the dead.

Pure physical exhaustion led her to crash, facedown on the sofa, almost as soon as she'd closed and locked the door behind Kevin. Apparently she had taken the time to grab a pillow from the bedroom and cover herself with the beautiful throw Sky had given her as a housewarming gift, though, because that was the composition of her makeshift bed when she awoke with a jolt to find a pair of dark eyes intently studying her the next morning.

Letting out a shaky laugh, she lifted a hand to rub Thor's cheek.

"And how was your first night in our new home?"

He responded with a swipe of his raspy tongue over her chin.

"You don't look as exhausted as I feel this morning," she noted. "Of course, you crashed in the middle of the party and I didn't get to sleep until everyone had gone."

He tilted his head as if to convey that he'd be able to make sense of her words if only she'd stop talking gibberish.

"I know what words you understand," she said. "But I need coffee this morning before you get your *R-U-N*."

Thor's head tilted in the other direction.

"And you probably need to go out," she realized, as she rose to her feet.

Out was another of the words that he knew, and he responded by racing to the front door.

"Not that way, this way," she said, turning toward the back of the house.

Thor reached the door before she did and waited for her to open it and give him the "okay."

"That is so much more convenient than having to walk down three flights of stairs to find a patch of grass," Nat noted, as she watched Thor commence an apparent effort to sniff every blade of grass in his new yard.

Leaving him to explore, she made her way to the kitchen.

Her single-serve coffee maker was already set up on the counter, the reservoir filled with water and one of her favorite pods at the ready.

Kevin, she guessed, unable to prevent the smile that curved her lips.

He really was a great guy. And a good friend. And she needed to learn to be grateful to have him in her life in that capacity and not yearn for anything more.

While her coffee was brewing, she went upstairs to exchange her boxer shorts and ribbed tank for proper running shorts and T-shirt. She brushed her teeth, pulled her hair into a ponytail and headed back downstairs for that first cup of java.

By the time Thor came back in from doing his morning business, her cup was empty.

As soon as she reached into the closet for her shoes, he raced to the front door again and sat waiting for her. She clipped on his leash, then opened the door and stepped out. She started at a slow jog, allowing them both a chance to warm up, and happened to arrive at Kevin's house just as he was closing his front door.

"Since when do you run?" she asked, noting that the shoes on his feet were specific to that purpose.

"Since my sophomore year in high school when I decided I wanted to move from the third string to the first on the football team."

"So you've been doing this a long time," she realized.

He struck a pose, twisting at the middle and flexing both his biceps. "How do you think I maintain my toned physique?"

"I figured you got enough of a workout carrying that massive ego around with you."

"Massive…what?" he said, making her laugh.

She was grateful that they seemed to be back on an even keel, able to joke and tease one another. And they fell into an easy rhythm together, Thor happily keeping pace between them.

"Do you know where you're going?" Kevin asked, when they reached the end of the street.

"Not really," she admitted.

"How long do you want to run?"

"Twenty minutes or so fits into my usual morning routine."

He nodded and veered off to the left.

As they completed a short circuit of the neighborhood, Nat noted that there were a handful of other runners out and about—including a new mom with a jogging stroller, who she watched with just the teeniest hint of envy. They also crossed paths with several other people walking dogs and a few more peddling bicycles.

At the end of the route, he left her at her door with a nod before continuing back to his own house.

And somehow, running with Kevin in the morning became a routine. As did walking in the evening. And when Nat mentioned that she needed some stuff for her new place, to make it feel more like hers, Kevin offered to take her to an antiques shop out by the highway. He helped her pick out paintings and art and a ridiculous set of banjo-strumming roosters that were actually salt and pepper shakers and made her smile every time she looked at them.

He helped her plant flowers in the garden at the front of her house and in boxes around her deck. And he took her to a craft show one weekend where she found a gorgeous handmade quilt in shades of purple and blue that she immediately coveted.

"If you want it, buy it," Kevin urged, as she trailed a hand over the soft fabric.

She shook her head. "Maybe, if my bedroom was blue. But I don't see it working with the sage green walls."

"So paint your walls," he said.

She blinked. "I can do that?"

He laughed. "It's your house, Nat. You can do what you want."

"Steven won't mind?"

"I might suggest you check with him if you wanted to slap wood paneling on the walls or paint a black-and-red checkerboard on the floor, but he's not going to care that you put blue paint over green."

So she bought the quilt—and then they went to the hardware store and studied paint chips until they found the exact shade she wanted. And when she was ready to paint, he was there to help her do it.

"I'm sorry about ruining your day off," Alyssa said, when she met Nat at the door, very early the following Thursday morning.

"It's not my day off yet," Nat said. "It's still the middle of the night."

"I'm sorry about that, too. Jay's parents promised that they'd be here for the girls when Delivery Day arrived, but they're out of town."

"The baby wasn't supposed to come yet," Jay chimed in.

"Apparently you forgot to give him that memo," his wife responded with saccharine sweetness.

"Him?" Jay asked hopefully.

"We'll know soon enough," Alyssa said.

"No explanation needed," Nat assured them both. "I'm happy to be here."

"Where's Thor?" Jay asked.

"I left him with Kevin—I didn't think you needed him underfoot as you were trying to get out the door."

"I'm sure he appreciated you knocking on his door at 3:00 a.m. Or maybe you were already there," Alyssa mused.

"I texted him first to give him a heads-up."

"Well, if Kevin wants to bring Thor over later, that's fine. I have no doubt Lucy and Clara will love him."

"Yeah, but then he'll get all the attention and I'm in desperate need of little-girl cuddles," Nat said.

"Let's see if you still feel the same way after fourteen hours with them."

"Fourteen hours?"

Alyssa shrugged. "Well, that's how long I was in labor with Clara—"

She sucked in a breath, then panted it out, breathing through the contraction.

"Lucy was twenty-two hours," she finished, when she could speak again.

"How far apart are your contractions?" Nat asked worriedly.

"Twelve minutes," Jay said, moving past with his wife's hospital bag.

"Nine," Alyssa corrected him.

His brows lifted. "Then we better get on the road."

She nodded and gave Nat a quick hug. "Thanks again."

Nat watched through the window as Jay guided his wife to the passenger side of their SUV, carefully helped her stretch the seat belt over her enormous belly to ensure she would be safe en route to the hospital, then raced around to the driver's side and shifted the vehicle into gear.

It always warmed her heart to see them together, to see how much in love they were with one another after half a decade and almost three kids together.

Nat had known Jay for almost as long as she'd lived in Haven. Before he'd hired her to work at Adventure Village, one of her regular charter clients was Blake Mining—the company his family owned. As a result, she'd been there through every stage of his relationship with Alyssa, from neighbors to friends to lovers.

It jarred her a little to realize that her relationship with Kevin had followed a similar track, although they'd first been friends and then lovers and now neighbors. But that's where the parallel ended, because she knew there was no happily-ever-after in their future. Thankfully, he seemed to have accepted her decision to end their personal involvement with no lingering hard feelings. And if she'd recently found herself wishing that he'd pushed back a little more, well, that was her problem.

She pushed the unwelcome thought aside to refocus on the

joyful events of the day. She remembered when Alyssa had
Lucy and then, two and a half years later, Clara. Now they
were adding another baby to their family, and Jay and Alyssa
had already told Nat that they intended to ask her to be a godmother to their children when they were baptized—further
proof that the lines between her professional and personal relationships with her boss and his friends had blurred so much
that she was no longer certain a line even existed, and she was
glad for it. She had a wonderful time with the girls, who were
thrilled to find "Auntie Nat" there when they woke up—and
even more overjoyed when they learned that Mommy had
gone to the hospital to have their baby brother.

"Are you sure you're getting a brother?" Nat asked, not
wanting them to be disappointed if they were wrong because,
as far as she knew, Jay and Alyssa hadn't wanted to know the
gender of any of their children prior to each of their births.

"We're sure," Lucy said confidently. "It's Daddy's turn to
get a baby that he can play with."

Though the logic was hardly unassailable, Nat had to smile
at their rationale. Because even if she'd never have a baby of
her own to play with, she was lucky to have wonderful friends
who happily shared their precious little ones with her.

Chapter Fourteen

Kevin showed up after lunch—with Thor, who was as happy to meet Lucy and Clara as they were to meet him.

"Did you think I needed reinforcements?" she asked, as she tidied up the dishes from the girls' meal.

"It was more that Thor was moping around, wondering where you were," Kevin told her.

"Yeah, he looks real interested in me," she noted dryly.

"Well, that's why I came with him," he said. "So you wouldn't feel too neglected."

After the kids and dog had spent a fair amount of time tumbling around the backyard, Nat rounded them up for quiet time. For Clara, that meant a nap, though the little girl insisted—between yawns!—that she wasn't sleepy.

With Lucy settled in her room with a stack of picture books, Nat changed Clara's diaper before she laid her down to sleep.

"You're pretty good at that," Kevin noted, as she slid a dry diaper beneath the little girl's bottom and quickly fastened the tabs.

"I was living with my sister-in-law when my youngest nephew was born," she reminded him. "So I got pretty adept at changing diapers. Though it's almost easier when they're babies, because they're a lot less squirmy," she said, tickling Clara's belly and making her giggle.

"I don't have the same hands-on experience," Kevin said, as

she pulled the little girl's pink denim short-alls back into place. "Both of my sisters moved away before they had their kids."

"You have two sisters?"

"Yeah."

"How did I not know that?"

He shrugged. "We don't usually talk about that kind of stuff."

Important stuff, he meant.

And that had been her choice.

Because she didn't want to complicate their physical relationship by mixing it up with personal stuff.

But they were also friends, and friends should be able to share with one another.

"I met one of your sisters a few years back," she recalled, after Clara was settled in her crib. "The one with the twin boys."

Thor, tuckered out from all his activity with the girls, settled beneath the crib for a nap, too.

"My younger sister, Eden. She and her husband, Phillip, run a boutique hotel in Back Bay."

"Back Bay—as in Boston?" she asked, making her way down the stairs so they could continue their conversation without disturbing the girls.

"Yeah."

"How old are their twins now?"

"Dawson and Sawyer turned nine just a few weeks ago."

"Wow."

He nodded.

"And your other sister?" Nat prompted.

"Gina. She's the oldest—an elementary school principal in Reno. Her husband, Domenic, is a trailer mechanic."

"How many kids do they have?"

"Two." He began scooping up the building blocks that were scattered across the carpet. "Paris is seven and Atlas is almost four."

"I guess you don't get to see either of your sisters or their families very often?"

"Not as often as I'd like," he confirmed. "But we FaceTime fairly regularly."

"What about your parents?" she asked. "Where are they?"

"They passed away."

"I'm sorry," she said sincerely. "I didn't know."

"It's okay," he said. "It happened a long time ago."

"What happened? And how long ago?"

"It was a car accident. Fourteen years ago. Seven weeks after my college graduation—and four days after my older sister and her husband got home from their honeymoon."

She wasn't surprised by the specificity of his response, because she understood only too well how the date of a life-changing event could become permanently etched in a person's mind.

"Steven had just finished his first year of college and Eden was looking forward to her final year of high school." He glanced around, as if for something else to tidy, before realizing the toys had all been put away.

Nat took a seat on the sofa and, after another few seconds, he did the same.

"Gina and Dom had planned to move into an apartment near Weston's Garage, where he was working at the time," he continued. "Instead, they moved into her childhood bedroom of our family home. I wanted to tell them to take our parents' room, but I couldn't bring myself to make the offer, to admit that they were gone. And I think that's why she never suggested it, either. It was as if we both thought that if we left their room exactly as it had always been, they might one day walk back through the door."

"Denial," she noted with sympathy. "The first stage of grief."

He nodded. "By the time the end of summer rolled around, Steven had decided that he didn't want to go back to school.

He wanted to get a job and stay home. I think we all drew into ourselves, our family, shocked by what we'd lost and clinging to one another."

"Obviously you managed to convince him otherwise."

"Gina did," he agreed. "She really stepped up and took over the mother role in the family. And Dom, bless him, didn't protest that they were putting their life together on hold until Steven and Eden were both ready to leave the nest. But Gina did it—she held our family together."

"I'm sure she had some help."

"Yeah. Dom was a rock."

"I wasn't just referring to her husband."

"I like to think I did my share," he allowed. "But there was never any doubt that Gina was in charge. She always was the bossy one."

Nat smiled at that. "It's interesting, isn't it, how different people handle loss in different ways?"

"Probably because we all have different life experiences."

"That makes sense," she agreed. "I always wondered why my mom moved out of California when my dad died. I know she got frustrated with the constant moving from one house to another whenever my dad was transferred, and yet, when she finally had the option of staying put, almost the first thing she did was move."

"Maybe because it was finally her choice," Kevin suggested.

"Maybe. Anyway, she lives in a retirement community in Phoenix now. She hadn't golfed a single game in all her life before she moved down there, now she's got tee times at least three days a week. She also plays bridge on Saturday nights and has afternoon cocktails every day with a group of neighbors."

"And isn't that proof that people really can change?"

"I guess it is."

"Certainly falling in love with Alyssa changed Jay."

"I can agree with that," Nat said. "Of course, if Jay had

backed off when you called dibs, Alyssa might be in labor with *your* third child right now."

"What are you talking about?"

"You think I don't remember how you guys almost came to blows because you thought your friend had moved in on the woman you had a crush on?" she said teasingly.

"He *did* move in on her," Kevin pointed out in his defense. "He knew her first."

"But I didn't know that," he said. "And anyway, it all worked out for the best."

"You've forgiven him?"

"I forgave him—and completely forgot that I'd ever had a crush on Alyssa—the night of Matt and Carrie's wedding."

"Because it was obvious to everyone there that Jay and Alyssa were head over heels for one another?" Nat guessed.

"Because you said *yes* when I asked you to dance—and then you let me take you home."

"I would have been stranded otherwise," she pointed out to him. "Because my date had already taken off with yours."

"I forgot that part," he admitted.

"I wasn't sorry to see them go," she said.

"Hard to believe that was almost six years ago."

The buzz of Kevin's phone cut through their introspection.

A smile spread across his face as he read the message displayed on the screen.

"A boy," he said. "Eight pounds, ten ounces, twenty-one inches with dark curly hair. They're going to call him Silas."

"Lucy and Clara have a baby brother." Nat felt tears sting the back of her eyes as she lifted her glass to swallow the lump of emotion in her throat.

She was overjoyed for her friends—and maybe just the teensiest bit sorry for herself.

"Hey, Gina," Kevin said, pleasantly surprised to see her name on the display before he connected the call. Though he kept in regular communication with both of his sisters, it was unusual for either of them to call for a spontaneous chat.

"I need a favor," she said without preamble, dispelling the notion that this was a casual call.

He could hear the tears in her voice and was immediately concerned, because his eldest sister had never been prone to emotional outbursts. Unlike Eden, who'd always been a drama queen.

"Anything," he immediately replied.

And he meant it.

"Can Paris stay with you for a little while?" Gina asked him now.

"Of course," he said.

"I'm hoping it will only be a few days, but…" She paused to draw a shuddery breath. "I really don't know."

"What can you tell me?" he asked gently.

"Atlas." Her voice hitched on her son's name. "He's sick. Really sick. A high fever and a weird rash. The pediatrician didn't seem to know what it was, so he sent us to a specialist who suggested that Atlas should be admitted to the hospital for further tests. It's not contagious," she hastened to assure him. "Paris is fine, but Atlas is at Renown Children's Hospital, and I can't be in both places—"

"I'm on my way," Kevin said, scooping his keys off the counter.

She didn't quite manage to stifle the sob. "I could have Domenic bring her to you, if that's easier."

"It's not," he said. "And I'm sure he'd rather be at the hospital with you and Atlas than making a six-hour round trip."

"Actually, I'm home right now," she told him. "I came home to pack a suitcase for Paris."

"I'll be there in three hours," he said.

Three hours was a lot of time to think and worry and pray. Because even a man who didn't regularly attend church—and occasionally questioned the existence of a God who could let bad things happen to innocent children—found himself appealing to the Deity when higher intervention was required. And while Kevin had confidence in the doctors caring for his four-year-old nephew, he figured a little extra help from above couldn't hurt.

He didn't question why Gina had called him rather than Steven or Eden. He had the most flexibility in his work and he lived in fairly close proximity, so he would have been more surprised if she'd hadn't reached out to him first.

He was climbing the stairs leading to her front door when it opened and his sister stepped out, closing it behind her. Before he could even offer a greeting, she threw herself into his arms, sobbing against his chest.

He held her while she cried, feeling helpless and wishing he could do more.

"Sorry," she said, when she finally managed to pull herself together and pull out of his arms.

"I wasn't completely unprepared for the tears," he said, "but I thought you'd at least let me get through the door first."

"I didn't want Paris to see me cry," Gina confided. "She's worried enough about her brother without seeing her mom fall apart."

"Is there any update?" he asked gently.

She shook her head. "Last I heard, they were running more tests. The poor kid's been poked and prodded so much, it's a wonder he's not black-and-blue."

She wiped her face and blew her nose on the tissue she carried. "How do I look?"

"Like your ragweed allergy is giving you some trouble."

"I'm not allergic to ragweed."

"Maybe you haven't been bothered by it in recent years, but it's definitely strong this year."

She finally clued in. "My face is blotchy and that's my

story?" He nodded and opened the door, gesturing for her to precede him.

Gina cleared her throat before calling up the stairs. "Paris, your uncle's here."

"Which one?" her daughter's voice called back.

"Uncle Kevin—the one I told you was coming. And it's a long drive back to Haven, so please don't make him wait."

"Can I get you anything?" Gina offered. "Coffee? Water?"

"I had both in the car."

"Bathroom?"

He nodded. "Yeah, I should probably use that before I hit the road again."

Gina gestured toward the main-level powder room, as if she might have forgotten that he'd been there once or twice—or two dozen times before. But he cut her some slack, because she had a lot more important things on her mind right now.

When he exited the powder room, Paris was finally making her way down the stairs, a backpack slung over one shoulder and a pillow in her other hand.

"Hi, Paris."

"Hi."

He couldn't blame her for her obvious lack of enthusiasm. She had to be worried about her brother, and now she was being shipped away from her family.

"Are you ready to go?"

"I guess," she said, shrugging the shoulder with the back-pack.

"Is that all you've got?" he asked.

"Not even close," Gina said, responding to his question before her daughter could. "Her suitcase is by the front closet."

He turned to look at the bag that would have been tagged as oversize by any major airline.

Apparently Gina thought Paris might be with him for a while. Or maybe the suitcase was stuffed with teddy bears.

He recalled that his niece had quite a collection—to which he'd been a regular contributor over the years.

"Mom packed it," Paris said. "Because apparently I can't be trusted to remember a toothbrush."

"Or the kitchen sink."

That earned him a small smile.

He almost suggested that she could leave the pillow as he had plenty of extras at his place, but he decided that if she wanted some comforts from home, she was entitled to them.

Unless one of those comforts was an iPod full of Taylor Swift tunes. Because he was not spending the next three hours listening to the pop star lament the loss of her seemingly endless string of boyfriends—not even for his favorite niece.

When Nat took Thor for his habitual evening walk on Tuesday, she was surprised to note that Kevin's truck wasn't in his driveway. As the person in charge of scheduling at AV—with the final stamp of approval given by the boss—she knew he wasn't there. Or not working there, anyway.

Sometimes members of the staff challenged their coworkers to games of laser tag or paintball or races to the top of the climbing wall, so it wasn't out of the realm of possibility that he might have gone to the park.

A second possibility was that he was hanging out with his brother, helping him with some of the updates Steven wanted to make on his new property.

A third was that he was on a date.

As she continued her leisurely stroll down Juniper Street, she decided that he was most likely on a date.

And good for him, because that was exactly what she'd wanted when she told him that they should see other people.

So why did the thought of him with another woman make her stomach feel tight and achy?

Or maybe it was the leftovers that she'd reheated for dinner that were responsible for her discomfort. Maybe a week was too long to keep pasta in the refrigerator.

When she got to the end of her usual route, she considered taking a different path back to her town house—one that wouldn't take her by Kevin's house again. But curiosity got the better of her.

This time, his truck was in the driveway.

And apparently he had brought home a female with him—though the willow-slim blond-haired girl sitting on his step was not at all what she'd imagined.

Thor, already almost as familiar with Kevin's town house as his own residence, started up the driveway, wanting to say "hello" to Kevin notwithstanding the fact that he'd been a no-show for their evening walk.

"Who are you?" the little girl demanded, when Nat let Thor drag her a few steps closer to the house.

"My name's Natalya."

The girl's gaze narrowed. "I don't know you. You're a stranger."

She nodded. "I don't know you, either. But I'm a friend of Kevin's."

"You mean, *Uncle* Kevin?"

"I guess I do."

"He went inside to get me a juice box."

"Okay." Nat considered continuing on her way, but there was something about the girl that tugged at her.

"What's your dog's name?" she asked now.

"Thor."

"That's a boy's name."

"It is," Nat agreed.

"Does he bite?"

"No." Nat could answer that question confidently, having watched the dog interact with any number of people and other pets without showing any hint of aggression.

"Can I pet him?"

"I'm still a stranger," Nat reminded her. "Don't you think you should check with your uncle first?"

"Check with your uncle about what?" Kevin asked, coming out the front door with the promised juice box—and a plate of grapes—in his hand.

"Can I pet Thor?" the little girl asked in response to his question.

He glanced at Nat then, a smile creasing his face. "Hi."

"Hi."

"I see you've met Paris," he said.

"Not officially."

"Well, this is Paris, my niece. Paris, this is Natalya, a friend of mine."

"Can I pet Thor?" Paris asked again, more interested in the dog than the woman.

"As long as Nat says it's okay," Kevin decided.

"Sure," she said, making her way up the walk before unclipping Thor's leash.

"Your older sister's daughter, right?" she asked Kevin, while the dog and child took a few minutes to get acquainted before falling madly in love with each other.

He nodded.

"She's visiting...for a few days?" Nat guessed.

"At least a few days," he confirmed. "Maybe longer."

"You sound a little apprehensive," she noted. "Have you never spent any one-on-one time with your niece before?"

"Sure, but never when she's been dumped on me because her little brother's in the hospital," he said, in a tone that reflected worry for his nephew.

"I can see how that would put a different spin on things," Nat said sympathetically. "Is he very sick?"

His expression was bleak. "Yeah."

She reached for his hand and squeezed it gently. "I'm sorry."

"Me, too."

"You'll let me know if there's anything I can do to help?" she prompted.

"This is helping already," he said, gesturing to where Paris and Thor were rolling around on the grass, the little girl responding with giggles every time the dog licked her face.

"Well, you know where to find us if she needs another doggy fix," Nat reminded him, giving his hand another squeeze before releasing it.

He nodded. "Thanks."

As Nat and Thor continued their short trek home, she realized that her stomach didn't feel tight and achy anymore.

Chapter Fifteen

When Nat reviewed the schedule of the day's events Wednesday morning, she saw that Kevin was scheduled to supervise a corporate team-building exercise that afternoon. Aware of his current circumstances, she reached out to ask if he was still able to come in or if she should find someone else to cover his shift. He replied with a quick message assuring her that he'd be there.

Nat was in the lunchroom when he came in with his niece just after noon, carrying trays laden with hot dogs and fries and onion rings and soda from the snack stand.

Paris nodded to Nat, a shy acknowledgment of greeting. But when she realized that Thor was at Nat's feet, all shyness disappeared.

"You hungry?" Kevin asked, nudging the tray of food toward Nat.

She surveyed the contents. "You know I don't eat hot dogs. But I do eat onion rings," she said, stealing one from the top of the basket.

"Can Thor have a treat?" Paris asked, with a fry in her hand.

"Food like that isn't good for dogs," Nat explained, sliding a plastic snap-top container closer to the girl. "Those are his vet-approved treats. You can give him one of those if you want."

She picked out a treat and Thor sat at attention, showing that he was a good boy.

When Paris had eaten her fill—and slipped three more treats to the dog—she asked to be excused.

Kevin nodded and handed over the bucket of tokens he'd obviously promised her.

When Paris stood up to head to the arcade, Thor rose, too, looking at Nat as if for permission.

"Do you want Thor to keep you company?" she asked Paris.

The girl's face lit up. "Sure."

"Go on," she said to Thor, who trotted happily after Kevin's niece.

"Don't leave the arcade," Kevin said, speaking firmly to her back. "This is a big place with lots of people in and out, so I need to know where you are at all times."

"I won't leave the arcade," she promised.

"Probably not for the next three weeks, considering the number of tokens you gave her."

"She wants to try *Mario Kart*—if she's not a good driver, those tokens'll be gone in half an hour."

"So…how did things go last night?" Nat asked, when Paris was out of earshot.

"Not great," he admitted.

"Did she have trouble sleeping in a strange bed?"

"She slept fine once she got to sleep. But her bedtime routine was thrown into chaos when she realized that her mom forgot to pack—in a suitcase the size of Rhode Island—a single pair of her pj's."

"The poor kid."

"Poor me," he said. "I'm the one who had to deal with her meltdown—and the one who was at the mall in Battle Mountain when it opened this morning."

"You could have saved yourself the trip to Battle Mountain and gone to Mother Hubbard's Cupboard."

"Mother Hubbard's Cupboard?" he echoed blankly.

"It's a children's clothing store on Main Street."

"And how was I supposed to know it was there?"

"Because it's on Main Street," she said again. "And you've apparently lived in this town your whole life."

"But I've never before needed to go shopping for kids' clothes," he pointed out to her.

"Well, if Paris runs out of socks, you now know where to get more."

"I also know how to operate a washing machine, so unless Thor eats all of her socks, I think we'll be fine."

"Thor doesn't eat socks."

"Just shoes."

"That only happened once," she felt compelled to point out in Thor's defense. "It was one pair of shoes. Actually, it was only one shoe of a single pair."

But it had been her favorite pair of army green Converse high-tops, and she hadn't been happy.

She also hadn't forgotten to close the closet door after that mishap.

"Anyway, I trust your excursion to the mall was successful? Paris found something she liked?"

"She got three nightgowns—each in a different color with a different Disney princess on the front."

"You're such a softie," she said, but with a smile intended to take any sting out of the words. "What else did you buy?"

"We only went for pajamas."

"That doesn't answer my question," she noted.

"A sparkly hairband, a pair of leggings printed with unicorns with sparkly horns—because they matched the hairband— and two teddy bears dressed in hospital scrubs," he finally confessed.

"*Two* teddy bears?"

"One for Paris and one for her brother." He shrugged. "Her idea."

"And a thoughtful one. How is Atlas? Have you heard anything new from your sister?" Nat asked.

"She called this morning—when we were on our way back from Battle Mountain. She didn't go into much detail, because I warned her that I was driving and she was on speakerphone, but she said the doctor is pretty sure Atlas has Kawasaki disease."

"I don't know what that is," Nat admitted.

"I didn't, either," Kevin said. "But I didn't want to ask with Paris listening intently to every word of our conversation, so I looked it up when we got back. Apparently it most often targets kids under the age of five, but because its symptoms are the same as so many other conditions, it's often misdiagnosed. And if untreated, it can cause serious complications."

"But they made the right diagnosis this time, didn't they?"

"I called Gina back when we got home, and she said the doctors are fairly certain that's what it is. They've given him something called an IVIG to bring down his fever and lower the risk of heart problems."

"Heart problems?" She was stunned. "In a *four-year-old*?"

He nodded.

"No wonder his parents are freaked out."

He nodded again, obviously shaken, too.

"If the treatment doesn't bring down his fever within thirty-six hours, they'll give him another dose."

"And then?" Nat asked cautiously.

"The doctors suggested that he might be home in two weeks and make a complete recovery within six."

She exhaled a quiet sigh. "That's a relief."

He nodded his agreement.

"And Paris will stay with you while he's in the hospital?"

"That's the plan," he confirmed. "But I don't think she's happy about it."

"She's had a lot of upheaval in her life the past couple of days," Nat noted. "And, on top of all that, she must be worried about her brother, too."

"I'm sure she is," he agreed.

"Well, bringing her here seems to have taken her mind off things."

"What kid doesn't love video games, right?" He sipped his Coke. "But I can't give her an endless supply of tokens and leave her to hang out here all day, every day, for the next two weeks."

"Well, you could, but it's probably not a good idea."

"Anyway, I was thinking we might plan a movie night at home tonight, since there isn't anything suitable playing at Mann's," he said, naming the local second-run theater.

"I bet she'll love that," Nat said.

"Any chance you want to join us?" he asked hopefully.

"I want to," she said. "But…it's Wednesday."

"Right. I forgot. I mean, I forgot that today is Wednesday." He swallowed another mouthful of soda. "The last thirty-six hours have been a blur."

She could see that was true.

And she was grateful that he'd accepted her response with no further explanation required. Because the veterans group relied on her to be there Wednesday nights, and she'd never let them down.

But Kevin was her friend, and she was afraid that she'd let him down far too many times over the years.

He didn't ask much of her—even this favor wasn't much— and she wanted to be there for him. To prove to him that, everything else aside, their friendship mattered to her.

"What time do you plan on starting the movie?"

"Probably around seven. I'm trying to keep to her usual bedtime schedule as much as possible."

"Okay," she said. "I'll give Jake a call to see if he's available to facilitate the meeting tonight. And if he is, I'll see you at seven."

Nat texted later that afternoon to ask Kevin if he had popcorn. He assured her that he did, but she still brought over Red

Vines and M&M's (plain and peanut—because she forgot to ask if Paris had a nut allergy).

"Supplemental snacks" she called them.

"So what are we watching?" Nat asked, following Kevin into the kitchen, where the corn was popping while Thor wandered off to find the little girl.

"Paris is scrolling through the Disney+ listings to figure that out."

"You have Disney+?"

"I do now," he said. "Since she's going to be here more than a few days, I need something to keep her occupied."

"And you figured the streaming service would be cheaper than buckets of tokens at the arcade?"

"More convenient, anyway," he said. "Since I have to work from home and she has to be here with me. She brought schoolwork with her, of course, and the plan is for her to do that in the morning while I'm at the computer. But I don't want her to be left twiddling her thumbs if her assignments don't keep her occupied very long."

"Makes sense," Nat agreed.

"You said I could pick the movie, right?" Paris called out from the living room.

"I did," her uncle confirmed.

"Anything I want?" she asked.

"Sure," he said, drizzling melted butter over the popped corn.

"Anything age appropriate," Nat felt compelled to interject.

"It's Disney," Kevin noted. "Isn't everything on Disney age appropriate?"

"Obviously you haven't scrolled through the guide."

"I signed up for the service an hour ago."

"Well, today's Disney's offerings include a lot more than *Snow White* and *Cinderella*," she told him.

"I know that much," he said. "There's also the four *Toy Story* movies and three about *Cars*."

"*Three Toy Story* movies."

He frowned. "I'm pretty sure there was a fourth one. In fact… Paris?"

She bounded into the room. "Is popcorn ready?"

"It is." He held up the bowl. "But first I have a question."

"Okay."

"When I was at your place last Christmas, what was that movie we watched? The one with Bunny and Ducky and Duke Caboom?"

"*Toy Story 4.*"

He looked at Nat as he handed the bowl of popcorn to his niece.

"Okay, technically, there was a fourth one," she conceded. "But it doesn't exist in my world."

"In your world?" he said, amused.

"That's what Mom says, too," Paris chimed in. "She says the fourth movie is—" she wrinkled her nose, trying to remember "—non-canyon."

"I think you mean non-canon," Kevin said.

She nodded. "Yeah, that's it. She says they should have stopped after *Toy Story 3*, when Andy gave his toys to Bonnie."

"Exactly," Nat agreed.

"My sister's agreement is hardly a conclusive argument," he said.

"Are we going to talk about *Toy Story* all night or actually watch a movie?" Paris asked, with more than a hint of impatience.

"We're going to watch a movie," Kevin promised.

"The question is—what movie?" Nat wondered.

She was surprised Paris hadn't picked one of the latest animated offerings but instead opted for *Night at the Museum: Battle of the Smithsonian.*

They all settled on the sofa together, Paris seated between the two adults, Thor at her feet. He'd taken an immediate liking to the girl that Nat didn't think was solely based upon the fact that she dropped one or two pieces of popcorn on the floor every time she reached into the bowl.

Thankfully the dog was well-trained enough that he looked at Nat to ensure it was something he could have before he wolfed it down. And though she knew she'd be the one to deal with his popcorn farts the next day, she let him enjoy what fell in front of him.

"What did you think?" Paris asked, as the credits began to roll.

"It was better than I expected," Kevin admitted.

"I enjoyed it," Nat said, rising from the sofa to gather the discarded candy wrappers and empty soda cans.

"We probably should have watched the first one first," Paris noted. "But this one's my favorite movie."

"Why's that?" Kevin asked.

"Because it's got Amelia Earhart in it."

"How do you know about Amelia Earhart?" her uncle asked curiously.

"From this movie," the girl admitted. "But then I looked her up on the internet and got a book about her from the library. Did you know she was the first girl to fly solo across the Atlantic Ocean?"

"I seem to recall hearing something about that," her uncle said.

"And then she tried to fly around the world and disappeared."

"I heard that, too," he confirmed.

"I'm gonna fly airplanes someday," Paris announced.

"I thought you wanted to be a ballerina."

She rolled her eyes. "Maybe I did when I was five."

"Now you're seven and ready to conquer the skies?"

"I can do it," she insisted.

"I have no doubt you can do anything you set your mind to," he assured her.

"Anyway, there are lots of girls who are pilots now," she said.

"I know," he said. "In fact, Nat's a pilot."

She frowned. "But she works with you at Adventure Village."

"That's one of her jobs," Kevin said.

The little girl's brow furrowed. "How many jobs does she have?"

"Three. Or maybe four."

"That's a lot of jobs."

"I have two jobs," Nat interjected to set the record straight as she returned with a damp cloth to wipe the sticky remnants off Kevin's coffee table. "I work full-time at Adventure Village and part-time at Mountain Charters."

"You're really a pilot?" Paris asked, evidently impressed.

Nat nodded. "Flying was my main job when I came to Nevada, but when I was hired at AV, it was tough to juggle regular hours at the park and long stretches out of town. So now I fly the minimum hours to maintain my qualifications, preferably via short flights that ensure I can get back to Haven—and now to Thor—the same day."

"Plus you volunteer at PAWS and with the veterans group," Kevin pointed out.

"Those aren't jobs."

"What's PAWS?" Paris asked.

"It's an organization that trains animals to provide emotional support to people who need it. The letters in PAWS stand for Pets Assisting Wounded Servicemembers."

"Do you train the dogs?"

Nat shook her head. "No. That would be a job. I just help with the little tasks—walking and grooming, that kind of thing."

"Are there lots of dogs at PAWS?"

"There's usually a group of ten to twelve being trained at any given time."

"Can we go see the dogs, Uncle Kevin?"

He looked at Nat.

"Sure," she agreed. "One of the most important things the dogs at PAWS need to learn is to be comfortable in different settings and with new people."

"Can we go tomorrow?" Paris asked.

"I'll be there in the morning," Nat said.

"If you want to go in the morning, you need to get ready for bed right now," Kevin said.

"Okay." She started to race off, then turned around to give Thor a quick hug. "See you tomorrow."

Kevin walked Nat to the door. "Thanks for coming tonight. And for bringing the snacks."

"Well, you can't have a movie without snacks."

He managed a smile. "Seriously—thank you."

"It was fun."

"Did you really think so?"

"I really did. Your niece is a sweet girl and she's lucky to have you."

Then, because it seemed appropriate, she offered him a hug.

When his arms came around her, returning the gesture, her heart gave a little sigh inside her chest, tempting her to linger.

Instead, she pulled back and offered him a bright—friendly— smile. "See you at PAWS tomorrow."

"What's your problem with Natalya?" Jake asked Raelynn, as she helped him tidy the kitchenette in the community center after their meeting. Ordinarily, he'd be helping Nat, but in his friend's absence, he was on his own and grateful that Raelynn had stuck around—which he knew she wouldn't have done if Nat had been there.

"What makes you think I have a problem with Natalya?" she hedged.

"The fact that you didn't immediately deny that you have a problem with her is a pretty good indication."

Raelynn lifted a shoulder. "I just don't like her type."

"Her type?" he echoed.

"You know—the art critic who's never picked up a paintbrush."

"If that was supposed to clarify things for me, it didn't," he told her.

"I just don't think a woman who obviously has no experience in combat has any right to sit with a group of veterans and listen to them talk about their pain."

"Like everyone else who was in this room tonight, Nat served her country," Jake said.

"What'd she do? Draft the paperwork to send troops to the frontlines?"

"Actually she flew Super Hornets for the navy," Jake said.

"No shit?" Raelynn said, obviously taken aback by this revelation.

"No shit," he assured her.

"Well, flying jets is a pretty cushy job compared to boots on the ground of the front lines," she said, clearly unwilling to give an inch.

"It might seem so," Jake agreed. "Though I'm surprised— and a little disappointed—that you'd be so quick to judge someone without having walked in her shoes."

"Her shoes wouldn't fit my prostheses."

He nodded, acknowledging the validity of her point. "Not all of us carry scars that are visible to the world, Rae. It doesn't mean we don't have them."

"You're right," she acknowledged begrudgingly. "And maybe I was too quick to judge her. She just seems so together… compared to some of the others. Compared to me."

"And isn't that the illusion we all try to create for others?"

He handed Raelynn the box of leftover pastries, confident that he'd also given her some food for thought.

* * *

"Am I calling at a bad time?" Nat asked, when Alyssa picked up the phone Monday afternoon.

"If it was a bad time, I wouldn't have answered," Alyssa said. "What's up?"

"I'm looking for a chocolate chip cookie recipe and there are thousands on the internet, but I only need one. Preferably a tried-and-true one."

"I have one," her friend confirmed. "But if you want cookies, why not just pick them up at Sweet Caroline's?"

"Because it's not really about the cookies so much as the baking," Nat confided.

"You've finally decided to test that fancy new kitchen?"

"Actually, I'm going to be baking cookies at Kevin's house—with his niece."

"Aww, that's sweet—but sad about her brother," Alyssa noted, confirming that Kevin had filled in Jay about his niece's visit and he, in turn, had communicated the relevant details to his wife.

"Yeah. Kevin's been trying to keep her busy—and distracted—and I've been helping out here and there when I can."

"From what I understand, here and there has been almost every day."

"Recipe?" Nat prompted.

"I'll send a picture of it to you, so you'll have the list handy at the grocery store to ensure you get everything you need."

"Is it an idiot-proof recipe?" Nat asked hopefully.

Alyssa laughed. "It's the recipe I've been using since I was twelve years old, so I'm pretty sure you can handle it. But if you have any questions, call me back."

Nat found most of the ingredients in her own pantry—including a couple of aprons that she was certain she'd never used before but thought might come in handy.

Shortly after she arrived at his place, Kevin excused himself to take a phone call. While he was occupied, Nat and Paris got busy, cross-referencing the recipe with the ingredients before starting to measure and mix.

Nat also took a minute to pull her hair back into a ponytail to reduce the likelihood of any stray strands ending up in the cookie dough, and then Paris insisted on doing the same with hers.

"What happened to your head?" Paris asked, as Nat was scraping butter out of the measuring cup and into the mixing bowl.

"My—oh." She self-consciously touched the back of her hand to the five-inch scar near her hairline—the reason that she usually let her long bangs cover her forehead. "That's an old injury."

"What happened?" the girl asked again.

"I was in an accident."

"A car accident?"

"No."

"What kind of accident?" Paris pressed, apparently not picking up on any hints that Nat didn't want to talk about it.

"Your uncle told you that one of my jobs is as a charter pilot. Well, in that job, I fly people to business meetings or vacation destinations. But before I decided to become a charter pilot, quite a few years ago, I flew jets for the navy."

Paris's eyes went wide. "Like in the movie *Top Gun*?"

"You've seen *Top Gun*?" she asked, surprised that a seven-year-old would know a movie that had been released more than thirty years before she was born.

The girl nodded. "It's one of my mom's favorites."

"Yes, like *Top Gun*," she confirmed.

"That. Is. So. Cool."

Nat managed a smile. "It was very cool. But during a training exercise, I had a little mishap," she said, not wanting to go into too much detail and say anything that might instill a fear of flying in the future pilot. "My parachute got blown off course and I ended up crashing into a tree.

"And that—" she pointed to the scar on her forehead "—is what happens when you crash into a tree."

The scar was also evidence that she'd somehow lost her helmet when she ejected—or at least before she crashed—though she had no memory of that, either.

Paris leaned forward to peer more closely at the remnants of the old injury. "Does it hurt?"

"Not anymore. In fact, most of the time, I don't even remember that it's there," Nat confided.

Kevin's niece was silent for a minute before she asked, "Did you get hurt anywhere else?"

She nodded. "Yeah. But I'm all better now."

"I'm glad," Paris said. Then she bent her knee to show Nat a white horizontal line on her knee. "I've got a scar, too."

"What happened there?"

"My stupid brother knocked me over and I fell on the sidewalk."

"How many stitches?" she asked, understanding that battle wounds could be a source of pride even for kids.

"Four," Paris said proudly.

"Wow," Nat said, suitably impressed.

"How many did you get in your head?"

Twenty-four.

"A few more than that."

Paris reached into the open bag to pilfer a chocolate chip.

"He's not really stupid," she said, as she nibbled on the sweet morsel. "Atlas, I mean."

"We all get annoyed sometimes with the people we love," Nat told her. "It doesn't mean we don't love them."

The little girl nodded at that, just as Kevin called from the next room.

"Paris—your mom's on the phone."

"Be right back," she promised Nat, before racing out of the room to take the call.

"Well, this is a sight I never thought I'd see," Kevin mused, making his way into the kitchen.

Nat glanced up. "What?"

"You with an apron around your waist and a mixing bowl in your hand."

"The apron's to protect my clothes and the mixing bowl is for the cookie dough."

"I'm just saying—it's a very sexy look."

"An apron?"

"*You* in an apron," he clarified. "Of course, in my fantasies, you're not wearing anything but the apron. Or maybe the apron and heels." His lips curved. "Red stilettos would be nice."

"But hardly an appropriate wardrobe choice for baking cookies with your niece."

"In my fantasies, you're *not* baking cookies with my niece."

"At the risk of bursting your fantasy bubble, I can assure you that you're never going to catch me in an apron and heels."

He wriggled his eyebrows. "I bet I *could* catch you, if you were wearing heels."

She rolled her eyes. "Which might be why I don't wear them."

"You wore heels to Matt and Carrie's wedding."

"Do you really remember what I was wearing? Or are you guessing, because most women wear heels when they dress up?"

"I remember what you were wearing." He took the bowl out of her hands and set it on the counter, then took a step closer, deliberately invading her personal space. "And I remember—in very vivid detail—undressing you. Starting with the high-heeled sandals with the skinny straps that wrapped around your ankles...then moving on to the little black dress that hugged every sexy curve…and finally, the front-fastening black lace bra and matching bikini panties."

The heat in his gaze caused her breath to stall in her lungs.

She swallowed. "We agreed that we weren't going to do this."

"We're not doing anything," he pointed out.

"But you're looking at me…as if…"

"As if…*what*?"

"As if…you're thinking of kissing me."

"Maybe I am," he said. "There's no harm in thinking, is there?"

"No." Of course there wasn't, but she took a half step back anyway, and found her instinctive retreat blocked by the counter.

"Are you thinking about it now, too?" he asked.

She couldn't seem to think about anything else—including any of the reasons that this was a bad idea.

She also couldn't seem to tear her gaze from his lips.

She knew how they'd feel, how they'd taste.

He'd taken another half a step closer, breaching the scant distance that she'd managed to put between them. And his hands were clamped on the edge of the counter on either side of her now, boxing her in.

But he didn't make another move.

He didn't cross the line between thinking about kissing and actually kissing.

She was the one who did that.

Chapter Sixteen

It was barely even a kiss…and it never had the chance to become more before three quick beeps sounded, indicating that the oven had reached its programmed temperature.

The sound jolted Nat back to the present and saved her from making a bigger mistake.

She deliberately pulled away from Kevin and spotted Paris standing in the entranceway, Kevin's cell phone in her hand.

"Mom wants to talk to you again," she said to her uncle.

He stepped back and accepted the device without missing a beat.

Nat resisted the urge to lift a hand to fan her overheated face. Instead, she smiled at Paris.

"Grab a couple of spoons and start dropping dough onto these trays so we can get them into the oven."

"Shouldn't I wash my hands first?"

"Right. Of course."

Paris went to the sink to lather and rinse, then she dried her hands on a tea towel.

"Like this," Nat said, dipping a spoon into the bowl to scoop up some dough, then using a second spoon in the other hand to scrape the dough off the spoon so it dropped onto the tray.

Paris picked up the other two spoons on the table and copied Nat's actions.

"So…are you Uncle Kevin's girlfriend?"

"No." She scooped up another spoonful of dough. "Just a friend."

"But if you're a girl and his friend, doesn't that make you his girlfriend?"

"If that was the only requirement, then your uncle has more girlfriends than I can count," Nat said dryly.

"Does he kiss all of his girlfriends?"

"I have no idea."

"Because I saw him kiss you just now."

Well now, how was she supposed to respond to that?

Certainly Nat wasn't going to confess to Kevin's niece that *she* had kissed *him*.

And she wasn't sure if it was good or bad timing that the subject of their conversation chose that moment to walk back into the kitchen.

"What are you guys talking about?" Kevin asked.

"You don't want to know," Nat told him.

At the same time, Paris said, "Kissing."

He looked at his niece. "What do you know about kissing?"

She lifted a shoulder as she dropped another blob of cookie dough onto the sheet. "I know a little."

His gaze shifted to Nat, who just shook her head as she slid the baking sheet into the oven.

"Henry kissed me on the playground once and he said that meant he was my boyfriend," Paris said.

"How old are you?" Kevin asked.

"You know I'm seven," she said. "You sent me a birthday card in February with the number on it."

"Isn't seven kind of young to have a boyfriend?"

The little girl shrugged again.

"Do you want Henry to be your boyfriend?"

"I don't mind."

He frowned. "Because you don't have to let him kiss you, if you don't want to be kissed."

"I know."

"So I guess you must like this boy."

"He's alright," she said. "It's not as if I'm gonna marry him or anything like that."

"So I don't have to mark a wedding date on my calendar?"

"Not yet."

"So how did you get on the subject of kissing?" Kevin asked.

"I saw you and Natalya kissing," Paris said.

"Did you?"

She nodded. "But she says she's not your girlfriend."

"Because she's not my girlfriend."

Paris's brow furrowed. "But you like her, don't you?"

"Sure, I like her."

"And you like Uncle Kevin, don't you, Natalya?"

"Sure," she agreed.

"I think you should be boyfriend and girlfriend," Paris said. "And then you can get married and have a baby and your baby will be my cousin, just like Dawson and Sawyer are my cousins. But you should have a girl baby, because I've already got two boy cousins."

"Your uncle Kevin and I are not getting married and we're definitely not having a baby." The words came out more sharply than Nat intended, as evidenced by the quizzical look that he sent in her direction.

"But you just admitted that you like the other," Paris pressed, undaunted.

"It's a long road from liking someone to wanting to get married and have a baby with them," Kevin said, responding to his niece in a more reasonable tone as the oven timer beeped again.

And thankfully, any further inquiries were forgotten when Nat pulled the tray of cookies out of the oven.

* * *

She'd been flustered by the whole kissing conversation. So much so that she'd made herself scarce over the next few days, leaving Kevin to his own devices with Paris—and then feeling inexplicably guilty about the fact.

The little girl was his niece, his responsibility. But Nat liked the kid, and she liked spending time with both of them. And when they were all hanging out together—with Thor, too—it was almost like they were a family.

It was the closest she'd ever come to having a family of her own—stealing moments here and there with other people's kids. And she didn't mind. But she also knew that she needed to be careful, to remember that it wasn't real and couldn't last.

But for now, she figured Kevin had muddled through several days of cooking for his niece—when Nat saw Paris at AV, the girl told her that he'd been making meals, and not just macaroni and cheese out of a box but real food—and deserved a break.

So she stopped at The Trading Post to grab a few things on her way home Friday afternoon, then picked up Thor and made her way to Kevin's house.

"I brought dinner," she said, holding up the grocery bag in her hand when he answered the door.

"Almost as nice a surprise as you," he said, stepping back to allow her entry. "Though that looks like dinner with some assembly required."

"I'll do the assembly," she promised.

"To what do I owe the pleasure?"

"I figured you deserved a break, after cooking for Paris all week."

"Well, I hope you've got everything you need in that bag, because I stocked my fridge last weekend, and it's pretty much empty now. Who knew that a seven-year-old kid could eat so much?"

"She's a growing girl," Nat noted, kicking off her shoes before following him to the kitchen.

"Tell me about."

Nat had peered in the living room on her way past, but hadn't seen Kevin's niece sprawled across the sofa—her usual location and position. "Is she upstairs? Do you want me to go tell her it's dinnertime."

"She's not here," Kevin said. "Steven decided that he wanted the title of 'Fun Uncle' and took her to Elko to stay in a hotel with an indoor pool and waterslide."

"I should have called first," Nat realized, feeling foolish. "It's your first free night in almost two weeks, and I've interrupted."

"You haven't interrupted anything," he said. "I have no plans. And, as I already mentioned, no food in the house. So if you leave—and take your unassembled dinner with you—you'd be consigning me to not only boredom but hunger."

"You could always head over to Diggers' for a bite to eat—and a flirtation with Blair."

He shook his head. "I don't feel like going out tonight."

She noticed that he didn't say he didn't want to flirt with Blair, just that he didn't want to go out.

And that was fine. Really.

Because she was just here as a friend—offering to prepare a simple meal because he had a lot going on in his life and needed a break.

"Now tell me what I can do to help," he suggested.

"I offered to make dinner for you," she reminded him. "You don't have to do anything."

"Maybe I don't have to, but I'd like to."

She shrugged. "Okay. For starters, you can get me out a cutting board, a knife and a frying pan."

He gathered the requested materials while she unpacked the groceries.

"Fajitas?" he guessed.

She nodded as she programmed the oven to heat the tortillas.

"Paris is going to be sorry she wasn't here."

"You might want to hold off on making such bold claims until you've eaten," she warned.

"I have complete confidence in you," he assured her, as she began to slice the peppers.

"Well, fajitas are pretty simple to make," she acknowledged. "Though my real specialty is gourmet PB & J."

He got out a bowl for her to put the sliced vegetables in. "How do you make a gourmet PB & J?"

"You add crispy bacon and grill it."

He looked dubious. "You shouldn't mess with the classics."

"You wouldn't say that if you'd ever tasted my gourmet PB & J," she told him, peeling the onion.

"Are you offering to make it for me sometime?"

"I haven't finished cooking this one yet, and you're already angling for another free meal?"

"I make a decent arrabbiata sauce," he told her. "Maybe the next time I cook some up, I'll invite you to come over and sample it."

"I wouldn't say no to that," she assured him, setting aside the sliced peppers and onions. "And I might, in return, be willing to reciprocate with my gourmet PB & J."

While Nat finished prepping and then cooking the steak and veggies, Kevin grated the block of cheese and set the salsa and sour cream on the table.

"Do you want a glass of wine with dinner?" he asked, as she took the warmed tortillas out of the oven.

"Actually, I'll have a beer, if you've got one to spare."

"I'm sure I do," he said, reaching into the fridge and pulling out two bottles.

So they ate fajitas and drank beer, and over dinner she told him about the plans she'd made for the following weekend to ensure Steven wouldn't hold the "Fun Uncle" title for long. Then they watched the original *Night at the Museum* movie—because Paris had recommended it—and it was nice.

Not just the movie, but the whole evening with Kevin.

But when she said goodbye at the door and kissed his cheek, she couldn't help but wonder if she'd ever be brave enough to let herself want something more.

"I have to agree with Paris," Kevin said, after his exhilarated and exhausted niece had gone upstairs to get ready for bed the following Sunday night. "That was. The. Best. Day. Ever."

Nat chuckled. "She did seem to have a good time, didn't she?"

"The. Best," he said again. "Seriously, you made her day today."

"It was really Jay who made things happen," Nat said.

"He didn't fly the plane."

"Probably a good thing, considering that he doesn't have a pilot's license," she noted. "But he did pull all the right strings."

"And for the thirty minutes that we were in the sky, Paris forgot about everything else."

"I'm glad," Nat said. "She needed the distraction from worrying about her brother."

"I don't think he crossed her mind once while she was in the cockpit."

"She was incredibly—surprisingly—focused. And curious. She had questions about every button and lever."

"And you answered them all with incredible patience."

"I don't often get to show off my knowledge," Nat confided. "Most of my passengers just buckle in and trust me to get them where they want to go."

"Do you think this wanting-to-be-a-pilot thing will fall by the wayside like her dreams of being a prima ballerina?"

"You know your niece better than I do," she said. "And it's not uncommon for kids—and even adults—to change their minds dozens of times before deciding on a career path. But based on what I saw in her eyes today, I think this could stick."

"It helps to have good role models," he noted.

"And uncles with friends who have access to private planes."

"That, too," he agreed.

"Anyway, now that she's flaked out, I'm going to head home to do the same."

When Nat had gone, Kevin wandered upstairs to check on his niece. She was wearing her Little Mermaid nightgown and her cheeks were still flushed from the excitement of the day, her lips curved.

No doubt dreaming of flying, he mused.

He carefully pulled the covers up, sorry that she'd ended up here because her brother was sick but also grateful that he'd had the opportunity to spend this time with her. And while the events of the day had clearly reinstated him as the favorite uncle, he found himself wondering if he was ever going to get to be a real dad—and if Nat would ever realize that she was meant to be a mom.

He was grateful to her, for everything she'd done for Paris over the past couple of weeks. At the same time, he was a little baffled that the woman who was usually all about boundaries could interact so openly with his niece.

But it gave him a glimmer of hope—foolish though he knew it might be.

Paris was sitting on the front step of her uncle's house when Nat and Thor were on their way home from their walk the following night.

"What are you doing outside? Ducking out of KP?" Nat asked teasingly.

Paris looked up, her brow furrowed. "What's KP?"

"Kitchen patrol."

"Oh." The girl shook her head. "There wasn't much to clean up, because we had pizza."

"Didn't you just have pizza on Friday?"

"Yeah, but Uncle Kevin said we could have whatever I wanted tonight, because it's my last night here."

"Is it?" Nat asked, surprised by this revelation.

Paris nodded. "My dad's coming to get me tomorrow."

Nat lowered herself onto the step beside the girl. "You don't sound very excited about going home."

"When I first got here, all I wanted was to go home," Paris admitted, stroking her hands over Thor. "But now I don't want to leave."

"I guess that means you've had a good time hanging out with your uncles."

"And with you and Thor."

The dog responded to his name by licking the girl's chin, making her smile.

"We've had a good time with you, too," Nat told her. "But I'm sure your parents have been missing you like crazy."

"They were too busy with Atlas to miss me," Paris said.

"I know it probably seems like that," she acknowledged. "Because your brother was really sick and they were worried about him, so he got all the attention. But that doesn't mean they weren't thinking about you and missing you."

"Do you think so?" Paris asked dubiously.

"I know so," she assured the girl. "Because I have two nephews who live in California, and even though I don't get to see them nearly as often as I'd like, I think about them all the time."

"Will you think about me when I'm gone?"

"I will," Nat confirmed. "And I'll look forward to seeing you when you come back to visit. But right now, I think you should take advantage of Uncle Kevin's offer and tell him that you want to go for ice cream."

The girl immediately brightened. "I *do* want to go for ice cream."

"Well, who wouldn't?" she agreed.

"Will you come to Scoops with us?"

"Absolutely," Nat agreed.

She took Thor home first, because although the shepsky was a big fan of ice cream—as Nat had discovered on a previous trip to the local ice-cream parlor when she'd glanced away from her half-eaten dessert to respond to a text message on her phone and, when she finished, discovered that her sundae was, too—she knew that it wasn't good for him.

Then she went to Scoops with Kevin and Paris—happy for the opportunity to spend a bit more time with the little girl before she had to say goodbye.

And when she finally did, Paris hugged her so tightly, Nat wondered that her heart didn't crack just a little.

Or maybe it did.

"I'm thinking about getting a dog," Kevin said, as he fell into step beside Nat on her usual after-dinner walk with Thor.

"I guess the house seems pretty empty now that Paris is gone," she remarked with sympathy.

He nodded, obviously missing the niece who'd gone home several days earlier.

"Well, dogs are great companions," Nat told him. "They don't talk back, they don't wrestle for control of the television remote and they don't steal the covers."

"All good points," Kevin agreed.

"They're also a big responsibility," she warned. "So before you do something impulsive, why don't you borrow a friend's dog for a few days to be sure it's what you want? The twelfth to the nineteenth of July works for me."

"That's a full week," he noted.

"Hmm… I guess it is," she agreed.

His mouth twitched at the corners as he fought against a smile. "You wouldn't be trying to finagle me into dog-sitting for you, would you?"

"What? Me? No."

"Yeah, nice try," he said, clearly not buying her protests.

"Okay, maybe," she relented. "I'm heading to California on the twelfth to visit my sister-in-law and nephews and I'm not sure I want to tackle a three-hundred-plus-mile road trip with a dog who snots all over my windows during a thirty-minute car ride.

"And I realize the easiest solution would be to ask Jake to take him while I'm gone, but considering the way Thor stressed out when I was packing up my apartment, I don't want him to see me pack a suitcase and then take him to PAWS—especially when he was already returned there once before."

"Yeah, that would be…*ruff*," he said.

"On the other hand, it might be less traumatic for him than spending a week in the company of a man who thinks he's a comedian," she decided.

"He has absolutely no idea what I'm saying ninety percent of the time, anyway. All he hears is 'wah-wah-wah-wah-wah-wah,'" Kevin said, imitating the muted-trombone sound of adult dialogue in the *Charlie Brown* cartoons, "interspersed with the occasional 'sit' or 'stay' or 'treat.'"

Thor immediately sat, stayed and looked up expectantly.

"See?" He reached into his pocket for one of the Nat-approved treats that he'd taken to carrying and offered it to her dog.

"He also knows 'down,' 'off' and 'out.'"

Thor tilted his head, obviously confused by what she was saying because he *was* "down," "off" and "out."

"Okay," she told him, and he rose to his feet to resume their walk.

"But sure," Kevin said, as they took the path leading to a nearby off-leash park. "Thor can stay with me while you're gone."

"Thanks."

While Thor ran around the enclosed area with his new friends from the neighborhood, Nat and Kevin continued to chat. It wasn't until they were on their way back to their respective homes again that Kevin ventured off the safe conversational path they'd been traveling to say, "I really can't thank you enough for everything you did when Paris was here."

"No thanks required. I enjoyed hanging out with her. And you."

"I guess being an afterthought is better than being forgotten," he said dryly.

"As if you could ever be forgotten," she chided.

"Anyway, I was thinking that I could make my arrabbiata sauce for dinner Friday night, as a gesture of my appreciation."

"No thanks required," she said again.

"Okay, then—how about a meal shared between friends?"

"I can't."

"I know you were adamant about us being just friends, but it seems to me that one friend wouldn't balk at sharing a meal with another."

"I can't," she said again, her expression as apologetic as her tone. "I have a date Friday night."

That was a shock. "Oh."

"Because I meant it when I said that we should see other people," she explained gently.

"Apparently," he noted.

She touched a hand to his arm. "You need to see other people, too, Kevin."

"I see other people," he assured her.

"Hanging out at Diggers' with your brother or Matt and Jay doesn't count."

"How about hanging out at Diggers' with Blair?" he challenged.

If his response surprised her, she quickly recovered.

"That would count," she agreed.

"So...who are you going out with on Friday?" he asked her.

"Does it matter?"

He shrugged. "Just making *friendly* conversation."

"Ian Payne," she finally responded.

"The doggy doctor?"

She sighed. "I really wish you wouldn't call him that, but yes."

"How long's this been going on?" he wondered.

"Nothing's going on," she said. "It's a first date."

"Well, I hope you have a good time."

She turned to face him when they reached the end of her driveway. "Do you really?"

"I want you to be happy, Nat,," he said sincerely. "I don't think you're going to be happy with the doggy doctor, but maybe you need to go out with him—and even a few other men—to figure out what I've known for a long time."

"What is it that you think you know?" she asked warily.

"That we belong together."

And then, without giving her a chance to respond—because he knew she'd certainly object to his pronouncement—he turned and walked away, determined, this time, to be the one who left rather than the one left behind.

Chapter Seventeen

It was the end of a long day at the conclusion of a long week, made even longer by the Fourth of July holiday the previous day. As in each of the past three years, AV had hosted a round-robin paintball tournament followed by a barbecue for charity and evening fireworks. In the past, Nat had always volunteered to work the barbecue with Kevin. This year, because she was still annoyed with him for his ridiculous "we belong together" assertion, she'd willingly relinquished that assignment to Sumera.

But she hadn't left the park early, which she should have done, and by the time she got home Friday afternoon, she wanted nothing more than to put on her pajamas and turn on the TV. Instead, Nat found herself standing under the shower to wash off the dust and sweat of her long day and mentally cataloging the contents of her wardrobe. Because Ian had mentioned wanting to try The Chophouse in Battle Mountain, and it definitely wasn't the kind of restaurant to which one wore jeans and a T-shirt.

After she'd toweled off and dried her hair, she stepped into the closet to rifle through the contents. She was tempted to FaceTime Sky or Alyssa to ask for their help—they were both so much better at this sort of thing than she was. But asking for help would open herself up to questions that she wasn't sure she was ready to answer.

"Okay, I'm going with the green dress," she decided. "But what about shoes?"

Thor responded to her question with a wide yawn.

"That's not very helpful."

She held up two pairs of shoes for his perusal. "I'm not sure I've ever actually worn either of these before," she admitted. "To be honest, I don't even remember buying them, which means that Margot probably talked me into doing so when we were out shopping together."

She thought she preferred the ones with the open toes, but that heel was at least an inch higher than the slingback, and considering that she and Ian were pretty much at eye level when she was wearing her Doc Martens, she opted for the slingback.

"What do you think?"

Thor, now stretched out inside her closet with his head on his paws, opened one eye.

The strap on her heel slipped a little as she turned toward the full-length mirror on the closet door.

"Hmm… Maybe these shoes aren't a good idea."

Thor continued to communicate nothing but disinterest in her dilemma.

But when the doorbell rang, he was immediately on his feet and racing down the stairs, barking.

"It's okay," she said, following at a more leisurely pace. "It's just Dr. Payne making a house call."

Thor barked again, clearly unconvinced that the person on the other side of the door wasn't an axe-wielding murderer.

She sent him a pointed look as she reached for the knob, and he immediately dropped to his haunches. Though he was fairly quivering with impatience, he'd been trained not to go through a door without permission, and he didn't move when she opened it.

Ian's eyes skimmed over her and his lips curved. "Hi."

She smiled back. "Hi."

Thor barked.

The vet grinned. "Hello to you, too," he said, reaching down to rub the dog's head. And the shepsky, always eager to lap up every ounce of affection that he could get, rolled onto his back, exposing his tummy.

Ian chuckled and complied with the unspoken request.

"He'll let you rub his belly all night," Nat said, "but my belly is hungry."

The doctor straightened up again. "In that case, we better go get you fed."

Nat picked up her purse, gave Thor a last pat on the head and walked out with the doctor—her first real date with a man who wasn't Kevin Dawson in more than three years.

Kevin had been certain Nat was bluffing when she said they should see other people. The fact that she had a date tonight with the new veterinarian in town proved he'd been wrong in that assumption.

But he wasn't overly concerned.

She'd dated plenty of other guys over the years, but none of them had stuck around for long. And afterward, always, Nat came back to him.

Still, there was something about *this* date that bothered him more than he'd expected.

Maybe because he'd recently overheard Harper Langdon and Jana Beatty in The Daily Grind, talking about the new doggy doctor and what a catch he would be. Harper claimed that she got quivers in her stomach whenever she took Fifi in for a checkup—and considering that Fifi was a fifteen-year-old overweight and diabetic cat, she needed frequent checkups. Jana had lamented that she hadn't been able to think about replacing her loyal canine companion of twelve years since his passing the previous winter, but the arrival of the new doctor had her thinking that it might be time.

He imagined that Harper and Jana would be commiserating over their lattes tonight if they knew the object of their admiration was dining with Natalya.

But he wasn't sitting in his living room with the blinds open so that he could see every vehicle that drove past, he assured himself. He just hadn't yet gotten around to closing them.

He glanced absently at the display when his phone rang, then did a double take when he saw her name on the screen.

Over the years, they'd exchanged a lot of text messages, but rarely did they talk on the phone. And never when she was on a date with someone else.

Had something gone wrong?

Had she kicked the doggy doctor to the curb and needed a ride home?

He snatched up the phone.

"Hey," he said, deliberately casual.

"Am I interrupting anything?" Nat asked.

"No. What's up?"

"I need a favor."

"Okay."

"Can you stop by my place and let Thor outside around ten o'clock? I thought I'd be home before then, but now I'm not sure."

"I can do that," he agreed, resisting to urge to ask, "Home from where?" because he wasn't sure he wanted to know.

"Is this awkward?" she asked. "Should I have called someone else?"

"It's fine," he said, even as he wondered if he was being a good friend or a complete fool.

And then, because apparently he couldn't resist torturing himself, he asked, "Are you going to be home to give him breakfast?"

Her laugh was strained. "I sincerely hope so."

Worried that she might be able to hear his teeth grinding, he deliberately relaxed his jaw.

"Well, text me if you're not," he said. "I can drop by again in the morning to take him for a run and feed him afterward."

"You have no idea how much I appreciate this."

"What are friends for?" he asked tightly.

"It's not what you think, Kev."

"You have no idea what I'm thinking."

"You're right," she finally said. "I'll be home as soon as I can, but the ER seems to be a popular place on a Friday night."

That gave him pause.

And what might have been heart palpitations.

"The ER?" he asked, immediately concerned.

"Not what you were thinking, huh?" she said lightly.

Definitely not.

"What happened? Are you okay?"

"What happened is that I'm clumsy." Her tone was rueful. "And I think I'm okay—just waiting for the doctor to confirm."

"But…I thought you had a date tonight."

"I was supposed to have a date tonight," she confirmed. "But we didn't even make it to the restaurant because I twisted my ankle."

"Is he there with you now? Or do you need me to come and get you?"

"He's here," she said. "He just stepped out to take a call, but he'll bring me home when the doctor gives the okay. I just need you to check in with Thor, so he doesn't feel as if he's been abandoned."

"I could go over now and spend some time hanging out with him, if that's okay with you."

"It's definitely okay with me," she assured him. "And he'd love it, thanks."

"Not a problem," he said. "Let me know if you need anything else."

"I will."

He ended the call and scooped his keys off the counter.

Was he a horrible person because he was glad that her date was a bust?

He hated to think of Nat in pain and stuck at the hospital, but not as much as he hated to imagine her enjoying a romantic meal with another man, possibly with wine and candlelight—and whatever might come afterward.

As soon as he climbed the steps to Nat's porch, he heard Thor race to the door, barking excitedly, eager to greet his person.

When Kevin stepped inside, the dog wagged his tail, but he was already looking past him. Looking for Nat.

"Sorry, buddy," Kevin said. "She's not with me."

Thor plopped down on his butt and looked up at Kevin, doing that canine head tilt thing that dogs tended to do when humans just weren't making sense.

"Do you want to go out?"

That was language the dog understood, because he immediately made his way to the back door and raced out into the yard when it was opened.

Kevin stepped out onto the deck, watching as the dog sniffed the grass, pausing every now and then for a longer sniff before moving on again and finally relieving himself on the tree in the far corner.

When he was finished, he sniffed around some more, then trotted back to the deck.

"Nat said it was okay for me to hang out here with you for a while," he said to Thor, leading him back inside. "And I figure I can watch the game here just as easily at home—or I could if Nat would get a decent-sized screen."

The dog wagged his tail, as if in complete agreement.

Kevin settled on the sofa and picked up the remote, and Thor lay down by his feet.

The game was over and highlights were replaying on TV when light flashed through the blinds as the doctor's vehicle pulled into the driveway. Thor, who'd been snoring softly, must have been awakened by the purr of the engine, because he was immediately up and racing to the door.

"Hold on a second there," Kevin said, snapping the leash on the dog's collar so that he wouldn't rush Nat when she walked—hobbled?—through the door and potentially cause another mishap.

He heard the murmur of voices from the porch, followed by Nat's soft laughter.

Rather than make her fumble for her key, Kevin twisted the dead bolt and pulled open the door.

"Oh," she said, apparently startled to see him there.

He was startled, too. First by the crutches tucked under her arms, and second by how stunningly hot she looked.

Of course, he always thought she looked good, but it seemed as if she'd pulled out all the stops for the doctor tonight. The dress she wore wasn't immodest—the long sleeves covered her arms to her wrists and the skirt fell to her knees—but the fabric clung enticingly to her curves and the deep green color really brought out the color of her eyes.

Thor barked to remind the humans of his presence.

"I see you," Nat assured him, laughing. "Just let me get over the threshold and I'll make a fuss."

Then to Kevin, as she maneuvered through the door, she said, "Thanks—for everything. But I really didn't expect you to hang around until I got home."

"I know, but Thor wanted some company while he watched the game."

"Did he?" she asked, a smile playing at the corners of her mouth.

"He also wants you to get a bigger TV."

"We'll have to chat about that," she promised.

Then she seemed to remember that her date was standing beside her, because she hastened to make the introductions. "Ian, this is Kevin—my neighbor, coworker and friend."

And occasional bed buddy, Kevin wanted to add, though he suspected that if he did so, it would be a very long time before he was reinstated to that status. As if the six weeks that had passed since she'd declared their relationship hiatus wasn't a long enough time already.

"Kevin, meet Dr. Ian Payne."

The two men shook hands, sizing one another up, while Nat fussed over Thor, as promised.

"You really didn't have to stay," Nat said to Kevin again, a not-at-all-subtle effort to nudge him along now. "I told you that Ian would bring me home."

"But I didn't know if you'd need a hand when you got here—because of your foot."

"Sprained ankle," she said.

"And I was hardly going to leave her at the door," the doctor said mildly.

"Well, I didn't know that, did I?" Kevin said, matching the other man's tone.

"I guess not," Ian acknowledged, with a tight smile.

"I appreciate your concern," Nat said, sounding more weary than grateful. "But you can both go now. I can handle it from here."

"You'll end up in the hospital with a broken neck if you try to negotiate the stairs with those crutches," Kevin warned.

"I'll use the banister for support. Or I'll sleep on the sofa," she said, when he opened his mouth to argue against her original plan.

"Let me give you a hand," Ian offered solicitously.

"It's probably better if I do," Kevin interjected. "I know where she keeps her pajamas."

Ian's expression remained carefully neutral, except for the muscle that clenched in his jaw. "I'm sure you're tired, Natalya, and I've got an early morning, so I'm going to say good-night."

"Good night," she replied softly, almost apologetically.

"Is it okay if I give you a call tomorrow—to see how you're doing?"

"I'd like that," she said.

"Then I'll talk to you tomorrow."

The doctor looked at Kevin then and nodded brusquely.

"It was good to meet you, Owen," Kevin said.

"You, too, Calvin," Ian replied.

Nat waited until the door closed behind the doctor, then she spun—as best she could manage on the crutches—to face Kevin. "Why didn't you just lift your leg and pee in the foyer?"

"Because I don't lift my leg to pee," he said mildly. "I think that's just something that dogs do."

"Well, my dog showed better manners than you."

"What are you talking about? What did I do?"

"Let's start with the fact that you were introduced to Ian not five minutes earlier and then pretended not to remember his name."

"He called me Calvin," Kevin pointed out in his defense.

"*After* you called him Owen."

"You're right," he acknowledged. "It was petty and immature and I'm sorry."

"*And* you implied that there's something between us."

"*Implied?*"

Her cheeks flamed. "Also, you don't have the first clue where I keep my pajamas."

"Only because you never wear pajamas when we're in bed together. Should I have told him that?"

"Aargh! You. Make. Me. Crazy."

Thor's head swiveled between them, a plaintive whine emanating from his throat.

"*I* make *you* crazy?" he countered. "How do you think I felt when I got a phone call asking me to check on your dog because you were out with another man?"

"Not *another* man," she told him. "Just a man—because you and I. Are. Not. Together."

Thor's sudden bark startled them both.

"And now you've upset my dog," she said accusingly.

"I wasn't the one yelling."

Nat maneuvered herself over to the sofa and dropped onto the cushions. "It's okay, baby," she said, scratching the dog behind his ears. "I just needed to yell at Kevin for a minute because he's being obtuse and unreasonable."

"You forgot petty and immature," he said.

"No, I didn't," she assured him, as she continued to soothe Thor with her gentle touch.

Kevin perched on the edge of the sofa beside her. "I'm sorry."

She shifted her attention from the shepsky to him. "Are you?"

"I know that I should be."

She managed a smile. "At least you're honest."

He smiled back, even though he knew she was wrong.

He wasn't honest.

If he was, he would have told Nat how he felt about her a long time ago.

But that was a truth he kept carefully hidden, because he knew that if he did tell her, she'd run—sprained ankle or not—as far and fast as she could.

Chapter Eighteen

In the end, Nat did let Kevin help her upstairs. After his half-hearted apology, he asked if she would let him stick around to give her a hand, and she relented, because she knew that she'd sleep much better in her bed than on the sofa. But she didn't tell him where to find her pajamas, because just the thought of Kevin sifting through bras and panties that he'd previously taken off her body was enough to have her yanking open the window to let the cooling breeze to blow through her bedroom.

He came back again first thing in the morning and insisted that she stay in bed while he took Thor for a run. Afterward, he fed the dog and made scrambled eggs and toast and coffee that he served to Nat in bed.

"I could have come downstairs for breakfast," she said, when he returned for the empty tray.

"Didn't the doctor tell you to stay off your ankle?"

"Yes, but he didn't confine me to bed."

"Fine. If you want to go downstairs, I'll carry you down the stairs."

"I don't need to be carried," she protested, when he reached for her. "And I want to get dressed first."

"Okay, then. Let's get you dressed."

"I can do that on my own," she told him. "No *let's* required."

"It's not like you've got anything I haven't seen before."

She pointed to the door. "Out."

He went out, but she knew he continued to hover outside the door while she fumbled around, first finding her clothes and then putting them on.

When she gave him the all clear, he insisted on carrying her down the stairs to the sofa, where he propped her ankle on a pillow and brought her a glass of water and a bottle of Advil.

"Who would've thought that you'd be a nurturer, Kevin Dawson?"

"Shh," he said. "Don't go spreading rumors that might ruin my bad-boy reputation."

"You're not nearly as bad as you want people to think."

"Shh," he said again.

"Okay, I'll shush," she said. "After I thank you for everything you've done."

"I figured it was the least I could do, after the way I behaved last night."

"You were pretty obnoxious."

"In my defense, I don't like to see someone I care about hurt."

"It's only a sprained ankle." But she'd heard the sincerity in his voice, and her own gentled. "I've had worse injuries."

He thought of the scars on her body, each one a visible reminder of the physical trauma she'd endured. And what about the scars he couldn't see? Because he knew she had her share of those, too.

She'd talked about her decision to eject during that RIMPAC exercise as if it wasn't really a big deal, and she'd assured him that she'd been trained to know what to do. But after she'd told him about the accident, he'd done some internet research of his own. What he'd discovered was that there was no such thing as a routine ejection, because there were numerous variables that had to be factored into the equation and conditions were never ideal. Which meant there was always the possibility for things to go FUBAR, as they'd done when she'd pulled that handle.

"I know," he acknowledged now. "But in the almost seven years that I've known you, I've never known you to be injured—or even sick."

"I had a cold once...three or four years ago, I think."

"A common cold, huh? I guess you are human."

"I hate being incapacitated."

He suspected she was remembering the weeks—maybe even months—that she'd been in the hospital after the training accident in Hawaii. Because he was pretty sure a person didn't just walk out of the hospital after surgery to remove a tree branch from their torso. Not even a badass like Natalya.

"Will it make you feel better to order me around? You can supervise while I do whatever needs to be done."

"I can manage," she said. "Honestly, what will make me feel better is if you go to work because I can't."

"You really don't like accepting help, do you?"

"I don't like needing help," she admitted.

"Well, you're on holidays next week, right? So you can rest at home with your foot up."

"Not quite how I planned to spend my vacation."

"That's right—you wanted to go to California to see your sister-in-law and nephews."

She nodded.

"Were you planning to drive or fly?"

"Drive," she said. "It would take almost as long to fly, by the time I got to an airport. Plus, I like the convenience of having my own vehicle."

"So you'll reschedule your trip," he said easily.

She sighed, because she really didn't have any other choice.

"Which means missing the boys' birthdays," she lamented.

"That sucks."

"Yeah. Especially considering that Margot cleared the date with me before she started planning their party."

"I guess it's kind of far to Uber?"

"Just a little," she agreed dryly.

"So I'll take you," he decided, perhaps surprising himself as much as her with the impulsive statement.

"I want to go so badly that I'd jump at your offer if I didn't know that you also work two jobs."

He shrugged. "I'm entitled to holidays, too."

"But I can't imagine Jay would be happy about both of us taking holidays at the same time."

"We've hired extra summer staff, so there are plenty of other employees who can pick up the slack," Kevin said confidently.

"But if you take me to California, who will look after Thor?"

"I guess we'll just have to see how he handles an extended road trip."

She shifted so that she was sitting sideways on the sofa and lifted her leg onto the extra cushion Kevin had put there to elevate her foot. The ankle was already feeling a lot better—so long as she didn't put any weight on it. And while she wanted to believe that she'd be able to drive again in only a few more days, she knew it would be foolish to attempt a three-hundred-plus-mile journey. Especially when Kevin had offered to do the driving so that she didn't have to.

She was still wary about the plan.

Not the more than five hours in a car with Kevin, but the five days at her sister-in-law's house with him.

It was a lot of time to spend with someone, especially someone with whom she'd had a very personal relationship. But considering that her only other option was not going, she pushed those concerns aside.

After checking the time displayed on her phone, she dialed her sister-in-law's number.

"Good timing," Margot said, when she answered the call.

"Unless you wanted to talk to the boys, because I just tucked them into bed."

"I figure I'll have lots of time to catch up with them in a few days."

"For a second, when I saw your number on the display, I worried that you might be calling to say you weren't coming."

"I'm definitely coming," Nat said. "So long as you're okay with me bringing someone else along."

"I hope you're referring to Thor, because the boys are counting on it."

"I am bringing Thor." Hearing his name, the dog lifted his head and wagged his tail, making her smile. "But I was hoping you'd have room for another guest of the human variety."

"Male or female guest?" her sister-in-law asked curiously.

"Male," she admitted. "Though his gender isn't as important as the fact that he's willing to drive because I can't."

"Why can't you drive?" Margot asked, immediately concerned. "What happened?"

"I sprained my ankle."

"How did you manage *that*?"

"Long story."

"I've got time," her sister-in-law assured her.

"Well, it starts with me wearing slingback shoes that I'm pretty sure you made me buy."

"You had a date?" Margot guessed, her tone hopeful.

"I had a date," she confirmed. "A first—and probably last—date."

"Because you sprained your ankle on your date?"

"At the very beginning of our date—as in, walking to his car."

Her sister-in-law giggled. "I'm sorry," she immediately apologized. "I mean, I'm sorry you're hurt, but the circumstances are kind of funny."

"Thankfully, my date was with a doctor," Nat continued. "Well, a DVM, actually."

"So...a vet?" Margot pressed her lips together, obviously trying to hold back another giggle.

"Yeah."

"And did he play doctor—or veterinarian—with you?"

Nat rolled her eyes. "He wrapped ice around my ankle and took me to the clinic for an X-ray."

"A medical clinic or veterinarian clinic?"

"Medical clinic. And while I was waiting to see an MD, he went to the hospital cafeteria and returned with veggies and dip, a couple of sandwiches and a bowl of green Jell-O."

"Appetizer, entrée and dessert?" her sister-in-law guessed.

"Yeah."

Margot sighed. "That's actually kind of romantic."

"It was," Nat agreed.

Or it should have been.

Except that the whole time that she'd been sitting there with Ian, she'd found her thoughts skipping between the throbbing pain in her ankle and cursing Kevin. Because, in a way, it was his fault that she was at the hospital. Because she'd only agreed to go out with Ian to make the point to Kevin that they needed to see other people. And that's why she'd been wearing the stupid heels.

"So why do you think it was a first—and last—date?"

"Because Kevin was waiting in my living room when we got home."

"And finding another man in your house didn't go over well with your date?" Margot mused.

"It was a little awkward."

"I can imagine the scene—former lover meets potential future lover."

"Anyway, Kevin knows how much I was looking forward to the trip to California, so he offered to drive."

"Hmm."

"No. Don't start hmm'ing and reading between lines that aren't there."

"I'm not supposed to wonder what it means that you're coming to California with a man with whom you've had an off-and-on-again relationship for the better part of six years?"

"More off than on," Nat said. "And completely off now."

"Completely off except for the fact that he's making a cross-country road trip with you?"

"It's hardly cross-country," Nat pointed out. "More like across-one-state-line."

"Hmm," Margot said again.

The trip to California was an experience that Kevin was glad he had a chance to be a part of, though he could have done without the gassy mutt in the back seat. But according to Nat, that was his fault because he'd given Thor the last bite of his hot dog when they'd stopped for lunch.

But they arrived at her sister-in-law's house right on schedule, and it was a kick to see the way her family embraced her—and how she transformed in their presence.

It reminded him of the way she'd been with Paris—a little less guarded, a little bit softer and somehow even more appealing.

"Kevin seems really great," Margot remarked, after the kids were tucked into bed and the man in question had taken Thor for a late-night walk.

The dog had been getting far more exercise than he was accustomed to since their arrival in Auburn three days earlier, but Nat knew that Kevin was trying to stay out of the way so that she could maximize her time with Margot, and she was grateful to him for it.

"He's a good friend," Nat confirmed, reaching for the glass of wine her sister-in-law had poured for her.

"You're still sticking with the friend thing, huh?" Margot

asked, sounding amused. "Despite the obvious and sizzling chemistry between you?"

"We *are* friends," Nat insisted. "And I don't want other stuff muddling that up."

"I know you were hurt by Christopher—"

"Ancient history."

"Is it?" her sister-in-law pressed.

"Absolutely."

"Then why haven't you been involved with anyone since the divorce?"

"Weren't we recently talking about the fact that I was sleeping with Kevin, on and off, for almost six years?"

"Sleeping with. Having sex with. Those were the terms you used," Margot noted. "And none of those indicate any kind of emotional engagement."

"I guess emotional engagement isn't my thing," Nat said lightly.

"Should I call the fire department? Because someone's pants are on fire."

"Forget about the fire department and tell me what's been going on with you," she suggested.

"What makes you think anything's going on?" Margot countered.

"My first clue was the way you snatch up your phone every time it chimes with a text message."

"Okay, there is something that I wanted to talk to you about. Actually…someone. And I'm hoping that you'll get a chance to meet him while you're here."

"I'm listening," Nat said.

But instead of talking, Margot reached for the wine bottle and topped off each of their glasses before she said, "You know that your brother was the love of my life."

Nat nodded, because she did know.

Because she'd always envied the relationship between her

brother and sister-in-law—until Alexei's devastating diagnosis changed all their lives, proving to Nat once again that loving someone was a precursor to losing them.

"But it's hard…being a single mom," Margot continued. "Being alone."

Nat reached across the table to squeeze her sister-in-law's hand. "I can only imagine."

"Honestly, I don't know that I would have made it through the first year after Alexei's death without you."

"I'm not sure how much help I was, but I was glad to be here with you and Alex—and eventually Levi."

"You were my rock," Margot insisted. "But then you had to get on with your own life—and we did, too."

Nat hadn't wanted to leave. Partly because she hadn't known where to go or what to do. It was as if her life had stalled like the engines of her F-18.

But when she heard, through the ever-reliable grapevine, that Christopher was getting married again—only weeks after their divorce was final—and that his bride-to-be was already pregnant, she knew that she couldn't stay in California. It would be too painful to run into her ex and his new wife— and especially their baby.

Auburn wasn't such a small town that she needed to worry about frequent encounters, but the fact that they might cross paths at any time would make her anxious every time she left home.

So she'd done what she needed to do at the time—and though she missed Margot and Alex and Levi like crazy, she knew it had been the right decision for all of them.

And maybe it did sting a little to imagine her sister-in-law with a man who wasn't Alexei, but no more so than it stung to imagine her spending the rest of her life alone, because Nat didn't want that for her, either.

"So…tell me about him," Nat urged Margot now.

"His name's Kabir. Kabir Sharma."

"*Major* Sharma?" she asked.

"Actually, it's Lieutenant Colonel Sharma now. But I didn't know you knew him."

"I met him once, I think. I know he was a good friend of Alexei's. And that he lost his wife…just a few months before Alexei died," Nat suddenly remembered.

Margot nodded. "I think that's one of the things that drew us to one another initially—commiserating over the common bond of widowhood."

"You're in love with him," Nat realized.

"I didn't say anything about love," her sister-in-law immediately protested. "I just said that I wanted you to meet him, because I didn't know that you already had."

"You wouldn't want me to meet him if you didn't have some pretty deep feelings for him."

"You're right," Margot acknowledged. "I didn't want to fall in love again…not after losing your brother." She swallowed. "Alexei was…everything…to me."

"I know," Nat said, her own throat tight.

"And I don't know that I'll ever love Kabir with the same certainty and intensity that I loved Alexei, but I think…I think I do love him."

"Then I'm sure I will, too," Nat said.

"You're really okay with this?" her sister-in-law asked cautiously.

"With you moving on with your life? Of course."

Margot stared into her wineglass. "I was afraid you'd think I was dishonoring your brother's memory."

"I know Alexei will live on in your head and your heart for as long as *you* live," Nat said. "And of course he lives in my heart, always. But your memories aren't going to keep you warm at night. They're not going to give you a shoulder to cry on. And they're not going to help you raise two little boys who need a father figure."

"Kabir *is* really great with them."

"So what's your hesitation?"

"Alexei was their dad. Alex barely remembers him and Levi never even had a chance to know him. And I'm afraid that if I let Kabir become a bigger part of their lives, they're going to start thinking of him as Daddy and…and the last bit of Alexei will be gone."

Nat considered that for a minute, aware that her sister-in-law's concerns were causing her real anguish.

"I don't think you need to worry about the title so much as the fact that they need someone to fill that role. Because Alexei is always going to live on in his sons—in Alex's eyes and unruly hair, and Levi's smile and knobby knees."

Margot laughed. "Alexei did have knobby knees, didn't he?"

"It's why he hated to wear shorts—even as a kid," Nat confirmed.

Then they laughed together, until their laughter turned to tears. But even that felt good, because crying was part of the healing process, and it proved to Nat that her sister-in-law was finally ready to move on with her life.

And that Margot was a much braver woman than she.

Chapter Nineteen

Kevin enjoyed watching Natalya interact with her sister-in-law and nephews, and especially seeing a more relaxed and carefree version of her. It was obvious that they had a close relationship, notwithstanding the geographical distance that usually separated them, and because he knew Nat's time here was limited, he tried to stay out of the way as much as possible.

He kept himself busy with Thor and Alex and Levi and quickly discovered why Nat was so head over heels for her nephews. The boys were active and inquisitive and messy and loud and everything else that little boys should be.

But right now, it was late and they were settled in bed, leaving Kevin and Thor to their own devices. Margot had been opening a bottle of wine when he got back from his evening walk with the dog, and she'd immediately reached into the cupboard for a third glass. He'd declined the offer, not wanting to intrude.

Instead, he took the shepsky out back, so that Thor could nose around the yard while Kevin relaxed on one of the loungers on Margot's deck until the sky was dark—a blanket of black velvet dotted with twinkling stars that reminded him of camping vacations taken with his parents and siblings a long time ago.

Remembering those happy times, he realized that he hadn't checked in with Gina in several days and decided to give her a call.

After the usual exchange of pleasantries, he asked, "How's Atlas doing?"

"Great," Gina said. "In fact, looking at him now, you'd never guess that he'd been sick. Not that I'm never going to forget those weeks he spent in the hospital, but I'm glad to know that he's already put them behind him."

"Has Paris reconnected with all of her friends?"

"She's at a sleepover at Cassie's tonight."

"Then I guess all is right with the world again."

"Or her little corner of it, anyway," his sister agreed, making him laugh.

"I really can't thank you enough for everything you did for her—for us—when Atlas was in the hospital," she said, her tone serious now.

"No thanks required," he assured her, echoing the words Natalya had said to him. "All I did was spend some time hanging out with my favorite niece."

"She's your only niece," Gina noted dryly.

"Which might be why she's my favorite."

His sister chuckled. "Speaking of your favorite niece… She told me that you have a girlfriend."

"Did she?"

"She said her name's Natalie and she's a pilot."

"Her name's Natalya," he said. "She *is* a pilot, but she's not my girlfriend."

"Do you kiss a lot of girls who aren't girlfriends?" his sister wanted to know.

"She told you about that, too, did she?"

"I think I got a detailed recounting of every minute that she spent with you in Haven—and it sounded as if Natalya was there for a lot of those minutes, too."

"Well, Nat also works at Adventure Village and she lives down the street. In fact, she's renting Steven's town house."

"Wait a minute—she's your on-again, off-again?"

"What are you talking about?"

"Ha! You think you're the only brother I have in Haven? Steven keeps me up to date on all the stuff that you don't."

Of course, Thor chose that moment to bark, startled by the hoot of an owl in the darkness.

"Is that a dog?" Gina immediately wanted to know. "Is that her dog? Are you at her place now?"

"No, I'm not at her place," he said. "Actually, I'm in California."

"What are you doing in California?"

"Enjoying the stars in the sky."

"There are stars in Nevada, too," she pointed out.

"Then you should take a walk outside and enjoy them."

"I'm your big sister," Gina reminded him. "I'm always going to worry about you."

"And I'm always going to love you," he said, as he registered the sound of the patio door sliding open behind him. "But for now, I'm saying good-night."

He disconnected the call without giving his sister a chance to respond and glanced over his shoulder to see Margot on the deck.

"I wondered where you'd disappeared to," she said. "I didn't expect to find you in the dark."

"It wasn't dark when I sat down," he said. "And then, when it got dark, it seemed a shame to turn on the lights and dim the stars."

"I didn't mean to eavesdrop," she said, perching on the edge of the chaise lounge beside the one he occupied, "but I couldn't help overhearing the last bit of your telephone conversation."

"And you're wondering who I promised to always love?" he guessed.

"Yeah."

"My sister."

"I suspected it was probably someone like that, but I wanted to know that I wasn't misreading the situation between you and Nat."

"I'm sure she told you that there's no situation."

"She did," Margot agreed. "But I know her well enough to know when she's lying."

"Has she turned in already?" Kevin asked, uneasy to think that Nat might overhear his conversation with her sister-in-law.

"Yeah. I helped her to bed before I came outside—and belatedly realized that it might not have been a good idea to let her mix wine with whatever she's taking for her ankle."

"I'd guess, whatever effects she was feeling, were solely a result of the wine. After the first couple of days, she stopped taking anything for her ankle."

"She's always been stubborn about working through the pain," Margot acknowledged. "Even after..."

"Hawaii?" he suggested, when her words trailed off.

"She told you about that?"

He nodded.

"Did she tell you about her divorce?"

"Just the basics."

"Including the fact that the ink was barely dry on the divorce papers before her cheating ex was exchanging vows with the bimbo he cheated with?"

"Pregnant bimbo and former friend," he noted.

"Yeah. The blows just kept coming."

"It was a rough year for both of you."

She nodded. "But we got through it together."

"You're obviously very close."

"And we don't get to see one another nearly enough, which is why I'm so grateful to you for bringing Nat out here this week."

"I was happy to be able help," he said.

"You'd do anything for her, wouldn't you?"

"Is it that obvious?"

"Probably not to everyone," Margot said.

"And definitely not to her."

"She might be afraid to see it."

"Nat?" he scoffed. "She's not afraid of anything."

"That's what she wants you to believe. What she wants everyone to believe. She's tough, because she's had to be. Because she's lost so much—and so many people she's loved. So if she's reluctant to open her heart again, it's no wonder."

"But still a source of frustration."

"I'm sorry for that."

"It has nothing to do with you."

"I think it does," Margot said. "Because Nat was here with me when Alexei died. She was still recovering from her own injuries and reeling from the breakdown of her marriage—and then she saw me completely fall apart."

"I'd say that was understandable, considering the circumstances," he noted.

"Maybe," she allowed. "But I think, to Natalya, it was just further proof that loving someone meant opening yourself up to the possibility of heartache."

"Is this your way of warning me off?"

"Not at all," Margot denied. "Because she talks about you a lot. Probably more than she realizes. And I know that might not seem like much of a consolation prize, but it proves that you matter to her."

"Why are you telling me this?" he asked curiously.

"Because I'm leading up to asking for a favor," she admitted.

"What's that?"

"Promise me you won't give up on her."

"I never could," he assured her.

"Then I'll look forward to seeing you again."

Nat was grateful to Kevin for driving her to and from California—especially as she knew she wouldn't have been able to make the journey without him. But a five-hour road trip at the beginning and end of a five-day visit was a lot of time to spend together, and by the time they got back to Haven, she needed a break.

Not because he'd been in the way at her sister-in-law's house, but because he hadn't. Because he'd fit effortlessly with her family, and she hadn't been prepared for that. Because she'd found herself imagining (and not for the first time) what her life might be like if Kevin was part of it—not just for now but for always. And that was a dangerous path for her thoughts to wander.

She needed to remember what her life was like without him in it every minute of every day, because he wasn't always going to be there and it would be a mistake to let herself count on him. So she'd spent the better part of the next week avoiding him—as much as she could, considering that he still showed up at her house every morning to take Thor for a run, and then again after dinner to ensure her dog got his evening walk.

As soon as she was able to move around without the aid of crutches, she released him from his dog-walking assistance and resumed her efforts of avoidance. Unfortunately, she couldn't avoid him any longer.

Today was the baptism for Jay and Alyssa's three kids, which meant that Kevin and Nat—as the chosen godparents—had to be center stage with them throughout the ceremony. And now their respective names were on each of the children's baptismal certificates, forever linking them not just with Lucy, Clara and Silas but with one another.

Nat had been stunned—and deeply moved—when Jay and Alyssa asked her to be godmother to their children. Of course, they'd assured her that they both planned to live until they were at least one hundred years old, so the ceremony was really just a formality.

"I know it was a long day," Alyssa said, when she settled in the rocking chair in the baby's room to nurse her hungry infant. "But I'm glad we waited to do all the kids together."

"Are you sure Silas is the last?" Nat asked.

"I'm sure," her friend said. "And Jason's got an appointment next week to guarantee it."

"How does he feel about that?"

"It was his idea," Alyssa said. "We had already decided that—boy or girl—baby number three was going to be our last. And since I did all the heavy lifting of pregnancy and childbirth, Jason decided that he could endure a little snip. Though he winces every time I use that word."

"I'll bet you have a lot of fun with that one."

"You know me so well," her friend said with a grin, as she carefully removed the baby from one breast and shifted him to the other.

The first time Nat had accidentally walked in on Alyssa nursing, when Lucy was only days old, she'd been embarrassed and apologetic. But the new mom had been completely unfazed, assuring her that after exposing all of her most private parts during childbirth, showing a little nipple was nothing.

And since Alyssa was right about it having been a busy day—with the parents mingling throughout a house filled with family and friends—Nat didn't feel guilty about stealing some one-on-one time with her friend when she finally had a quiet moment.

It filled her heart with joy that she'd been invited to play even a small part in the life of this child and his sisters. And, at the same time, there was an emptiness inside her that she knew could never be filled, because she'd never have a child of her own.

"Can I steal a five-minute cuddle with my godson before I have to head out?" Nat asked, when Alyssa finally lifted the slack-jawed baby onto her shoulder to burp him after his meal.

"Of course you can have the cuddle," Alyssa said, passing the baby to her friend. "But why are you rushing off?"

"Thor's been on his own at home all day—he needs some attention. And his dinner."

"You should go get him and bring him back."

"As much as I know he'd love that, you've got enough going on here and a lot of other guests who are probably grumbling that I've been monopolizing your time."

"You're the godmother," Alyssa reminded her. "The right to monopolize is embedded in the title."

"I'll keep that in mind," she promised, touching her lips to the sleeping baby's forehead before passing him back to his mom.

She made her way through the crowd, ensuring that she said goodbye to Jay and Lucy and Clara before heading out. She looked for Kevin, too, because it was the polite thing to do. But he seemed to be deep in conversation with Ben Channing and so she slipped out without a word to him .

As she made her way toward home, the ache in her heart eased a little.

It was strange, she thought, that she hadn't realized how much she needed a home until she had one.

Not just a place to store her clothes and make a cup of coffee in the morning, but a place where she got to decide what color to paint the walls and what flowers to plant in the garden.

Every time she turned into her driveway and saw the cheerful faces of the pansies, she couldn't help but smile. And every time she slipped her key into the lock and heard the clatter of Thor's nails on the floor as he raced to greet her, she felt a burst of happiness in her heart.

Even cutting the grass gave her pleasure, because it was her grass.

Except that it wasn't really.

It was rented grass—only hers temporarily, until Steven decided the market was right to sell the property.

But if he wanted to sell it, why couldn't she buy it?

The question popped into her head for a second time without warning.

And though she tried to dismiss the idea again, the question—and the possibility—lingered in her mind.

"You left without saying goodbye," Kevin said, when Nat responded to his knock on her door a short while later.

"You were talking to Jason's dad. I didn't want to interrupt."

"Is that the real reason?" he asked, offering a doggy biscuit to Thor, who was sitting patiently beside Nat in anticipation of one of the treats Kevin usually carried in his pocket.

"What other reason would there be?" she said, as her dog scampered off.

"You tell me," he said. "You're the one who's been avoiding me since we got back from California."

"I couldn't avoid you if I tried," she said. "We work at the same place, live on the same street and we just spent the past several hours together at the baptism."

"Something happened in California."

"Lots of things happened," she said lightly. "It was a busy week."

"Something happened between us," he clarified.

"I don't know what you're talking about."

"If I did something wrong—if I got in the way or interfered somehow, just tell me."

"You didn't do anything wrong." She looked at him then, waiting patiently for the explanation she knew he deserved, and sighed. "In fact, you did everything right."

"I don't understand."

"My sister-in-law is one of my best friends and my nephews mean the world to me, and the limited time that I have to spend with them is precious. So precious that I didn't want to give it up, even though I knew that everything would be different and awkward with you there.

"Except that it wasn't different and awkward. You stepped up to help Margot in the kitchen, filling in where I couldn't because of my ankle. You kicked a soccer ball around the park with the boys and sat on the floor in the living room to build Lego with them. In fact, you fit so perfectly with my family, I think they were more unhappy to say goodbye to you than to me."

"I'm...sorry?" he said cautiously.

"You didn't do anything wrong," she said again. "It was me. I let myself get caught up in the illusion that we were all part of one big happy family, and I just needed some time on my own to remember that we're not."

"Maybe we're not," he acknowledged. "But we could be."

Now she shook her head. "You want the fairy tale, Kevin. And I can't give it to you."

He took her hands in his. "I want *you*, Nat. You have to know that."

"You won't find your happily-ever-after with me."

"And I won't find it without you," he told her sincerely.

Her gaze shifted away. "What if I told you that I can't have children?"

He squeezed her hands gently. "I'd ask why you thought you needed to keep that fact a secret from me for so long."

She looked at him, clearly stunned by his matter-of-fact response. *"You knew?"*

"Not for certain—until now," he admitted. "But I'd managed to put most of the pieces together."

"Unfortunately, I lost some pieces as a result of that training exercise in Hawaii," she confided. "That's why I'll never be able to have a child."

"I'm sorry, Nat."

She lifted a shoulder, as if it didn't matter.

But he knew that it did.

Because she wouldn't have tried to keep the truth from him for so long if it didn't matter a lot.

"I accepted it a long time ago," she told him now. "But I understand that not being able to have a child is a deal-breaker for some people."

"I'm not your asshole ex-husband, Nat."

"I know."

"It doesn't change anything for me," he promised her. "There are absolutely no deal-breakers when it comes to being with you."

"It might not be a deal-breaker for you, but it's a deal-breaker for me."

Chapter Twenty

"Do you mind if I join you?"

It was a good thing Nat was already sitting down, because when she glanced up and saw Raelynn standing beside her table at Sweet Caroline's the following Wednesday afternoon, she would have been knocked off her feet.

"Of course not," she said, gesturing to the empty seat across from her.

"Thanks." Raelynn set her coffee and doughnut on the table before lowering herself into the chair.

"I don't think I've ever seen you here before," Nat said, cautiously venturing forward with the conversation.

"It's a recent addiction," Raelynn admitted. "I got hooked on these Boston cream doughnuts at the meetings. I justify it in my mind as a pregnancy craving, but Tim just shakes his head, because he knows that I've always had a sweet tooth."

"There's no better fix for a sweet tooth than Sweet Caroline's," Nat told her. "So you should get as much of it as possible while you still can."

"Are you saying the rumors are true? That Caroline is selling the business?"

"Already sold, from what I've heard."

"Damn." The other woman shook her head. "I'm really going to miss these doughnuts."

"We all have our weaknesses," she acknowledged.

"What's yours?" Raelynn asked. "Because I don't believe for a minute that you only came in here for a cup of coffee."

She gestured to the plate beside her cup. "Raspberry bliss bars."

"There's not a single crumb on that plate."

"And that should tell you everything you need to know about how good they are," she said.

"I'm not sure that I've ever tried one," Raelynn said.

"You'd know if you had," Nat assured her. "They're crumbly and chewy and sweet but with just a hint of tartness."

"Sounds like bliss," the other woman agreed. "So why aren't there ever any in the box of pastries you bring to the meetings?"

"There's usually one," Nat said. "And I usually pilfer it before anyone else walks through the door."

Raelynn chuckled. "So maybe you are human, after all."

"Why would you doubt it?" she asked, noting the remark was startlingly similar to one Kevin had once made.

The other woman shrugged. "You just seem to have it all together. And everyone looks at you like you're superhuman. Like the bionic woman."

"You're the one with the high-tech parts," Nat pointed out.

"Yeah, lucky me," Raelynn said dryly, but her words lacked the edge Nat was accustomed to hearing in her voice.

She lifted her cup to sip the dregs of her now-cool coffee while Raelynn bit into her doughnut.

"I actually saw Jake here a few weeks back."

"A rare sighting," Nat said. "He doesn't have much of a sweet tooth."

"It was the day you skipped the meeting, so I think he was here picking up pastries for the group."

"That would explain it," she agreed.

"He told me that you flew Super Hornets for the navy."

"A long time ago," Nat said dismissively.

"A long time ago that seems like yesterday, I'll bet," Rae-lynn said.

"Sometimes," Nat agreed.

"You miss it?"

"Sometimes," she said again.

"I miss the army every day," Raelynn confided. "It was my sense of purpose, and when I lost that…"

Nat nodded, understanding everything that the other woman couldn't put into words.

"Well, I've got a new purpose now," Raelynn said, laying her hand on the still-subtle curve of her belly.

"You're lucky," Nat said softly. Sincerely.

"You got any kids?"

A lump rose in her throat. "No."

It was hardly the first time she'd been asked the question, and she'd learned long ago not to let it faze her. But for some inexplicable reason, this time, her eyes filled with tears.

She glanced away, but evidently not before the other woman noticed, because Raelynn swore under her breath.

"I'm an insensitive jerk."

"No, you're not," Nat denied. "It's a common enough question."

"And one I'll bet you always respond to with just that one-word answer."

"No one wants to hear my sad story."

"I do," Raelynn said.

And so Nat told her what she'd never told anyone else, aside from her mother and sister-in-law and, much more recently, Kevin.

Christopher knew, because the doctors at the VA hospital thought her husband had a right to know the extent of her injuries—to know that she'd never be able to bear the children they'd dreamed of having one day.

And though she'd never shared any of the details with him,

she knew that Jake had figured it out—probably when she started bawling her eyes out the first time she got to hold his infant daughter in her arms. So she figured his wife knew, too, because Jake and Sky didn't have any secrets from one another, and that was as it should be.

"The engines of my F-18 failed in a training exercise over Hawaii. I couldn't save the plane—had to eject. Ended up losing consciousness and crashing onto a tree that decided to fight back by shoving a branch right through me and pretty much destroying my uterus."

"Jesus."

Nat nodded. "Facing death is one of the quickest ways to find God."

Raelynn swallowed another mouthful of coffee before she ventured to ask, "Did you want kids?"

She managed a jerky nod. "I wasn't at the stage in my life where I was ready to have a baby, but yeah, whenever I thought about my future, I always pictured kids in it."

"Life really sucks sometimes."

It wasn't an empty platitude but a simple truth they both understood only too well.

"You don't usually say much at the meetings," Raelynn noted.

"I'm there to facilitate discussion, not monopolize it."

"Is there anyone that you talk to?"

"There was a psychologist that I had regular sessions with for the first couple of years after I left the navy, when I was living in California. Then I moved to Haven. She still reaches out to me, once every few months or so, just to check in. I tell her that I'm doing okay, and that's the end of it for another few months."

"Do you think she believes you?"

"I don't think she'd still call if she believed me."

"I don't have any credentials," Raelynn said. "But I've been told I'm a pretty good listener, if you ever wanted to talk to me."

"I thought you didn't like me."

The other woman shrugged. "Apparently I've changed my mind."

Nat was playing with some of the new recruits—and Thor—when she saw Ian arrive at PAWS. They'd exchanged some text messages and had a few telephone conversations since their aborted date, but there had been no talk of rescheduling.

Of course, she'd still been on crutches until recently.

And since he'd made all the previous overtures, she decided it was her turn. Leaving Thor to play with his new friends, she headed toward the barn into which she'd seen him disappear.

Ian grinned when he saw Nat walking toward him. "The crutches are gone."

"The crutches are gone," she confirmed.

"How's the ankle?"

"Fine. Or at least better," she said. "Much better."

"Glad to hear it," he told her. "And really happy to see you."

"It feels good to get back into my usual routines."

"I'm sure Thor would agree with that."

"He'll be happier when we get back to running, rather than the walking we've been doing the past several days. Thankfully my neighbor's been really great about taking him out for real exercise while I've been recuperating."

"We should all have such helpful neighbors," Ian agreed.

"So what's going on with this little guy?" Nat asked, gesturing to the pup on the exam table.

"Girl," Ian said. "This is Scarlet. Named after the Scarlet Witch, or so Connie informed me."

"She does like her Marvel characters."

"So I've come to realize. Anyway, Connie noticed that Scarlet was having a little trouble keeping up with her pals when they were playing, so she asked me to check her over." He tucked the end of the stethoscope into the pocket of his lab coat, then reached into a bin on a shelf to give the pup a treat. "She seems to have a bit of a heart murmur."

"That doesn't sound good."

"I'll need to run some tests to figure out the origin," Ian said. "It's not good, but it's not necessarily debilitating, either."

He carried Scarlet to a nearby enclosure and set her down on top of the blanket. She immediately curled up and went to sleep, and he turned his attention back to Nat.

"Now that you're back on your feet, any chance we can re-schedule our aborted date?" he asked hopefully.

Nat hesitated, because what was the point of dating anyone when she wasn't looking for a relationship?

But Sky insisted that she needed to go out with someone else to prove that she wasn't hung up on Kevin, and maybe her friend was right.

"I'd like that," she finally responded to doctor's question.

And if it was a lie, well, it was only a little white one.

And hopefully, by the time they went out, it would be the truth.

"Dare we try seven o'clock on Friday again?" he asked.

"I think we dare," she said. "But this time, I'm going to wear flats."

The doctor chuckled. "Good idea."

"Did I come at a bad time?" Sky asked, when Nat responded to her knock on the door late Friday afternoon.

"Actually, you came at the perfect time," she said, dragging her friend over the threshold.

"Why's that?"

"Because I have a date with Ian tonight."

"Oh." Her friend sounded not only surprised but disappointed.

"I thought you wanted me to go out with him."

"I did," Sky confirmed. "I do. I mean, as long as it's what you want."

"I said *yes*, didn't I?"

"Apparently."

"Anyway, I could really use some help figuring out what to wear."

Sky followed her friend upstairs to the walk-in closet of the master bedroom. "Wow. You could fit a sofa in here."

"I probably could," Nat agreed. "But why would I want a sofa in my closet?"

"To stretch out and look at all your clothes." Sky glanced at the sparse rails. "Or all the clothes you should have when you have a closet this big."

"I mostly wear jeans and T-shirts to work at the park, and a uniform when I fly. I don't need much more than that."

"Bite your tongue," Sky said. "A person needs options. Colors. And shoes!" She looked around. "Where are all your shoes?"

Nat gestured to the half-dozen boxes neatly lined up on the floor.

"Oh, honey, we need to go shopping."

"My next day off," Nat promised. "But right now, I need you to find something in here that I can wear tonight."

"Okay." Sky directed her attention to the task at hand. She lifted a hanger off the rail and held it closer to the light. "This one's nice."

"It's also the one that I was wearing the last time we went out—or almost went out."

Sky returned it to the rail and pushed it aside to examine the next garment.

"A little black dress works for almost any occasion."

"That one's pretty old," Nat said.

"It's classic," her friend insisted.

"The last time I wore that was Matt and Carrie's wedding. I'm not even sure it fits me anymore."

"Matt and Carrie's wedding, huh?"

She nodded.

"So that would have been the first night that you and Kevin…" Sky deliberately let her words trail off.

Nat sighed. "Yes."

"That's the real reason you don't want to wear this dress, isn't it? Because you'll never be able to put it on again without thinking about Kevin taking it off you."

"Yes," she said again.

"Okay, the LBD is out… What about this one?"

Nat suspected that her cheeks were in the process of turning the same crimson color as the dress in her friend's hand.

"I wore that one to the AV Christmas party last year."

"And?" Sky prompted.

"Kevin did *not* take that one off me."

In fact, they'd barely made it across the threshold before he was hiking up her skirt and taking her against the door.

She'd been every bit as impatient as he was, scattering his buttons across the ceramic tile floor when she tore open his shirt to put her hands on him.

Her friend's brows winged up. "Are you going to tell me more or let my very active imagination fill in the details?"

"I'm *not* telling you more. And I'm *not* wearing that dress tonight."

"Okay," Sky relented. "Though I have to say, I'm not sure this walk down memory lane is helping to get you in the mood for your date with Dr. Payne."

"I'm very much looking forward to having dinner with Ian."

"Have you been rehearsing that line all day?"

Nat felt her cheeks flush. "It's true."

"If you had a sofa in here, this is the point in our conversation where I'd take you by the hand and lead you over to it so that we could sit down and have a heart-to-heart."

"I don't need a heart-to-heart—I need to figure out what I'm going to wear tonight."

"I know I'm the one who pushed you to go out with Ian, but now I'm thinking it was a bad idea."

"What changed? Did you catch him kicking puppies in the barn?"

Sky rolled her eyes. "The problem isn't Ian—who I still think is a terrific guy—but that you're obviously head over heels for Kevin."

"I'm not," Nat assured her friend. "And in light of recent events, I'd appreciate you refraining from any mention of heels."

"Okay, then," Sky said, taking her friend's cue and returning her attention to the contents of her closet. "Unless Kevin took you shopping and you did it in the change room, this one should be a safe bet, because it's still got its tags attached."

"I bought that at an end-of-season sale last year," Nat admitted, looking at the plum-colored sheath with a critical eye. "Fifty percent off."

"Were you shopping with Kevin?"

She rolled her eyes. "No."

"Then I think we've got a winner," Sky said, and handed her the dress.

"You look every bit as stunning as the last time we tried this," Ian said, when he arrived to pick her up for their date.

Nat smiled, pleased by the compliment. "Hopefully you'll get to look at me across a candlelit table rather than a brightly lit emergency room tonight."

"Do they put candles on the tables at Diggers'?" he asked.

The twinkle in his eye told her he was joking, and his sense of humor was one more thing she liked about him.

And she *did* like him.

Not to mention that her dog loved him.

So what if her heart didn't bump against her ribs when he smiled at her?

It was normal for feelings to change and grow over the course of a relationship, and this was just their first date.

And even if this night didn't lead to anything more, it would hopefully make the point to Kevin that he needed to move on with his life without her.

Ian took her to The Chophouse, as had been the plan for their original date. Nat had dined at the upscale steakhouse in Battle Mountain only once before—a few years back when she and Kevin were trying the dating thing. But she was determined not to spend any more time thinking about Kevin tonight. Instead, she would follow the advice of folk musician Stephen Stills and give her complete attention to the one she was with.

As the hostess led them to their table, the scent of grilled meat made her stomach grumble in anticipation of the fabulous meal she knew would come. The dining area boasted lots of stone, wood and leather; the tables set with gleaming silver and sparkling crystal. Soft overhead lighting was supplemented by flickering tealight candles in shallow bowls, adding to the romantic ambiance.

They were seated at a curved leather banquette that necessitated sitting almost side-by-side rather than across from one another. Perhaps the seating was designed to up the romance ante, but it seemed to Nat much less conducive to conversation.

Ian took his time perusing the wine list, his remarks about the various offerings indicating that he had some knowledge about the vintages. But when it came time to choosing a bottle for the table, he deferred to her preference.

She opted for a Napa Valley cabernet and they shared a garlic-parmesan pan bread appetizer followed by Caesar salads. For her main course, Nat chose the peppercorn striploin with roasted cauliflower and her date ordered the tenderloin with spicy shrimp and baked potato.

While they ate, they talked about any number of topics,

from books and movies to local politics and Thor's apparent crush on a fluffy white poodle that he'd met at the dog park. Ian also told her a little bit about his marriage—and divorce—explaining that he and his ex-wife had married fairly young, both of them career people not interested in having a family. Then, after twelve years of marriage, she suddenly changed her mind, and when he wouldn't give her the baby she wanted, she divorced him in favor of someone who would.

Nat confided that she'd been married, too, and that her marriage had ended much more quickly when her husband realized that being married to a military pilot wasn't as romantic in real life as it was in the movies. That led to more conversation about her time in the navy and her eventual transition to civilian life.

The whole conversation was comfortable and easy—and proof to Nat that there was no chemistry with the doctor.

"Well, that meal was a step up from a dry turkey sandwich, don't you think?" Ian asked, as Nat dipped her spoon into her chocolate crème brûlée with fresh raspberries.

"Several steps," she agreed.

"Still, we've got an interesting first-date story," he remarked.

"Says the man who didn't spend the two weeks following on crutches."

He nodded his head in acknowledgment of the point. "I will admit, this evening has gotten off to a much better start."

"I've had a really nice time," Nat said.

"Why do I sense that there was an unspoken *but* at the end of the sentence?"

"The meal was fabulous," she assured her. "And you were wonderful, but—"

"It's the kid thing, isn't it?" he guessed. "A lot of women can't understand why a man might not want to procreate."

"It's *not* the kid thing," she assured him. "It's just that I've been sitting here for the last ten minutes, between bites of this amazing crème brûlée, thinking about what comes next."

He seemed puzzled by her remark. "We could go somewhere for an after-dinner drink—or to a club, if that's more to your liking."

She shook her head. "It doesn't matter where we go or what we do, we're eventually going to end up back at my place and you're going to want to kiss me good-night."

"And you don't want me to kiss you," he realized.

"I'm sorry."

He shrugged. "You don't have to apologize for not being attracted to me."

"I should be," she said. "I want to be. You're an attractive man, interesting and charming and funny, but... I'm just not feeling it."

"Is there someone else?" he asked.

"No. Yes." She sighed. "I don't know."

"The helpful neighbor," he guessed.

"I'm sorry," she said again.

"No need to be," he said. "I'm sure I'm not the first man to step up to the plate and go down swinging."

She managed a regretful smile. "The baseball analogy is another mark in your favor, so if you tell me you're an A's fan, I just might have to reconsider my stance on the good-night kiss."

"I'm from Fort Worth, Texas," he reminded her. "It's the Rangers for me all the way."

"Well, thanks for dinner, anyway," she said, making him chuckle.

"So my boyfriend *finally* picked up on the hints that I've been dropping *for months* and took me to The Chophouse for dinner last night," Sumera said, as she settled into a vacant seat across from Nat in the lunchroom at AV the following afternoon.

"Did you enjoy it?" Nat asked.

"It. Was. Fabulous. The atmosphere, the food, the cheesecake. Ohmygod—" she closed her eyes and sighed "—the cheesecake."

Nat had to laugh. "It's worth the trip to Battle Mountain just for the cheesecake."

"Is that what you had last night?"

Nat was aware of Kevin on the other side of the room, rummaging through the tool cabinet.

Was he close enough to hear their conversation?

Did he care?

"Actually, I had the chocolate crème brûlée," she said.

"So you *were* there," Sumera said. "I thought I saw you, but you were on the other side of the restaurant, so I wasn't one hundred percent sure."

"I was there," she confirmed.

"And was that the hunky doggy doctor you were with?"

She wondered if she could actually feel the weight of Kevin's gaze on her or if she was just imagining it.

"Yes, I was there with Dr. Payne."

"So…how was *your* date?"

"It wasn't really a date," Nat said.

"Since when is dinner in a fancy restaurant *not* a date?" her coworker wanted to know.

"Since we decided to be friends."

"Did you decide that before or after you slept with him?" the other woman asked teasingly. "Because you never really know if you're compatible until you do."

Kevin apparently found whatever he was looking for in the utility cupboard, because he closed it with more force than was probably necessary.

"Someone's got a burr in his butt today," Sumera noted with a frown.

"I didn't sleep with Ian."

Though Nat's response was to her friend's question, she hoped she'd spoken loudly enough that Kevin could hear, but he gave no indication that he'd done so as he walked out of the lunchroom.

Sumera wiggled her eyebrows. "But did you have sex with him?"

"That would be another *no*," Nat said, tossing the remnants of her lunch into the garbage on her way out the door.

She found Kevin in the arcade a short while later. He was working on something that looked like a circuit board that he'd taken out of one of the machines.

She took a couple steps closer.

He didn't even glance in her direction.

"Maybe it wasn't Alyssa who cheated," she said lightly. "Maybe you manipulated the scores to put her on top of the *Tetris* leaderboard."

He responded without looking at her. "I can't manipulate the scores. I can wipe the memory to clear them, but I can't change them."

"Well, I'll get back on top eventually," she said. "I just haven't had a lot of time to play in recent weeks."

"Is that why you're here now? Because the *Tetris* machine is over there," he said, pointing to the opposite wall.

"That's not why I'm here now," she said.

He slid the board back into the console and began to replace the screws in the panel.

"I'm here because I wanted to talk to you," she said, ignoring the fact that he hadn't asked.

"So talk," he said.

But he still wasn't looking at her, which made it difficult to gauge his mood.

On the other hand, the tension simmering in the air was a pretty good indication that he had—to use Sumera's term—a burr in his butt.

"I just wanted you to know that I didn't sleep with Ian."

He rose to his feet and tucked the screwdriver in his back pocket. "You said that already."

"I said it to Sumera," she acknowledged. "This time I'm saying it to you."

"Why?" he challenged. "Why should I care who you sleep with when you made it clear that whatever was between us was nothing but sex?"

"Because the sex part aside, I thought we were friends."

"Yeah, well, this friendship thing isn't really working out for me."

His tone was cool, almost dismissive, and it made her uneasy.

"I don't understand," she said. "Where is this coming from? Why now?"

"Because I don't think either one of us wants a front-row seat to watch who or when or how many people the other might be dating," he said. Then he shrugged. "But that's just my opinion. Maybe I'm wrong and you do want to know what I did last night."

The edge in his tone sounded like a warning—and one she intended to heed.

"No, I don't think I do," she decided.

"I had a date with Blair," he said, blatantly ignoring her response.

"Oh." She pressed the heel of her hand to the center of her chest, as if that might assuage the ache in her heart.

His eyes, when they fixed on hers, were dark and stormy. "Aren't you going to ask if I slept with her?"

She shook her head. "No."

"Why not?" he challenged.

Because suddenly, she didn't want to know.

Suddenly, the thought of him kissing the other woman, touching the other woman, left her feeling absolutely gutted.

And not just Blair, she realized, but *any* other woman.

Not that she could ever admit that to him.

Especially not after she'd deliberately pushed him away— and into the other woman's arms.

"Is it because I'm free to date—and sleep with—whoever I want?" he continued, pressing her to respond. "Because there are no strings between us, right?"

"Right." She nearly choked trying to force the word out of her throat.

"So it wouldn't bother you to know that I was so hot for her, we didn't even make it to the bedroom the first time? That we did it against the front door—just like me and you did it the night of the Christmas party?"

She was certain it would have hurt less if he'd taken the screwdriver out of his pocket and plunged it into her heart.

He took a step closer, his eyes glinting with a dangerous light. "Do you remember that night, Nat? Do you remember how you screamed out my name as I buried myself deep inside you?"

She closed her eyes, as if that might block the erotic memory— or at least the pain of him using it against her.

"I hate you," she whispered.

"Yeah, well, that makes two of us," he said, and walked away.

Chapter Twenty-One

He owed her an apology.

And the truth.

Hearing Sumera tease Nat about her date with the "hunky doggy doctor" had pushed his buttons and he'd walked out of the lunchroom before he could say something that he would regret. But instead of reading his mood and leaving him the hell alone, Nat had followed him into the arcade.

Literally cornered him.

And like a cornered animal, he'd lashed out.

And he'd hurt her.

Maybe—for a moment—he'd felt a certain grim satisfaction to know that he could hurt her as she'd hurt him.

The difference was that Natalya would never intentionally cause someone pain, and he'd done so on purpose.

And he hated himself for it, maybe even more than she did.

She usually walked Thor after dinner, but she was always home by eight—unless she had the late shift at AV, which he knew she didn't because she'd left the park before him. So at eight thirty, he walked up to her front door.

Before he could lift a hand to knock, he heard Thor barking, alerting Nat to his presence. He guessed that she peeked through the sidelight to see who was there, because when she opened the door, her face was carefully blank.

The dog, seemingly oblivious to the tension between the humans, waved his tail in happy welcome.

Nat skipped over the usual pleasantries, instead asking, "Didn't we say everything we needed to say to one another already today?"

"Except for one thing… I'm sorry."

"Why are you apologizing to me?" she asked. "Are you sorry that you had sex with Blair? Or that you felt compelled to shove the details in my face?"

"I'm sorry that I lied," he said. "I didn't have sex with Blair. Not against my front door or anywhere else."

A small pleat formed between her brows. "So why did you tell me that you did?"

"Because I wanted to get a reaction out of you," he admitted. "I wanted to know that you cared enough to react."

"You know I care."

It was true, he did know she cared.

She cared about him, and he loved her with every fiber of his being.

Yeah, unrequited love really did suck.

After another minute, Nat stepped away from the door, a silent invitation to enter.

When he stepped into the foyer, Thor immediately sat in front of him, looking at him expectantly.

"Sorry," Kevin said to him. "I didn't bring any treats with me today."

The dog, visibly disappointed in his human friend—*join the club*—slunk off to the living room.

"Apparently I've got a lot to be sorry for today," he mused ruefully.

Nat didn't look amused.

"And maybe I needed to know that you hated the idea of me in bed with Blair," he said, picking up the thread of their conversation again, pushing for a little more.

"Do you really need me to tell you that?" she asked him.

"Maybe I do."

"Fine. I hated the idea of you in bed with Blair," she admitted. "But I have no right to—"

He touched his fingers to her lips, silencing the rest of her words.

"Let me just bask in that for a moment, okay?"

She pushed his hand away. "You want to bask in my irrational jealousy?"

"I'm interpreting your irrational jealousy as a subconscious—or is it unconscious—admission that you have feelings for me."

"Subconscious. I think," she said. "And of course, I have feelings for you. You're one of my very best friends."

"Then why are you trying to cut me out of your life?" he challenged.

"I'm not trying to cut you out of my life," she denied. "I'm just trying to reestablish the boundary lines that we let get blurred."

"Honey, those boundary lines weren't blurred, they were decimated."

"You're right," she agreed. "And we never should have let that happen. We never should have let our physical relationship affect our friendship."

"Why do you keep insisting that what we shared was nothing more than sex?" he challenged.

"Because you keep trying to make it the foundation of something more."

"So if it's just sex," he continued, "then you could get naked with any man to satisfy your needs?"

"I'm not indiscriminate in my choice of sexual partners," she said, a little primly. "But otherwise, yes, I'd say that's accurate."

"Okay," he said, nodding. "So tell me—how many other guys have you slept with in the past twelve months?"

She scowled. "How is that any of your business?"

"It's not," he admitted. "Just like the number of other women that I've slept with isn't any of yours."

"Agreed."

"But I'm going to tell you, anyway."

She shook her head. "I really don't want to know."

"It's zero, Nat."

She seemed taken aback by his admission, but quickly recovered. "If that's true, it might be because there aren't any single women left in Haven that you haven't already slept with."

"It's zero," he said again, pointedly ignoring the latter part of her remark. "And I'm willing to bet that your number's zero, too."

"Which proves exactly *nothing*," she told him.

"It proves that we somehow found ourselves in an exclusive relationship without meaning to."

"I never wanted a relationship at all," she reminded him.

"And yet, here we are."

"*No.* We're not *here.* We're not *anywhere.* We're not *anything.*" Her tone was vehement, almost angry, even.

But there was a hint of something else in there, something so surprising, it took him a minute—and the memory of something Margot had said to him—to put his finger on what it was.

…she's lost so much—and so many people she's loved. So if she's reluctant to open her heart again, it's no wonder.

Thor must have picked up on Nat's agitation, too, because he abandoned his doggy bed and padded over to her, butting his nose against her thigh, as if to let her know he was there. Her hand automatically dropped to the dog's head to give it a rub, soothing him—and maybe soothing herself, too.

"You're scared," Kevin realized.

"I'm *not* scared," she denied.

"You're afraid of opening yourself up to a real, honest relationship."

"Maybe you're the one who's afraid of a real, honest relationship," she countered. "Maybe that's why you keep coming back to me—because you know that our relationship isn't going anywhere and that's your comfort zone."

"That's a creative argument. Totally invalid, but creative," he said.

She folded her arms across her chest, set her jaw.

"Do you want to know the real reason that I keep coming back to you?" he asked her. "Because you're it for me, Natalya. You're the one—*the only one*—I want to be with, not just for now but forever."

Her expression softened with something that he feared might be pity.

"Kevin—" she began.

"No," he interjected. "You can question your feelings all that you want—and we both know that you do—but you don't get to question mine.

"I love you, Nat. I don't know when I fell. I can't pinpoint an exact date or time, but I know that it happened, and I'm tired of pretending that my feelings are less than what they are because they might make you uncomfortable.

"I've been dealing with them for some time, and now you're going to have to deal with them, too."

"I don't have to do anything," she said defiantly.

Thor's head swiveled between them, a whine sounding low in his throat.

Kevin nodded. "You're right. You can continue to pretend we're just friends. That when you show up at my house in the middle of the night, it's because you want a friend to help you scratch a particular itch.

"But I'm done pretending that someday I'll find the strength to turn you away and move on with my life without you. Because when I say that I love you, it's forever, Nat.

"And if it takes until forever for you to figure out that you feel the same way, you should know that I'll be right here waiting for you."

Her eyes glittered with something that, if she was any other woman, he might have suspected were tears. But she wasn't any other woman, she was Nat, and he'd never seen her cry.

"I don't know how I'm supposed to respond to that."

His anger drained away, leaving him empty and weary.

"I have no expectations, Nat. I just wanted you to know how I feel." He patted Thor on the head and started toward the door.

"Kevin."

He paused, waiting.

But that was all she said.

And it wasn't nearly enough.

"You look like hell," Jake said, when Natalya carried the tray of cups and plates into the kitchenette after their usual Wednesday-night meeting.

He hadn't intended to speak so bluntly, but he was worried about her.

"Thanks, that's exactly the look I was going for."

The flippant response was typical Nat.

The flat tone was not.

He tipped her chin up, forcing her to meet his gaze. "Whose ass do I need to kick?"

"No one's." Despite his grip on her chin, she managed a slight shake of the head. "This is all on me."

"What's on you?" he asked, letting his hand drop away.

"I should have seen it coming. No—" she shook her head again "—I should have stopped it from happening."

"I'm going to need more information, Nat."

She sighed. "Kevin."

Her response didn't help him fill in the blanks.

"You should have stopped Kevin from happening?" he asked dubiously.

"I should have known it was a mistake to get involved with him," she clarified, as she began to load the dishes into the dishwasher. "Except that we weren't supposed to be involved. It was just chemistry. Sex."

"Ah," he said, picking up the thread of the conversation again. "You and Kevin had a fight."

"No. Well, yes. But that was at work. And we're usually good about keeping the personal separate from work, but maybe that was my fault. And then he came over later to apologize for not sleeping with Blair and followed that up by saying his number was zero and—"

"Whoa! Hold on a minute." He signaled time-out with his hands because the thread had slipped completely out of his grasp again. "He apologized for *not* sleeping with another woman?"

"No, he apologized for saying that he did when he didn't," she clarified. "And then… He told me that he loves me."

"You can't have been surprised by the words," Jake said gently.

"I knew he had feelings for me," she acknowledged. "But I was completely honest with him from the beginning that our relationship was never going anywhere."

"Oh, Nat," he said, shaking his head. "You might *think* you were honest with him, but I'm not sure you were even honest with yourself."

"I can't give him what he wants," Nat said brokenly.

"You mean you can't give him what you assume he wants," he guessed.

"He wants a family."

"Family isn't a rigid concept, Nat."

"I know that."

"Does he know what happened in Hawaii?" Jake asked gently.

She dropped a detergent pod into the dispenser and closed the door. "He does now."

"And how did he respond when you told him?"

"He said my inability to have children doesn't change how he feels about me."

"And that scared you," he guessed. "Because you were trying to push him away, never anticipating that he might be willing to accept you, exactly as you are."

"I thought your wife was the one with the psychology degree."

"I've learned a lot, being married to Sky," he told her. "But I know how you're feeling because I know *you*—and because I've been right where you are, afraid to trust that anyone could really know me and love me, anyway."

"You got lucky."

"I got very lucky," he agreed. "But only after I found the courage to take a chance on love."

"Well, I guess you're braver than me."

"You can do this," Jake said. "You just have to give Kevin—and yourself—a chance."

She shook her head. "I can't."

"Don't you think you owe him that much?"

"Why do I owe him anything?"

"Because you love him," he said simply.

"I don't." She shook her head again. "I *can't*."

"You can and you do, or you wouldn't be so tied up in knots about this."

"Love sucks."

"Sometimes it does," he agreed. "And sometimes it's the only thing that makes life worthwhile."

"I don't want to end up with my heart broken."

"He loves you, Nat."

"Which is no guarantee that he won't break my heart."

"You're right. But love isn't a microwave—it doesn't come with any kind of guarantee."

She managed to laugh. "A microwave? That's your analogy?"

Jake shrugged. "You got the point, didn't you?"

"Yeah," she admitted. "Love doesn't come with any guarantees—which is all the more reason not to buy into the concept."

But despite her satisfaction of having the last word, Nat couldn't help reflecting on her conversation with Jake long after the meeting.

If he was right—and she wasn't yet willing to concede that he was—she had to wonder how it had happened.

How had she let herself fall in love with Kevin?

She'd known what a risk it would be to open up her heart, which is why she'd done everything in her power to keep it firmly closed behind reinforced barricades.

But somehow, he'd found the key.

Or maybe he *was* the key.

Either way, he'd gotten in.

When had it happened? Last week? Last month? Last year? Did it matter?

Now she was paying the price, yearning for something that she knew she couldn't have, wanting to believe in a future that she knew could never be.

And if it takes until forever for you to figure out that you feel the same way, you should know that I'll be right here waiting for you.

His words echoed in her head, tempting her with possibilities and infuriating her at the same time.

Because who said something like that?

What kind of person put their life on hold for another?

It was a ridiculous promise to make—a promise she couldn't ask him to keep.

And so, when she'd taken some time to sort out her thoughts and feelings, she decided to respond. To finally make him give up the ridiculous notion of a future for them together so that he could move on with his life without her.

But she wanted the home field advantage to stay in control of the conversation, so she sent him a text message, asking him to come over.

Per her request, he was at her door at eight o'clock Friday night.

"Where's Thor?" he asked, when he wasn't greeted by the shepsky's usual joyful bark.

"I put him in the backyard," she said. "He doesn't like when we fight."

Kevin's brows lifted. "Are we going to fight?"

"It's not outside the realm of possibility."

"Maybe you should get started, then, and give me a chance to figure out what we're fighting about," he said.

She scowled. "Stop that."

"What am I doing?"

"You're being clever and charming and making it hard to stay mad at you."

"Why are you mad?"

"Because you pushed to change things that I didn't want to change."

"Then I guess you're going to have to stay mad, because I'm not sorry," he said.

"Well, I've been thinking about what you said, and I've got something to say, too."

"I'm listening."

"You said that I wasn't allowed to challenge your feelings, but I have to. Because I know how much you want to have a family and your chances of having a family with me are zero. You wanted me to give you that number the other day—well, there it is."

"I do want a family," he confirmed. "But the most important part of the family I want—the only essential part—is *you*."

She closed her eyes, fighting back the tears that threatened. "How do you do that?"

"Do what?"

"Always manage to say just the right thing to cut through all my defenses."

"I'm only telling you the truth that's in my heart."

"And if I let myself believe it, I'd be depriving you of the opportunity of ever expanding that family."

"That's not true," he said. "There are other options—if you're willing to consider them. Adoption, for example."

Her throat tightened.

She loved the idea of adopting a child.

In fact, she'd planned to suggest just that to Christopher when she learned of the extent of her injuries, but he never gave her the chance. And then she thought she might go ahead with the process on her own, when she was ready, but she'd worried that an unmarried woman with occasional episodes of PTSD might not be an ideal candidate.

"Are you?" he prompted gently.

She managed to nod in response to his question.

"Good," he said. "Because I happen to believe that couples who can't have children were made to be matched with children who don't have families."

"Adoption isn't an easy process," she warned. "And there are no guarantees that we'd be approved or ever get a child."

"We will," he said confidently.

"You can't know that."

"I can," he said. "Because there is no one who was meant to be a mother more than you."

"This is not at all how I envisioned this conversation going," she admitted.

"Do you want to yell? Throw something?"

"I'm keeping those options in reserve," she told him, as the words Raelynn spoke a few weeks back echoed in her head now. "But someone I know once told me that we all deserve to love and be loved, and that the really lucky ones find someone who can love all their parts—even the broken ones."

"Does that mean you're finally willing to believe that I love you—every part of you—and want a future together?"

"You've put forth some persuasive arguments," she acknowledged.

"I have some more arguments in favor of setting date for our wedding," he told her.

"I thought you were willing to wait until forever."

"I said I would if I had to," he acknowledged. "And I meant it. But I'm hoping your invitation to come here today is a sign that I won't have to."

"I want a life with you," she admitted. "And I want that life to start as soon as possible."

He finally drew her into his arms and lowered his head to touch his lips to hers.

"And I want this house," she added, after he'd kissed her.

His brows lifted. "You have this house."

She shook her head. "I'm renting it. That's temporary. I want to put down real roots, here, with you."

"Are you saying that you want to buy this house?"

"I do," she said.

She'd received a divorce settlement from Christopher. Guilt money, she'd figured, and she'd wanted no part in assuaging his guilt. But Margot had urged her to take it, to do something with it for her future and forget about the cheating husband in her past.

So Nat had taken it and invested it, and now she knew that she wanted to invest it in her future with Kevin.

"We've already made this house a home together," she said. "We painted the walls and planted the flowers together, so I figure we might as well live in it together—you and me and Thor."

"I can get behind that plan," he said, tightening his embrace. "But you seemed to have skipped over something."

"What's that?"

"You haven't yet told me that you love me."

"You know that I do," she told him.

"I'd still like to hear the words."

She lifted her arms and linked her hands behind his head. "I love you, Kevin Dawson. I can't tell you exactly when or where I fell, I only know that I did. Completely head over heels.

"You are the most amazing man I've ever known. You are patient and steady and kind—not to mention that you totally rock my world in the bedroom and occasionally other places around your house and mine. And even the supply room at Adventure Village once.

"I never imagined that I'd fall in love again. I didn't ever want to fall in love again. But you didn't give me a choice. And one of the things that loving you has made me realize is that nothing I've ever felt before is as deep and real—or as terrifying—as what I feel for you.

"Not only can I imagine spending my life with you, it's what I want, more than anything else that I've ever wanted. I want to live with you and raise a family with you—if we're lucky enough to be given that opportunity.

"But mostly I want to grow old with you. You are the first person I want to see every morning and the last person I want to see every night, because I will love you every day of my life from now until the end of time."

"That was a pretty impressive speech," he remarked, his voice thick with emotion. "Almost as if you've been practicing."

She shook her head. "I asked you to come over here to tell you why we couldn't be together," she reminded him. "You made me see that I was wrong, so that's all straight from the heart— a heart that's already yours every bit as much as it's mine."

"And mine is yours," he said.

"Good, because I kind of like the idea of a winter wedding."

"Glad to hear it," he said, and pulled a square-cut diamond solitaire out of his pocket.

"You have a ring," she said, stunned.

"I bought it a few months ago," he admitted. "I wanted to be prepared so that if you ever said *yes*, I could slip it on your finger before you changed your mind."

"I'm not going to change my mind," she said, holding out her left hand. "You're stuck with me now."

When the ring was in place, he kissed her again to seal the promises they'd made to one another.

"I do have one minor request," he said, after they'd finally come up for air.

"What's that?"

"Can you keep that bit about the supply room at AV out of our wedding vows?"

"It will be our little secret," she promised.

But she had no more secrets from him—the man she knew she would love forever.

Because falling in love with him was the best mistake she'd ever made.

* * * * *

Look for the next installment in
Match Made in Haven,
Brenda Harlen's miniseries for Harlequin Special Edition,
coming soon, wherever Harlequin
books and ebooks are sold.
And catch up with previous books in the series,

Snowed In with a Stranger
The Rancher's Christmas Reunion
Her Not-So-Little Secret
Countdown to Christmas
Captivated by the Cowgirl

Available now!

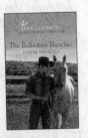